ECOSYSTEM

JOSHUA DAVID BELLIN

For my children

Book One: Sward

The fact that, of all organic beings, man alone is to be regarded as essentially a destructive power, and that he wields energies to resist which, nature—that nature whom all material life and all inorganic substances obey—is wholly impotent, tends to prove that, though living in physical nature, he is not of her, that he is of more exalted parentage, and belongs to a higher order of existence than those born of her womb and submissive to her dictates.

—George Perkins Marsh,
Man and Nature (1864)

THE ECOSYSTEM BREATHES.

I crouch at the edge of the forest, waiting. Waiting for its attention to shift so I can make my dash across the greensward. Waiting until I can Sense its thought in my bones.

There are no guarantees, Sarah, Aaron told me before I set out this morning. *There is only the Sense of things: eyes and ears and nerves and muscle. And,* he added, smiling, *a little bit of luck.*

The Ecosystem rustles, settling. I edge forward, my eyes focused on the patch of bright green turf just beyond the dense tangle of bushes and creepers. I breathe shallowly, lowering my heart rate to a relaxed, steady rhythm. The suffocating smell of vegetation surrounds me, but I detect no threat from the sultry air. The Ecosystem has lost sight of me in the tall grasses, failed to track me from the kill site. Its final assault will come at the edge of the village, where its anger runs deepest. Where there's nothing to attract its thirst for blood but me.

I rise to a sprinter's crouch, fingers braced against

moist earth. My heart pulses in my fingertips, and I hope that isn't enough to rouse the Ecosystem's ire.

The Ecosystem doesn't sleep, Aaron reminded me. *But it dozes. It sends signals from place to place, heightening some zones while dulling others. Always conscious, but not always mindful. Not always. Not everywhere.*

Not here, I think. I Sense. Not now.

Now.

My body uncoils, hurdling the fringe of under-brush that separates forest from lawn. My foot strikes the turf, but only long enough to propel me into my next stride. Stumble on the grabgrass and I'm dead. I cross the green in a random, zigzag pattern, hoping the individual blades can't anticipate my next move. I Sense snares exploding in my wake: a sinkhole, a clinging ten-dril, a venomous thorn. But the Ecosystem is sluggish, emerging from dormancy, too slow to catch me. I leap from living grass to the charred circle surrounding the village stone, and the vines the Ecosystem hurls at my back clutch nothing but air.

I trot across the boundary circle, bare soles crunch-ing on blackened turf, heart hammering in my throat. When cool village stone lies beneath my feet once more, I turn to the forest. The Ecosystem's many tongues erupt at the sight of me: winged cicatrix chat-ter, prowler monkeys hoot, bloodbirds screech. I smile, pull my first kill from the pouch at my belt, and dangle the dead thing before the forest's face.

"I am Sarah," I say to it, enunciating each word despite the raggedness of my breath, the heaviness of my heart. "You have taken what was mine, and now I take what is yours."

With an exaggerated motion, I twist the spine of the thing I killed until I hear a sharp *crack*. Then, while the Ecosystem howls in thwarted rage, I cross the stone terrace and enter the village.

AARON WAITS FOR me at the Sensorium. He leans heavily on his staff, a length of polished, fire-blackened wood wrested from the Ecosystem during his own days in the field. His gray hair hangs long and knotted beside withered cheeks; his dark eyes have begun to cloud. But when he sees me, his ancient face crinkles in a smile, and in a giddy moment, I hoist my kill above my head, feel its limp weight dangle from my hand. For as long as I can remember, he's been the closest I've had to a father or mother, and I'll do almost anything to see him smile.

"My child." He cradles my face in hands that smell of age and woodsmoke. His fingernails are long and split at the ends. No one dares touch me but him. "You are unharmed?"

"It was easy," I joke. "Just like you said."

He studies my face. "The Ecosystem did not recognize you," he says. "Your scent, your touch. You did well."

I recall my mad dash across the lawn, my taunt at hunt's end. It will recognize me now, I think.

But I don't say that to Aaron. I don't want to alarm him, much less risk his displeasure. I offer him my arm, and he lays a hand lightly on my bare skin. His hand feels cool and dry, with a tremor that's worsened noticeably in recent weeks.

We walk through the village, at his pace. His staff ticks against stone; his body under its furs is light and airy as a bird's. I wish I could have seen him in his prime, when it's said he moved like a shadow over grass.

"What was the first snare?" he asks.

"Bogsand," I answer. "I Sensed it from rods away. I doubt it was strong enough to hold me."

"And the next?"

"Stabbing nettle," I say. "Another easy dodge."

"Projectile?"

I nod. "But obviously, it missed."

A frown creases his cheek. "It fired?"

"Only when I was well out of range," I assure him.

He scrutinizes my face, his milky eyes uncommonly keen. "What of the bloodbirds?" he asks.

"Not until the end. And they didn't strike. I don't think they could smell me." His silence prompts me to continue. "I'll do better next time, Master. Avoid the snares, not just manage them. I promise."

I brace for his reprimand, but he says nothing. We resume our walk. The only sounds are his staff striking stone, the aura of cicatrix droning in the trees. Already, I feel the warmth fading from the thing I killed.

At the intersection to the great hall, Aaron stops and squeezes my arm. "You are young, Sarah. The Sense yet grows within you. There will be time to correct the errors of today's hunt."

"Errors," I say.

"Enthusiasms," he amends. "As you grow in the ways of the Ecosystem, you will become more receptive to it, more obedient to its laws. Yet it will seek to nullify any threat it perceives from you, and it will be learning as you do."

"I will never become obedient to it," I say, with a coldness I instantly regret.

But he doesn't appear offended. His fingers quiver as he touches my cheek once again.

"We will celebrate today," he says. "Celebrate our newest Sensor. Sarah, the brave and strong."

And though it's been years since he first called me that, my face warms as it always has with the pleasure of his words.

I'M FIRST OF the Sensors to return. Not surprising, as my circuit was the shortest, my track the safest. The others have gone deep into the Ecosystem, to places I've only heard of, realms I can only imagine. In time, if I'm successful, I'll seek out the same places, where the game is thickest and the dangers greatest. In time, if I live, I'll train the next generation of Sensors, as Aaron has trained me.

But tonight, I'll celebrate. The village will celebrate. They will celebrate me.

We will meet in the great hall, the entire community assembled as one, except for the few threshers assigned to guard the periphery against the Ecosystem's attacks. In the stone hearth, the firestarters will light the blaze that is the Ecosystem's chief grievance against us, that and the cutting tools with which the threshers keep the forest from encroaching on the pavilion of stone. As the flickering shadows grow against the vault's stone walls, the Sensors will step forward to be acknowledged by the mass of commoners. In their identical uniforms of close-fitting brown fur, cut short to expose muscled arms and long legs, the members of the Sensorship will stand like statues: aloof, unsmiling, their Sense of the Ecosystem isolating them from the community they're sworn to serve. And for the first time, clothed in the matching outfit I wore on today's hunt, I will stand with them. I'll stand straight and still as the rest, though my heart will tremble with excitement.

Then Nathan, as Conservator of our order, will deliver the customary address, reminding the populace of how the Sensorship came to be. In his deep and commanding voice, he'll speak of the days of old, when humans were numerous and powerful, when their towns and trails covered the land. He'll speak of towers that climbed to the skies, things like giant birds that flew across earth and water and air. He'll tell us of devices that enabled one man to hail another across the globe, ghostly screens that enabled one to see another's face no matter the distance between them. We who've known only the Ecosystem these past hundred generations will find the picture laughable, but none of us will laugh. Even the village children will stand silent and solemn, seeing in the shadows stirred by Nathan's voice visions of a time that once was, a time that can never be again.

And then, his voice sunk to a whisper, Nathan will speak of the Ecosystem's rise. He'll tell how, unseen and undreamed of by those who claimed earth's dominion, the planet's innumerable threads of life knitted themselves into one, the first dim flickers of awareness burgeoning over time into full angry consciousness. He'll speak of cities overwhelmed by jungle or swallowed by monsters from below, farmlands turned to lakes of poison and parklands roamed by deadly predators. He'll spare no detail, yet his words will fall far short of reality. It was a planetary outpouring of grief and rage, a coordinated attack that swept human civilization from the face of the earth. It gave rise to the world we know, a world in which the Ecosystem rules and we who were once its masters huddle in its shadow.

But it didn't destroy us all. Its desire was thwarted, and so its anger festers to this day. For among the few of our kind who were left, there arose a fraction who discovered within themselves a hint of the Ecosystem's will, an ability to hear its dark whispers. These were the first Sensors, and as they gathered the survivors around them, there arose the first villages of stone, the first walls and firewells, the first masters and apprentices. Down to the present day, the Sensors have used their power for good, their Sense of the Ecosystem freeing them to roam the forest in the daily hunt for food and fuel. They've served their people selflessly, renouncing all ties that might distract from their vital calling: ties of love, family, children. We know nothing of how other villages fare; for all we can tell, we're alone. But so long as the Sensorship stands, we will not fall.

When Nathan finishes, the commoners will applaud, though they'll have understood his words only the way a blind man understands what it means to see. As the village's newest Sensor, I'll be singled out for my investiture, receiving from Aaron's hand the token he received from his own master, and his master from the one before, and so on back to the beginning, something no one outside this line of masters and apprentices has seen. It will be small, and Aaron will pass it to me in secret, an item wrapped in fur for me to unwrap when I'm alone. His wrinkled face will smile as he bestows it on me, and his smile will call back to me the earliest of my memories, the morning when, looking up at his face as he now looks up at mine, I first heard from his lips the new name he'd given me. And I'll remember, too, what I learned many years later: that the name of *Sarah* was another's name first, that one so old as Aaron would never have taken a girl of three as his apprentice if not for the other apprentice he'd trained and lost. It will be a moment for the community to welcome me after a lifetime of preparation, a moment for me to mourn the one who came before, though I remember nothing of her except her name. It will be a moment for me to honor her stolen memory, and to hate the Ecosystem for taking her from me.

And then the village will feast on the thing I killed, the life I tore from the Ecosystem in retribution for the pain it has caused me. With a stone pestle, Aaron will smear its blood on my cheeks, and the firestarters will roast its flesh, each member of the community sampling a small bite before they consume the bushmeat caught by the other Sensors. Aaron, as Chief Sensor, will give a speech, and the name of *Sarah* will be spoken again and again, while the congregation grows drowsy with food and fire. And when he's finished, I'll walk to the center of the gathering, and I'll eat the one part of my kill saved for me, the first and only bite of food I'll be permitted this day.

I will eat its heart.

In itself, that will be nothing new. I've eaten the Ecosystem's heart every night since I first learned of the one who came before. It has tasted like gall in my throat, but I've choked it down just the same.

Only tonight, there will be a difference. Tonight, it will taste good.

THE VILLAGE OF stone echoes the tap of Aaron's staff as we make our way to the gathering hall. The path we walk is paved in stone, and the archways above our heads are reared in stone, and the huts we pass are built of stone, carved and beveled to fit tightly without mortar as they rise from circular bases to conical peaks. Smooth, cool stone, scavenged by those first Sensors from the ruins of the old world, reinforced over the years to ward off the living will of the Ecosystem. Interior walls run through the streets to baffle any creature that might slip into the village, but the periphery is unwalled, open to prevent the enemy from approaching unseen. The village sits on elevated land far from the marshes, where disease-carrying insects abound. From its outskirts comes the sound of the threshers, the rhythmic swish and chop of their stone scythes as they clear the insistent fingers of life with which the Ecosystem probes our defenses. To protect them from invisible dangers carried on the wind, an apprentice of our order, Sensitive to poisons but unready for the hunt, patrols the fringe. Today it will be Levi or Jarrod or Saul or Rachel. Just last year, I stood in their place. I recall myself, lazily Sensing snares that had long since ceased to be a challenge, peering impatiently into the forest for the day I would be set free. On occasion, I'd hear the threshers whistle at a passing girl on the pavestones, but their whistles died on their lips when I turned my eyes on them.

The lane we walk is lined with firewells, some aflame and smoking vigorously, others merely smoldering. They account for the gray haze that hangs over the village, as well as the pungent smell of woodsmoke that pervades the atmosphere. The firestarters have their own, elaborate patterns for igniting the wells, dug deeply to prevent the Ecosystem from launching a subterranean attack. We Sensors supply them with fuel, harvesting the Ecosystem's own produce to foil its will. The part of me that's Sensitive to its mind knows the roots of its anger, the intensity with which it broods on our offenses. The part of me that hates it—the same part—knows that, though it could do without us, we couldn't do without it. The Ecosystem is the source of what little we have. We couldn't destroy it utterly without destroying ourselves.

"See," Aaron says, pointing with his staff toward the gathering hall. "They come."

The lanes converge on the central building, a long oval of piled stone. Our village numbers nearly two hundred, of whom only nine are Sensors. The rest, young and old, stream toward the hall. They wear the loose furs of the village commoner, who require neither speed to outrace the Ecosystem's snares nor bare skin to Sense its intentions. A gaggle of teenage girls enters the hall, talking and laughing, long hair braided down their backs. Behind them slouches a posse of threshers. They've donned shirts for the occasion, but that's as far as they'll go to acknowledge my investiture. They crowd into the building behind the girls, jostling each other, ignoring a lone girl who trails the pack, her black hair unruly, her stick arms crossed over a flat chest. Her name escapes me, but I know I've never heard the threshers whistle at her.

At the door of the gathering hall, we meet the apprentice Sensors, all but Saul, who must be tending the remaining threshers. Levi, at sixteen the oldest of the three, bows stiffly to Aaron.

"A fine day for hunting, Master," he says. Jarrod and Rachel, fifteen and thirteen respectively, bow as well.

"An uncommonly fine day, my children," Aaron answers, and returns their bow, fluid for all his years. Though their exchange is ceremonial, it couldn't be truer today: clear vault of blue, gemfire sun, a Sense of life stirring as sharp as blood.

"Good day, Sarah," Levi offers to me. I note in his voice the same stiltedness I saw in his bow. His eyes roam enviously over my uniform and kill pouch.

"Good day," I say calmly.

Levi watches me a moment more before turning to Aaron.

"Did you hear, Master," he asks, "the flock of blood-birds that crossed the village this morning?"

"These ears are old," Aaron says. "They hear but little of what crosses the village."

Jarrod and Rachel shoot each other a smile. Not noticing, Levi forges ahead. "Such flocks are known to travel from leagues away to the site of a kill, are they not?"

"Too well known," Aaron says, "to pay them any mind."

"But such a large flock," Levi pursues.

"Let us forget for the moment the things that fly overhead," Aaron says lightly but with finality, "and remember our purpose in meeting here today."

Levi licks his lips but says no more. With his reddish hair and scruffy beard, he looks a bit like a bloodbird himself.

Aaron takes my arm as we enter the hall. The stone interior gleams in the light that spills through high arched windows. Stone tables and benches line the walls, leaving the central space clear for hobnobbing. The dominant feature is the ceremonial hearth, a circular pit adorned with a stone altar on which my kill will be roasted when the time comes. The stone's streaked with black from generations of investitures, though it's been five years since we last installed a new Sensor. Aaron steers me toward the circle of commoners who occupy the space before the hearth. "What do you make of Levi's tale?"

"Fairytale," I say. "I Sensed no more than common hunger among the bloodbirds."

"That is my Sense, too," he says. "But on this day, I judge the others wish to have a tale of their own to tell. They know you have surpassed them."

"I had a good teacher," I say distractedly, for we've reached the others, and the crowd presses around me.

I've had little contact with the villagers these past years. I know most by name, some by a scrap of personal history, none by close acquaintance. They chatter and jabber as they surround me, complimenting me on my first hunt, eyes widening at the dead thing at my belt. The hubbub of praise drones in my ears. Adept as I've become at picking out signals from the Ecosystem's clamor, I find it impossible to attend to their words, but I try to smile at each new face in the mob. Aaron stands by my side in case anyone attempts to touch me, but not even the youngest child dares.

I'm in the midst of showing off my kill for the fiftieth time when Chief Warden Daniel insinuates himself between me and my protector. Though his body's gone soft from indoor work and he'd be butchered by the Ecosystem before he took two steps beyond the charred circle, Daniel moves through the social setting as a seasoned Sensor moves through the forest: silently, stealthily, so in tune with all that surrounds him he nearly fades into the background. He wraps his ceremonial cloak around his belly and leans in to cut me off from the crowd. Even he, however, observes the taboo.

"I'd best offer my congratulations now," he says jovially. "Once Aaron launches into his panegyric, I doubt I'll get a word in edgewise."

My mouth opens to respond, with what I don't know. Luckily, Aaron comes to my rescue.

"We are honored to serve our village on this joyous

day," he says. "And Sarah, as you know, has proved an extraordinarily apt pupil."

"I for one never doubted she would," Daniel says, his fleshy face sweating with exertion or good cheer. "How many years has it been, Sarah, since you were identified for the Sensorship?"

"Fourteen," I say, thankful to have a direct question to answer.

"And yet you've just begun," he muses, "to learn the secrets of the world around us."

"Is there any way to learn those secrets," Aaron remarks wryly, "without walking in the world?"

"If there were, surely you'd be the one to find it!" Daniel guffaws. For a moment, it seems he's going to forget himself and slap Aaron on the back, and I bristle. But his fit of humor dies, and he tugs at the neck of his cloak.

"Well," he says. "I must prepare for the day's festivities. Congratulations once again, Sarah. I hope," and he inclines his head toward me, "you and I will have a chance to speak of your experiences soon."

I nod, though what a Sensor should speak to him about I can't imagine. It occurs to me I should say "thank you," but he's gone before the words have left my mouth.

"What was that all about?" I ask Aaron.

"I haven't the faintest idea," he says, with either a smile or a grimace. I'm about to press him when a shout goes up from the end of the hall nearest the door, and I see that the first of the senior Sensors has returned.

It's Esther, tall and lithe, her hair tied in a simple twist, her muscled arms swinging easily at her slim waist. A brace of the creatures she killed dangles from her back. I don't know her true age, but I imagine her to be roughly the age the other Sarah would have been had she lived. The crowd parts to let Esther through, then closes just behind, creating the impression that she's contained within an invisible bubble that enforces a distance of three feet in all directions.

She glides up to me and Aaron, bows slightly, receives his bow in return. Her eyes travel up and down my body, and I have the sense of being inspected by an intelligence as keen and unfeeling as the Ecosystem's own.

"Sarah," she says.

I nod.

"Welcome to the brotherhood."

I search without success for a trace of irony in her flat eyes and tone. She unties the kill from her shoulder strap, six long-legged birds with sharp bronze feathers. Tricky vultures, we call these things. Flightless. They run fast and scavenge the dead and almost dead.

"Hen and poults," she says. "We'd best be cooking them."

A villager with gloved hands gathers the birds from the stone hearth and removes them to the cleaning room, where the real cooking takes place. She'll pluck the carcasses and toss the feathers into the fire, where they'll shrivel and vanish with a coppery smell. Beaks and eyes and entrails will follow before the birds are skewered through their scrawny necks and hung over a much-used fire pit to roast.

I'm reminded of the kill at my belt. "Should I," I whisper to Aaron.

"Later," he reassures me. "When the others have returned."

"What's taking them so long?"

"Patience," he says. "You have waited fourteen years. Surely you can wait another few moments." His eyes dance behind their watery veil. "Laugh. Be sociable. The worst will be over soon."

I smile weakly and try to calm my heart as I did in the forest.

One by one, the elder Sensors return. Next is Nathan, tall and powerful, with a thick mane of hair silvering at the temples and a short black bow that makes him as deadly at a hundred paces as other Sensors are in close quarters. He must be over fifty, but his body belongs to a man half that age. He'll be Chief Sensor after Aaron, and though I know he's earned the right, I've never forgiven him for that. Draped over his shoulders is the single massive warhog he slew, hideous and black and spiked from forward-facing tusks to spinal plates, meat enough to feed the village for a week. It thuds to the hearth like an earthquake.

"We will speak later," he grunts, the first words he's said directly to me in all the years I've known him. As Conservator, it's his duty to hear each Sensor's report of the hunt, to study it for patterns, quirks, variations in the Ecosystem's strategies. I've no idea what I'll say to him. The rumble of his voice is for orating, not for chatting with another master's apprentice.

But I'm an apprentice no longer, I remind myself. I'm a Sensor. "I look forward to it," I say steadily, before he turns away.

Samuel comes next, shorter than the average Sensor, shorter than I am, but nimble of hand and Sensitive to the slightest shiver in the leafy understory. To my astonishment, he bears the bodies of three quetzalcoati, feathered marsupials with tapering, inquisitive snouts and banded tails, impossible to catch without venturing into the trees that are their homes. He smiles easily, as if daring the other Sensors to doubt him. To me, he winks and whispers, "Something special. For the celebration." My cheeks warm pleasantly. The villagers cluster around the strange things Samuel has brought. We share a smile at their *oohs* and *ahs*.

Time passes. The crowd around me waxes and wanes. Aaron tries to amuse me with reminiscences of mishaps past. As sunlight shifts from eastern to western-facing windows, the remainder of the Sensorship assembles: first Judah, then Adam, then Ezra, each of them bearing the thing that crossed their path, the creature they snared or brought down with bare hands before the Ecosystem grew conscious of their presence. All greet me with a bow or a curt nod. The room sweats with bodies. Those my age have forgotten our purpose and begun to treat the gathering as another opportunity to flirt. The threshers lounge and strut, the girls preen. Jarrod and Rachel chat while Levi sulks. The black-haired loner has vanished, or at least slunk to a corner where shadows blot her from view.

Still we wait. By evening, all but one of our number has returned: Barnabas, the youngest Sensor but for me, whose job today was to gather wood for the ceremonial fire. I remember his investiture five years ago, the blood streaming down his round face as he devoured the heart of his kill. A small thing, fox squirrel-size, allowing each villager only the tiniest pinch of meat. Though Barnabas turned Sensor five years ago, he's easily ten years older than I am, his training under Nathan having proceeded with unusual caution. Aaron will say nothing about it, but from gossip among the apprentices, I've heard that Barnabas grew too big and careless to exercise good Sense. I don't know whether to credit such tales. He's big, and on the village stone he might be counted clumsy, but he's survived five years flitting through leaf and branch and root that would have drained the blood of lesser men.

And yet, as time slips by and Barnabas fails to return, my heart misgives me. Jarrod and Rachel have snuck off to watch for him, while Nathan and Esther have left the hall more than once to Sense for any sign of his presence in the surrounding forest. The villagers have grown increasingly restless, talking loudly about anything or nothing at all. Daniel circulates, his face shining in the glow from the kindled hearth as he tries to buck up the crowd with yarns and sleight-of-hand. But nothing works. Conversation has dwindled to coughs and rustles and the dimness of twilight has settled on the forest when at last Aaron makes the decision to lay hands on the Ecosystem in an effort to locate the missing Sensor.

We exit into the muggy dusk. The rhythmic drone of the cicatrix sharpens in the treetops, winged carapaces in the millions producing a squeal that has always put me in mind of bone grinding against bone. The lightest of rains slicks the streets, shines mossy on Aaron's fur cloak. Remembering Levi's tale from the morning, I keep alert for any Sense of special malice. But there's nothing, only the Ecosystem's ever-brooding will. The commoners trail us for a distance before breaking off for the safety of home.

We make our way to the eastern edge of the pavilion, where Nathan's hut stands, where Barnabas lived when he was under his master's training. There'd been talk that he might have returned here to conduct some business before joining the celebration, but the house sits silent and empty. The ranks of forest trees appear denser than usual with the fading of the light. I can hardly believe that just this morning, I stood on the village stone and taunted goliaths that loom two hundred feet above my head.

Aaron hands Levi his staff, and with my assistance, he lowers himself to his knees at the edge of the charred circle, where dead grass meets living. I've never seen anyone do what he's about to, though I've heard of it. If he were still active in the field, searching for Barnabas in this way would carry considerable risk, for sustained contact with the Ecosystem will fix his imprint forever in its mind. But Aaron will never again venture into the wild. And so, though Nathan is Barnabas's former master, it falls to the Chief Sensor to reach out for word of the lost hunter.

Aaron's eyes close, and his palms fall to the turf, bony fingers clutching it to the roots. A tremor passes through his arms, whether from contact or age I can't tell. His head bows, and a supernatural calm settles over his features as he opens himself to the will of this far greater being. I kneel beside him, prepared to protect him if necessary. He shakes his head, gray locks swinging with the motion, and though my hands itch to touch him, I desist.

Then I Sense it.

The Ecosystem is awake, its mind focused on Aaron, its far-flung thought tapering to the single small figure who kneels at its feet. From deep within the ground, I Sense its pattern rearranging, querying this new life-form, deciding whether it's one of its own. With an angry shock, it recognizes Aaron for who he is: one who has trod wraithlike through the forest for the past fifty years, slipping just beyond the margins of its consciousness, ripping prey from its embrace with such skill it's never been able to identify him as the one who's cheated it of its children. But now it knows. His life force races through its mind, and all the fifty years of crimes he's committed against it are revealed in a flash.

The ground beneath Aaron's hands erupts, vomiting vines that clutch his wrists and shoulders. I react instantly, wrapping my arms around his chest to pull him free. But the grass is slick and the vines much stronger than I am, and I fall to my back on the charred circle with Aaron on top of me, living ropes twining his body. I Sense the tendrils changing direction, curling from his arms to his throat, but I'm pinned by a force far greater than his body and can't stop them. In the instant before they tighten around his neck, I realize that the vines have circled my arms along with his, and a prickling Sensation floods my body as the Ecosystem locks on me.

It knows me. It knows me all too well.

Then the vines part as Nathan and Esther hack at them with stone knives, greenish blood smearing their forearms. Sensor hands drag me and Aaron away from the sward, and I struggle to stand, choking on the soot and cinders of wet burned grass. The ground Aaron contacted continues to spit vines at random, but they're too far away to reach us, and they flail on the blackened turf like living whips.

Aaron hasn't risen, hasn't moved. I fall to the ground beside him, lay hands on his frail chest. Beneath my fingers, his lungs labor. His face is slack. Then his hand grips mine, and his eyes open.

"It has taken him," he whispers. "Barnabas is alive."

Nathan kneels beside me. "Alive, Master?"

Aaron nods. The grieved look on his face silences Nathan's next question before it's asked.

Barnabas is alive. The Ecosystem holds him in its jaws. It would be better for him if he were dead.

THE CELEBRATION IS ruined, my retribution destroyed. Days from now, we'll hold a private ceremony at Aaron's hut, where I'll receive the token from my mentor's hand. I'll grip it, know that it passed through the hands of the other Sarah, but the moment will have lost its shine. The heart of my first kill will have grown cold and rancid, and I'll eat numbly whatever Aaron serves in its place.

I will remain bereaved. I'll hunger still for its blood.

AARON TRIES TO console me, but I'm inconsolable.

"It could have been any day, child," he says. "The Ecosystem takes those who stray unwarily into its path, and cares nothing for the trials and joys of men."

I wonder. Wonder if it allowed me my small triumph only to make my defeat all the more crushing. In the brief moment the Ecosystem touched me on the sward, I felt in its breast a searing recognition too deep for one who'd completed only a single ceremonial hunt.

"Why must all the Sensors go out at once?" I wail, embarrassed by my own voice.

"You know the reason," he says.

I do. I know the community's need is too great, the Ecosystem's yield too precarious, to waste an entire day on an initiate's party. I know, too, that I asked the question only to hear Aaron's calming response.

He knows this as well. "Sarah," he says. "There will be another time. Every day we survive is a victory."

"I should not have survived," I mutter. "I should never have been born."

"Sarah!"

"It's true. You can't deny it's true."

He's silent for a long time. When he speaks, his voice has hardened. "We have lost a Sensor today, and the village grieves. Those of us yet living are called to action, not self-pity."

I bow my head, and am truly ashamed.

Aaron's words are no empty proverb. This morning, when the sun rises above the trees, the Sensors will meet. For the first time, I'll meet as one of them. Though Barnabas's fate was sealed last night when we returned to our homes without him, the decision won't be formalized until today. For that reason, Chief Warden Daniel will join our meeting and report our verdict to the populace. On my first full day as Sensor, I'll cast a vote to abandon one of my own to torment and death.

Our walk to the Sensorium seems slower than usual, and the others are there by the time Aaron and I arrive. I slide onto a bench beside Esther, who glances at me before returning her gaze to the space at the room's center. Nathan, Samuel, Adam, Ezra, and Judah are similarly remote. In shape and size, the Sensorium is like all the village structures except the gathering hall: an unadorned dome roughly twenty feet in diameter, with enough headroom to stand at the sloped roof's lowest point. But unlike the dwelling places, which contain stone tables and chairs and beds and firewell, the meeting-house holds nothing but concentric stone benches arranged around a central, cleared space. There are no windows, for Sensor business is our own. I've been here once before, but only as an apprentice, speaking at the Sensorship's behest. I doubt I'll take the floor this time.

The benches seat twenty or more, but today, counting Daniel, we number only nine. The Chief Warden has shed his ceremonial cloak in favor of the commoner's garb, his normally jovial face solemn in the room's semidarkness. The Sensors, by contrast, wear the same clothing and expressions they did last night. Looking at their erect shoulders and stoical faces, I almost permit myself to believe that yesterday was a dream. Aaron, however, shatters that illusion at once.

"We are here to discuss the matter of Barnabas," he says as he steps to the central circle, "and to decide among us what course to pursue."

There's a respectful silence, during which I let my eyes unfocus on the motes that hover in the gloom.

Nathan, as Barnabas's former master, rises from his place and addresses Aaron. "I ask, Master, that you report as completely as possible on our lost colleague, that we may cast our votes in full possession of the facts."

Aaron nods. I wonder how much of this is a formality, how much if any an actual request.

"The information I collected from the Ecosystem locates Barnabas nearly a three days' journey from our village," Aaron announces. I'm the only one who gasps. "He was taken on his outward voyage, transported by unknown agents to that distant place. He lies in swampland, his body submerged, his nose and mouth exposed. Meanwhile, his flesh is consumed by watermites."

Again, I stifle a gasp that's shared by no one else. Watermites secrete a resin that devours organic matter. Normally, they feast on aquatic plants and insects. Their work is slow but thorough.

"Thank you, Master," Nathan says. He sits, places his hands on his thighs, and stares ahead of him with an expression of calm forbearance.

Judah, master of Saul, stands next. "Master, is it your belief that the path our brother took is well guarded?"

"It is not guarded at all, beyond the normal mechanisms," Aaron says. "And that is what gives me pause." His gaze lifts to mine, and I can't help thinking his words are meant for my hearing in particular. "The Ecosystem appears to be inviting us to launch a rescue. And it appears confident that such an attempt will fail."

"You Sensed this?" Judah asks.

"No," Aaron admits. "Contact was broken before I could process all the pertinent information. I will say only that in my experience, the Ecosystem has never left a trail so poorly camouflaged. I therefore have reason to suspect that Barnabas's capture was strategic, and that we risk far more than we stand to gain should we seek his recovery."

"Thank you, Master," Judah says. He sits, and the silence of stone settles over the Sensorium as no one else ventures a question.

"We have not heard from all," Aaron says. "Is there more anyone would know, more anyone would say?"

The silence deepens.

"What of our council's newest member?" Aaron asks, his eyes once again finding mine. "Sarah," he says, and it's as if he can't say the name without the customary gentleness stealing into his voice. "There is much here that is new to you, much that may appear unwonted. Is there anything you would ask?"

I shake my head, then realize how rude that is, so I stand. I want to ask what he felt when he made contact, when he Sensed Barnabas's flesh being picked from his bones. "Thank you, Master," I say. "I understand."

I sit, feeling Aaron's gaze linger on my face.

"Very well," he says. "And what of our Chief Warden? Would he add anything to our deliberations?"

Daniel stands, but unlike the others, he wheels around his bench toward the central circle. Aaron reaches for his own seat and lands clumsily, perching on the edge of the bench with gnarled hands wrapped around his staff. Daniel takes his place in the speaker's position.

"Thank you, Aaron," he says quietly, his voice modulated to the size and occasion of the room. "It has been some time since I last addressed the circle of Sensors—and alas, I seem to address you only in circumstances such as these. Most of us recall the matter some years past, when I was called to speak of another Sensor lost to the forest, though still dear to our hearts."

I sit up at these words. We lost the Sensor Hanna

five years ago, though I didn't attend the meeting that time. Is this the loss of which Daniel speaks? I wish I could read as much in my fellows' words as I do in the forest's secret language, but humans are unlike anything else in the Ecosystem: though I can Sense their living presence, their minds are closed to me.

"But perhaps that is my purpose here," Daniel continues. "Like you, I grieve the loss of Barnabas. And yet, unlike you, I do not bear the heavy burden of decision. I know you would hasten to rescue your lost brother if there were any hope of his recovery. Perhaps you would seek to do so even now."

Nothing in the posture of the Sensors suggests any such intention, but Daniel carries on.

"Let me urge you to consider this matter from an outside point of view," he says. "Let me speak on behalf of the village, which cannot bear the loss of another of your circle. Much as we may wish it were otherwise, we have as yet no champion capable of withstanding the Ecosystem's will. Let your choice, then, be guided by wisdom as much as valor. Let it be a choice that honors your fallen brother's sacrifice, but not at the cost of further suffering and loss."

No flicker of movement hints that the circle of Sensors is swayed by his appeal, but I suspect it's achieved its purpose. Maybe it was as much a ceremonial gesture as Nathan and Judah's questions. Now we can cast the votes we would have cast anyway without appearing heartless in our own eyes.

"And let me say one word more," Daniel breaks into

my thoughts. "Just yesterday, the Sensorship was nine, and today it is reduced to eight. Of those eight, one, for all his wisdom, cannot any longer travel beyond the village. Another is newly come into her estate, and though we have great hopes for her future, she remains a learner still. Would it not be wise to look for those among the common folk who show signs of being blessed with the Sense? Would it not be well to deepen the ranks of those who will one day carry on your great and necessary work? I raise this as a suggestion only, and hope you receive it in the spirit of good fellowship that has ever existed between your office and mine."

He circles the stone bench and sits. Aaron doesn't rise, but he nods in acknowledgment of the Chief Warden's counsel. So far as I know, there's no law to prevent Daniel from offering advice to the Sensors, though I wonder at the audacity of his proposal. I look to Nathan's spot, thinking the Conservator might want to weigh in, but he remains stony and silent.

The business is soon concluded. Aaron calls for other commentary, then, hearing none, for a vote. It's unanimous. It must be, and so far as I know, it always is. Though my arm feels as if vines seek to drag it down, I put my hand in the air to be counted as one of them.

"It is decided," Aaron says gravely. "Our brother is lost to us. Nathan, it is yours to prepare what memorial you deem fitting. If, at the conclusion of a week's time, it is your will to do so, you may choose from among the village youth one in whom you see promise of the Sense. Of the other matter raised by our Chief

Warden, we will speak at a later day." His eyes travel the circle, and I wonder if I'm the only one who notices how very old and tired those eyes seem. "This council is adjourned."

We rise, and one by one, my elders file from the council room.

Aaron finds me at the doorway and takes my arm for support. We make our way from the Sensorium to the pavilion of stone, neither of us talking, the sound of his cane unusually heavy. We stop short of the charred circle and listen to the rhythm of the threshers, the call of the Ecosystem's teeming life.

"You thought our vote callous," he says.

"It was my vote, too."

"It is our charge," he says gently. "It is the life we chose."

"The choice wasn't mine to make," I say, and I'm not so gentle.

"Would you choose a different life now?"

"I don't know any other," I say. What life would I choose, now that I've tasted the fever of my first hunt, borne the yoke of my first ballot?

Aaron knows my mood too well to pursue the discussion. "What did you think of the Chief Warden's advice?"

"I'm not ready to take an apprentice."

"That, I believe, was his point. There have been too few new Sensors of late. Five years is too wide a gap."

"No one's come forward."

"None has been welcome," he says with a frown.

"That too, I take it, was the Chief Warden's meaning. We have perhaps been overly selective in the choosing."

"The Sense chooses," I say, a refrain from the Conservator's speeches. "Not the village."

"Yet the Sense may be encouraged," Aaron says distantly, "when the need is great." He faces me, but his thoughts seem elsewhere. "Times are changing, Sarah. It may be that the ways of the past will serve us no longer. It may be that we must find another way."

I search his clouded eyes, hoping to recall him from this strange spell. The forest moans, the shapes of bloodbirds flickering red in a shaft of sunlight, and I'm gripped by a terrible longing. "I want to hunt," I say.

"We are well provisioned from yesterday," he says. "The hunt can wait."

"The village will need wood and water. Barnabas," I remind him, "was supposed to bring firewood."

Aaron's reverie is gone, his eyes narrowed on mine.

"For wood only, then," he says. "And I will send Samuel as well." He clutches my arm, and for the first time since childhood, I feel an urge to break free. "Listen to me, Sarah. This is no time for anger. The Ecosystem will be awake, and aware. Slay no living thing. Find only the dead wood it has shed from its mind, and return swiftly."

I realize he's afraid: afraid of it, afraid for me. I refuse to be afraid.

"Do I have your word?" he asks.

I've never lied to him, which must be why the lie I tell now works so well. "You have my word."

He releases me, and I return to my home to prepare. When I cast a final glance back at his figure, I am struck by how lone and gray he appears.

Whatever Nathan decides, the memorial for Barnabas will be a small affair: a fire in the night, a bowing of heads. When we lost Chief Sensor Malachi, Aaron's predecessor, five years ago, we burned his body. But then, we had a body to burn. When we lost Hanna that same year, we lit a fire that consumed only wood long dead.

I can't bring back Barnabas. I don't know where to look. But I'll bring back a body. And I will watch it burn.

I SLIP OUT of the village like a wisp of woodsmoke. Samuel leaves with me, a bladder slung over his shoulder to collect water, but we separate instantly. The earliest Sensors discovered that two hunting as a team were far more vulnerable than one hunting alone: though each could mask his own trace, each drew attention to the other. Samuel's here only on Aaron's insistence, and only as a precaution in case I get into trouble.

"Be careful," he says needlessly, and vanishes into the woods.

It's amazing how quickly the village follows suit. Within moments, the forest closes around me, and all trace of stone fades into the green. I stand amid trees many hundreds of years old, their branches trailing lattices of moss, their bark carved into antic shapes like deeply wrinkled faces. Ferns with spatulate leaves form beds between tree-trunks, while a few downed giants wave earth-brown roots to the sky. The sun casts shafts through the canopy, illuminating cobwebs and the silken nests of insects. The tart smell of decay penetrates my nostrils. Everywhere, I hear the voices of the Ecosystem: drone of cicatrix, caw of bloodbirds, cough of prowler monkeys, buzz of horrornets. There's no path here, no refuge. Move or stand still, there's no place to hide. A commoner would lose his way in a twinkling, his life soon thereafter.

But not me. I sprint through the trees, my bare feet light on the undergrowth of leaf mold and moss, my Sense of the Ecosystem a fine needle quivering in my flesh. Every breath that fills my lungs, every hair that lines my arms carries signals so rich and diverse I would have drowned in them years ago. The Ecosystem is treacherous yet luminous, and I float through it like a ghost, never pausing long enough to take solid shape in its mind.

Anger drives me, steadies me. I didn't know Barnabas well, but my heart burns at what the Ecosystem did to him, what it's still doing to him. I know no kill of mine can take his pain away. But I hope that in the death of one of its creatures, the Ecosystem will feel something of what it inflicts on him, what it inflicts on us all. What we've suffered and lost at its hands.

It's midday before I lock onto suitable prey. I'm deep in the Ecosystem by now, so far from the village I seem to have entered a realm with no boundaries, only luxuriant vegetation and spike-straight trees and the rising tide of cicatrix wings. I've ignored the few creatures I Sensed so far: tricky vultures too clumsy to test my skill, a pack of warhogs too massive to drag home unassisted. Now, through long shanks of sunlight that illuminate a clearing, I see a lone killdeer, a doe just short of its yearling weight, with gangling legs and round forehead. It nibbles shrubs—poisonrose, histeria—that make its flesh deadly to humankind. But I'm not hunting for a meal, and I can afford to slay a creature it would down the entire village to eat.

The doe hasn't registered my presence. The mind of the Ecosystem dwells in all living things, enabling them to Sense us as we do them—but its mind is unfocused, spread too thinly to be alert everywhere and at all times. My mind, by contrast, is keen and sharp. If I'm wary, I should be able to spring my trap before the Ecosystem knows I'm here.

I circle the clearing, using the skills Aaron taught me: lowering my heartbeat and breathing, tightening my pores to mask my scent. A lifetime's worth of information streams from my prey, giving me its size, the toxic churn in its gut, the wobble in a hind leg gone partly lame. I'll have one chance to take it down, and if I fail, I risk rousing the Ecosystem's awareness. The strike will have to be swift, sure, and virtually bloodless. A perfect kill.

I ready my stone knife in my hand. My fingers fidget to find a grip.

Then the killdeer is bounding my way, unmindful that it's chosen the path of its hunter. As it leaps past, I plant the knife between its shoulder blades, one firm thrust and withdrawal, and it collapses, the channel from brain to limbs severed. I Sense the shriek of pain that races through the Ecosystem at this assault, but before it can gather my existence to its breast, I slit the killdeer's throat and watch the huge round eyes dull. Now there's nothing but a dead doe, and the one who killed it has slipped back into a blind spot in the Ecosystem's eye.

I hoist the carcass onto my shoulders. It's heavy, but I Sensed its weight beforehand and wouldn't have killed it if it was beyond me. Still, the return journey will be slow. Nighttime is distant, but there are things that come out at twilight I'd rather avoid. I can't delay.

I retrace my steps, the route visible to my Sense in the muted leaf-green of the forest. The still-warm body of the doe hangs around my neck, its head lolling on my chest, the acrid scent of its death enveloping me. Gore freckles my arms. The blood-encrusted mouth has fallen open, and I think once more of Barnabas, dying in the Ecosystem's watery grip, longing to duck his head and breathe deeply if only the reeds that bind him would permit it. It strikes me that while the Ecosystem can kill us as slowly as it pleases, we're forced to kill its creatures quickly to escape its notice. But I have years to kill. Years to make it suffer, one death at a time.

I'm halfway back when I Sense danger.

Immediate danger, not the generalized threat one always Senses in the Ecosystem. There's a whisper in the air, a foul taste on my tongue. I let the carcass flop to the ground, where it lies with bloody neck exposed and limbs splayed. Raising my hands, I flex my fingers in the wind, but the Sensory filaments that flow down my arms are too diffuse to judge properly. I close my eyes and finger the strands, reel them in as gently as I can, so gently that whatever lies on the other end can't guess my intention. The thing comes closer, clearer. At last, the Sense of it looms before me.

My eyes fly open and, kill forgotten, I dash back into the forest. I move quickly but warily, fighting a rising tide of panic. Fear will make me visible to the Ecosystem, and I have to remain unseen. I have to reach the thing it showed me, have to arrive ready to fight.

An instinct finer than sight or touch enables me to trace the path. It leads me to the spot I Sensed from leagues away, the thing I Sensed waiting. Still, when I pull up at the base of the sickenmore tree and squint into its midmost branches, I shudder at the sight of the abomination that rests there.

Even in sleep, it appalls me. The arachnard lies heavily on a stout branch, the flesh of its abdomen hanging in thick folds. One of its eight muscular legs dangles below; the others curl beneath its torpid body. Its color is between gray and purple, like meat left to spoil. A ridge of horns splits its broad, scaled face. From beak to backplate, the reptile's eight feet at least. Though it makes no sound I can hear, the Sense of its hunger roars in my ears.

And it's spun a web of its own. Thick lengths of sticky rope hang from the sickenmore's branches, careless loops nothing like a true arachnid's meticulous pattern. This creature relies on brute strength rather than stealth to capture its prey. The evidence of its success lies tangled in the web's serpentine coils.

Samuel, his head fallen, his arms spread as if caught in a desperate leap to the ground,

I CLIMB.

I don't think. If I did, I wouldn't find myself grabbing the lowest branches of the sickenmore tree, swinging myself to the next level. I would know that there are a hundred ways the Ecosystem can kill me once my feet leave the ground: an animate branch could skewer my chest, a spray of venom could paralyze my limbs, a signal to the sleeping arachnard could wake the monster to claim its second victim. If I touch any of the web's tripwires, I'll be as helpless as a fly. Staying in place is sure doom in the Ecosystem. Climbing a tree is suicide.

Yet I climb. My hands grip rough branches, my feet scramble for support. Unlike the man I'm trying to rescue, I have no practice at tree-climbing, and I'm no good at it. The only thing that might save me is calm, caution, my ability to Sense my surroundings and evade the Ecosystem's snares. But if I had any Sense, I wouldn't be doing this at all.

I reach the branch below Samuel's suspended body. The deep purple mark of the arachnard's sting smears his chest, the poison radiating like a network of veins. The strain on his arms is terrible. If I could free him from the strands that hold him, if I could support his weight as I descend the tree….

His eyes stare into mine.

I jerk back, almost lose my grip. Samuel's eyes are brown; I've always known that. But from this close, I notice the green flecks that catch the light within their depths. They're green like the moss that cloaks the trees, the slime that coats the pools. Their green echoes the green of the forest that kills him.

"Go," his lips form the word.

I shake my head, reach for the webs around his wrists. His eyes blaze.

"Too late," he says.

A visceral tug in the web tells me the arachnard has woken. Samuel's eyes pinion me, while at the same time they will me to flee.

"The Conservator," he says. "Warn…."

"The Conservator?" I repeat, uncomprehending. Then I realize what he means. He's leaving it to me to report the details of his final hunt.

"No," I say. "You'll tell him yourself. I'll free you. I'll…." My hands tug on the strands of the web, succeed only in gumming my palms. If I try much longer, I'll be snared too.

"Go," Samuel says again, his head drooping to his chest. Though I shake my head once more, I'm already backing down the tree, just as the arachnard swings its heavy bulk to the branch above us.

Its legs flail at me, fire clashing the back of my hand. Blood spatters my face, and in a nightmare of red I see the claw impale Samuel's body, watch his shoulders split as he jerks like a doll of grass and twig. The sickenmore has come to life at last, the trunk trembling and groaning, the branches I try to grasp telescoping so quickly I fear they'll suck my hands inside the trunk. I push off with my feet and launch myself into the air, how far from the ground I don't know and can't Sense. I crash backward through vines and branches, meet the earth in a collision that jars my skull. In my confusion, I discover that I'm soaked to the skin, realize I landed on Samuel's discarded water bladder. Maybe it broke my fall. But I don't allow the momentary daze to slow my escape. I spring to my feet and kick free of the roots that burst from beneath the soil in their effort to ensnare me.

I run. I look back only once. The arachnard's legs work busily, spinning its web around something I can no longer see.

The Ecosystem churns around me. Fully awake now, fully conscious, incensed. It's connected me to the dead killdeer, my hands on the web tree, my feet on the sward last morning and night. My tattered Sense is barely enough to dodge the vines that snap out from the branches overhead, the roots that unfurl from the ground. Sinkholes open at my feet, and it's only luck that enables me to stumble past. I hear the call of bloodbirds wheeling above the trees, scream as they divebomb my face. Serrated beaks peck through wet tangled hair to find my ears and scalp, the blood they draw sending them into an even greater frenzy of wings and talons and teeth. I fall, claw at the ground, stumble to my feet, fall again. Through a fog of fear, I realize that the Ecosystem's shifting subtleties have erased my trail, the woods closing around me. I can no longer Sense what pursues me, no longer Sense anything.

But I can feel the strong arms that lift me, the sharp breaths that accompany the runner's strides. I'm hot and wet and bruised, crushed against the bosom of the one who holds me, and for a moment, I think I'm in a dream. Then darkness wraps me, and I dream no more.

I WAKE FROM anger to anger. The anger of the Ecosystem I've always known. Aaron's anger is new.

"You defied me, child," he says, his voice quavering. "You lied to me, and defied me. And now another of our number is taken."

I can't argue with him. Samuel's eyes won't let me.

"You are banned from the hunt," Aaron says coldly, and Esther, her uniform wet from carrying me, nods in witness. "The council will meet to decide your fate."

He says no more, only grips Esther's arm and stands. The tap of his staff turns faint then dies.

Salt burns my cheeks where the bloodbirds bit me.

IN THREE DAYS, I'm recovered enough to leave Esther's house. I walk with a limp. Long cuts crisscross my legs, and my back is stiff and sore from my fall. An ugly purple welt marks my right hand, while the fingers of my left are so swollen, I can't bend them at all. Still I might be counted lucky, if being alive is luck.

I'm to meet with Chief Warden Daniel. Esther told me. Aaron won't speak to me.

The sun burns diamond-bright in a lapis sky. The Chief Warden's home is no larger or more sumptuous than any other, no better provisioned than the bare hovel I just left. Its sole distinction is that it sits alone on the western edge of the village, uncrowded by other structures. From the back of Daniel's hut, there are fewer trees to block the sunlight or attract the bloodbirds, a broader expanse of open green beyond the circle of stone. I've heard that Daniel can be seen from time to time resting on the stone bench outside his hut's lone window, gazing across the sward's lush vista to the forest giants beyond.

Today, though, he waits for me at the entrance to his home. I've been given no clue what to expect from this meeting, Esther having told me only, and brusquely, that

I was to speak the truth. The Sensorship hasn't convened to discuss my punishment, and whether today's interview with Daniel is a trial or a debriefing, I have no notion. Whether I'll leave his home bearing the kill pouch that signifies a title I've held for only five days—three of them spent on bedrest—I don't know either.

He smiles when he sees me. Smiles and, wearing the comfortable furs that tell me he's off-duty, ushers me through his doorway. I enter a room furnished with the usual appliances: bed, table, chair, hearth, firewell centered in the circular floor. Daniel's wife is long dead, having left him childless. When he dies or steps down, his home will become another's. We build little new, our energies focused on preserving what we have.

Daniel offers me a drink in a fired earthenware cup. The water's been kept cool in a hamper of stone dug below floor level, and my Sense tells me it's clean of infection. As I clumsily balance the cup between stiff left hand and tender right, it occurs to me that the surviving Sensors have been out during my convalescence, collecting the wood and water Samuel and I were to have brought home. My eyes sting as I raise the cup to my lips.

"It's good to see you back on your feet," Daniel says delicately, but his words call out the sob I've been holding inside for three long days.

He reaches for the cup, takes it without touching my fingers. My hands fly to my face, and my back shakes with an anguish I can't contain. I'm dimly conscious of Daniel's ineffectual attempts to comfort me, his hands jockeying the air around my shoulders. His efforts only remind me that I can now add shame and weakness to my growing list of faults.

Daniel waits for me to settle. If Aaron had shown any glimmer of the Chief Warden's sympathy, this scene would have been his to bear. I suppose I can be thankful it wasn't.

"I'm sorry," I say, wiping my cheeks. I wonder if my skin will ever feel smooth again.

"Think nothing of it," he says. "You have survived unspeakable horrors."

His kindly tone is a torment, but I'm determined not to cry again. "May I ask why you wished to see me?"

"No reason, really," he says. "Other than to assure myself you were on the mend. But now that you're here, perhaps you'll indulge me in a little secret of mine."

My heart skips at the word *secret*. But there's nothing inappropriate in his mild expression, nothing to knot my stomach or raise the hairs on my neck. I watch as he reaches inside his fur-trimmed vest, withdraws something too small to see. His fingers unfold, and I stare at the slim brown thing that rests on his palm.

It's a seed.

My skin tingles as the Sense of it races up my arm. I know what this thing is. If planted and fed, it'll sprout a heavy stalk, taller than me at full growth, bearing a single blossom of bright yellow petals that open to the sun. Stunflowers, we call them, carnivorous plants whose aroma can fell a bird in midflight and drop it into the waiting flower's mouth. I watch it warily, this germ of life in the Chief Warden's hand. Dormant now, but with the potential to grow.

Daniel smiles through my silence. "It's safe," he says. "The healers assure me."

"The healers." We have one or two such about the village. They're of little use when a commoner sickens, though they do array the bodies prettily for the burning.

"Your own Sense, then," Daniel says. "It must tell you a single seed poses no threat."

My Sense tells me no such thing. I recall Nathan's tales of the early years, tales of living plants brought home from the forest to be cultivated in clay pots and window boxes. We've heard what those plants did to the people who grew them.

"All life is subsumed in the Ecosystem," I say, my eyes glued to the seed case, which reminds me of a beetle with folded wings. "All life, once awoken, answers to its will."

"All life," he says, "except ours?"

"We're different," I mutter. "Higher. It's why the Ecosystem hates us."

"Yet the Sense suggests our affinity with it, does it not? Our affinity, or even our kinship?"

I've heard this argument before. Heard it, in fact, from Nathan, who warned the apprentices we might encounter it among the commoners. It's easily refuted. If we're truly one with the Ecosystem, why are so few of us gifted with the Sense? If we're its children, why does it reserve its anger for us alone? I don't need the past days' heartbreak to give me my answer. Allow the

Chief Warden's seed to grow, and it will become a terror to us all.

Before I can utter any of this, Daniel passes his right hand over his left, and the seed vanishes. I look up at him, as startled as a child at a wizard's trick, but he only smiles.

"I've kept this seed about me for years," he says. "As a reminder of a better time that was, a promise of a better time to come. I've dreamed of a day I might plant it without fear, tend it with delight. Or if not me, then one whom I've known."

"You don't know me," I say.

"Perhaps not," he says. "But I do know this, Sarah: you are not bound to the darkness. You of all people should know that a new life is possible."

He holds out a hand, not to touch me, merely to bid me rise. On the threshold of his cottage, he halts me with a look.

"The circle of Sensors will decide what punishment to mete out for your transgression," he says. "I have no voice in the matter. All I would ask, and this not as Chief Warden but as a neighbor and a friend, is that you bear your sentence with fortitude. If a new day is coming, we will have need of you, Sarah. Your strength, yes—and your hope as well."

With that, he leaves me. I watch as he descends the pavement behind his cottage, the trees of the Ecosystem towering above his puny figure. A vision sharper than eyesight catches a glint of blood-red wings against pale blue sky, and I wish I could find it within me to imagine the future he sees. But I can't.

The Chief Warden doesn't know me. Hope died in my heart a long time ago.

I WAS NOT quite three when the Sense first showed itself in me. I have no memory of that night, but Aaron has told me the tale: how, standing on the stone circle to which I'd wandered from the funeral pyre, I reached out to the invisible forest and grew silent, the baffled tears I'd shed drying on my cheeks. The wind blew my curls, the night sounds called my steps forward. He saw me shiver as the life of the wild flowed through me. And when I turned to him, he says it was as if the one I'd so newly lost shone in my eyes, her spirit a flickering flame in their tranquil depths.

He took me then, to breathe the flame into fullness.

But even after that night, it was months before my formal training began, before the Sensorship approved his application to take me on as his new apprentice. Months of observation and trial to make absolutely certain I was the one.

It has to be this way. The true Sense runs in few of us, and the risks of misidentification are great. Time wasted on an unworthy candidate is time lost to a legitimate Sensor who might have been. Claiming a child for the order has never been a guessing-game, a blind throw in the dark.

Never, that is, until now. A new day has indeed come, but it's nothing like Daniel promised. While I was sleeping off the attack in the woods, the Sensorship has voted to scour the village for replacements. The death of Samuel settled it, only five Sensors, subtracting me and Aaron, being left for the hunt. Against Nathan's objection, we've opened our ranks to unproven recruits, regardless of age or prior scrutiny. Most will fail, of course. All may fail. But for the indefinite future, a formerly elite corps will accept all comers: thrill-seekers, masochists, and just plain fools. And I, Sarah, will lead them.

On the day of the memorial for Samuel and Barnabas, Aaron seeks me out to report the council's judgment. My defiance, he tells me, has cost me my freedom: I'm forbidden to hunt until I've won back the Sensorship's trust. When that may be, what that will take, he refuses to say. In the meantime, I'm to remain in his company and participate in the training of the new recruits.

The harshness of his sentence is like a slap from those gentle hands. I consider telling him about Daniel's seed, but shame stops my tongue. Though I know my punishment could have been worse—exile from the order being the fear that kept me up nights—only the reminder that it was my reckless anger that drew the Ecosystem to Samuel prevents me from railing against my fate. That, and Aaron's formal tone as he removes the kill pouch from my belt.

"You will report to the Sensorium tomorrow at day-break," he orders me. His hands, leathered with age, tremble as they undo the laces that hold the pouch to my side. "There we will begin the lessons."

My lessons, I think. Lessons in humiliation and mortification.

But I do as I'm told. The following day, dressed in the hunting garment I might never need again, I make my limping way to the Sensorium.

I could weep. The council chamber is full to over-flowing, but only because it's been converted to a nurs-ery. Jarrod and Rachel are present, as much prisoners as I am. As for the rest, I can't help thinking a random sweep of the village couldn't have yielded a less hope-ful crop. The youngest of those who answered the sum-mons dance across the benches as if the Sensorium is a playground. I wonder why their parents let them come, unless it was to get the friskiest of the bunch out of the house for a day or two. Among the older children, I spy hunchbacks and bowlegs, spastic runners always at the rear of the race and clumsy throwers always on the verge of catastrophic backfires. Teens have arrived, twin threshers named Caleb and Noah, along with the loner I noticed at my investiture. Her name, she mumbles as I make the rounds, is Miriam. At fourteen, the twins are tall and muscled, at home in their bodies. In stark contrast, Miriam holds herself awkwardly, shoulders rounded and stick arms wrapped across her chest. Plus, she's only a year younger than I am, and if she possessed any smidgeon of the Sense, it would've shown itself by now.

But here she is. Here they all are. And Aaron wastes no time welcoming them to the trials.

"I greet you," he begins, his voice unnaturally loud, "at the seat of the Sensorship. It cheers me to see that so many have come. Our need is great, and today's response speaks highly of your commitment to the village."

The thumb-suckers in the crowd exhibit no sign of commitment or even comprehension, but a few of the older enlistees nod and square their shoulders. Miriam displays her appreciation for the compliment by curling into an even tighter ball, her head nearly buried in her lap.

"The Sense," Aaron continues, "we have always understood as a gift freely given from birth. We have never sought to inquire whence it came, nor to predict its coming. But we have always known that when it comes, it must be nurtured. We hope, in calling you here, we have given some among you the opportunity to show us a clue we may have missed, a stirring you may have felt in yourself." Giggles from a pre-teen girl set my teeth on edge, but Aaron smiles almost sheepishly and goes on. "Has any of you felt this stirring of which I speak?"

Caleb and Noah's hands shoot instantly into the air, followed by three or four more tentative responses. Some of the littlest ones have their hands up as well, probably because they think they're supposed to. Miriam's fingers crouch by her cheek like a closed chrysalis.

"Good," Aaron says. "Today we will test to see if these hopeful signs be true."

He lays his walking-stick deliberately on the bench beside me, unclasps his cloak. The room has fallen silent, everyone from youngest to oldest watching him intently. It strikes me that these novices can have no idea what Aaron intends to do; for all they know, the test may involve feeding them to a flock of bloodbirds. To me, though, he seems to be stalling, as uncertain as I am where to start. He's laid his cloak beside his staff and is preparing to speak again when a voice comes from the rear of the room.

It's Miriam.

"How," she whispers, then clears her throat and goes on, "how will we know?" Despite the throat-clearing, her voice remains muffled, as if she's attempting to swallow her tongue.

"Ah," Aaron says, a grateful smile inching over his face. "That is a question perhaps best left to our newest Sensor. Sarah?"

I rise, wishing he'd prepared me for this. I take some heart in the fact that he refers to me as a Sensor, and not a fallen one. But I've never been asked to share the mystery of my Sense with anyone but my master, and I resent having to divulge it to a roomful of commoners and children. I try, though, in hopes of recovering Aaron's goodwill, to recall my earliest inkling that I was gifted in ways few around me were.

"What do you think of the Ecosystem?" I ask Miriam, gruffly.

"What do I...?" she stammers, mouth agape.

"When you think of the Ecosystem," I clarify. "What first comes to mind?"

She shakes her head, purses her lips. She's not up to this. And neither am I. I turn to Aaron, spreading my hands. I'm about to say something I'll likely regret when Miriam calls out, "Wait."

I wait.

"I think of hunger," she says.

"Hunger."

"Or food," she tries. "Being fed."

I move around the bench until I stand on the floor before her. "Are you fed?" I ask.

Miriam looks terrified. "The Sensors bring us—"

"That's not what I asked. Are *you* fed?"

She tries to look at me, fails. I wonder how much of the story of Samuel has reached the villagers, and in what form. Have I become monstrous in their eyes? Then Miriam's face unfolds like a bud come to life, and her lips set as she meets my gaze.

"I am fed," she says. "Yet still I hunger."

"Then," I say softly, as if I'm speaking to her alone, "there could be some whisper of the Sense about you."

I return to my seat, surprised to find my face warm. The room has gone even quieter than before. Caleb and Noah wear scowls of protest.

"There are many forms the Sense may take," Aaron breaks the silence, and the twins regain their air of easy superiority. "Each of you must find a way to tap it, if it lies within you. Yet there are tests we can conduct to determine its presence. These we will begin today."

At a signal from him, Jarrod and Rachel rise and shepherd the volunteers from the council-house. This requires some doing, as the young ones have discovered a new game, walking the circle of each bench then skipping to the next level and reversing course. Aaron remains seated on the bench I occupy, but at a distance from me, around the curve of the meeting-house floor. His hands clutch his staff, his breath appears labored. From standing? From speaking? Or from hearing what I said? I rise to exit the room when his voice stops me.

"You will run the tests." He speaks not to me but to the empty space before him. I watch his wrinkled lips move behind the tangle of shoulder-length hair. "You know what to do."

"And you, Master?"

"I will remain here," he sighs. "Call if you have need of me."

I bow to him as stiffly as if we've never met. I've reached the door when he calls out, "And, Sarah...."

"Yes, Master?"

He half-turns, a glint of his old humor visible in his eyes. "Try not to scare them all away on the first day."

The rush of relief nearly brings me to my knees. "I'll try, Master."

Only my fear of making a fool of myself prevents me from saying more. My steps are buoyant as I leave him, huddled over his cane in the empty room.

MIRIAM HAS THE Sense.

I'm sure of it, as sure as I can be after a week of the trials. You'd never know it to look at her, all angles and elbows like a fledgling tricky vulture, with a nest of ill-kempt hair perched on her oversize head. She hunches, avoids eye contact, tugs at her skirt as if to disguise her gawky limbs. Every time I see her fidgeting across the pavestones, I don't know whether to laugh or cry.

And yet she's gifted. Undeniably gifted. Almost freakishly gifted, considering she's sixteen and has zero training. While the other volunteers fumble through the preliminary tests, relying on mere chance and guesswork, she grows eerily calm, lifting her chin to the forest, her cheeks and brow softening to reflect the immensity before her. I know that look. I've seen it on the faces of all the Sensors who've preceded me, seen it on Aaron's face, marred though it is by time. More, I've felt it in my own face: the opening, the entering, the becoming. It's unconscious for me, as it is for all of us. I respond to the Ecosystem not because I will it, not even because I want it, but because a Sense deeper than willing or wanting draws it from me.

As it does from her. She stands on the pavestones by the charred circle, her gangly body almost graceful in its stillness. I approach her in this trance state, ask her to identify what hidden life drifts behind the darkling trees. She straightens, seems to gain not only height but years, and her voice thrums steady and deep, the voice of the Ecosystem itself. She doesn't guess. She knows.

"Bloodbird. Ghosthawk. Stabbing nettle. Fell-cat. Hellion. Cicatrix...." She rattles the names off, then looks at me, startled at herself. She didn't know she knew half these words until they spilled from her lips.

Though it's too early for a snare test, I spring it on her the third day of the trials. Leaving the others in the care of the inseparable Jarrod and Rachel, I roam the perimeter of the village with Miriam in tow, speaking to her of everyday things, her home and parents. She's by turns chatty and tongue-tied. I feign interest, hoping to distract her. I Sense the approach of a snare, a poisonrose vine, and steer our steps in its direction.

"And my little sister, Naomi, is six..." Miriam is saying.

Then she stops. "Oh," she says. Her body goes rigid, the reaction of one who's been stung. The vine lies concealed beneath the turf, but she's Sensed it. She's passed a test we normally wouldn't administer until months into the training.

"It spoke to me," she says later, when I ask her how she knew. "As if it was posing a question. And before I had time to think, it told me the answer."

I remember. The first weeks of my training, when

the voice of the Ecosystem spoke constantly in my ear, telling me all the things I'd never known, all the things I'd always known. I ask her when she first remembers Sensing the Ecosystem's will.

"When I was four," she says without hesitation. "I watched a leaf fall from one of the giant ache trees. It spiraled to the ground, and I had the strangest feeling that I was spiraling down with it. As if a part of me had fallen when it did."

"And you told no one?"

A squall of blinking chases the dreaminess from her eyes. "My mother told me not to. She said I'd be forced to become one of the…one of you."

"No one's forced," I say, only half-believing. "But why now?"

"The need was great," she says lamely.

"The need's always great," I press. "Why now?"

That's one thing I like about Miriam, or about me when I'm with her. I'm under no obligation to be polite.

"*My* need was great," she says. "I watch the sunlight draping the treetops, and my heart yearns within me. The sounds of the forest call to me at night, and if I don't answer, I feel—"

"You don't feel," I say. "You Sense."

She nods solemnly, even sadly.

"You know you might die," I point out.

"I know I might live," she answers. And that's all there is to say.

I report Miriam's words to Aaron, who smiles. It's

only now that his smile has returned that I realize how lost I felt when it was shuttered inside.

"I will discuss this with the Sensorship," he says. "They will be pleased that our experiment has yielded at least one success. What hid her from us, I wonder?"

"Her family," I respond. "They kept her cloistered, fearing what she might become."

"But the girl herself has no doubts?"

"None," I affirm. "It seems the open search has given her the excuse she needed."

"Then we can be thankful to the Chief Warden for suggesting it," Aaron says. "Though privately, I had hoped for more."

I know what he means. By week's end, the original fifteen volunteers have dwindled to three: Miriam and two children, Rebecca and Esau, ages seven and nine. The pair in whom Aaron placed highest hopes, Caleb and Noah, have failed miserably. Truth be told, I doubted them from the start: their enthusiasm was so great, it seemed unlikely they'd have been missed as children. The first tests confirmed my suspicions. They're keen-eyed and sharp-eared, true: they can spot a bloodbird from twenty rods away, hear its caw long before it rises above the tree line. But ask them to tell you how recently it feasted (and on what), to calculate its flight path, to gauge its intention to strike, and they might as well be comatose. Within two days, their ineptitude has become obvious to everyone including themselves, and they've slunk away, their faces clamped in shame and disgust.

The results of Rebecca and Esau's tests are less conclusive. Both can close their eyes and picture a random element emerging from the Ecosystem: a tree-leaping quetzal, a rare hydra bird with brightly plumed decoy head to lure prey near its true head's snapping jaws. But both children are easily distracted, as children possessing the true Sense would never be. I have somewhat better confidence in Rebecca, who's younger and more finely attuned than Esau. But my prize pupil remains Miriam.

"She distinguished a sharkbug from a stinkbug at thirty paces," I tell Aaron. "And that while the creature was in flight."

"How did she know?"

"She Sensed its appetite."

Aaron mulls this over, nodding.

"And her Sensitivity continues to grow," I add. "Now that she's no longer holding back, it increases by the day. She'll be ready for more complex tests soon."

"I would never have thought it," Aaron says, smiling.

"I admit she's a bit of a wreck...."

"Not her," he says. "You."

My heart skips a beat. Since the death of Samuel, I've startled quickly at the slightest sign of Aaron's displeasure.

"Do not fear, child," he says. "I merely meant I had not known you would find such joy among the young."

I open my mouth to protest, *Miriam's not so young*, but stop when I realize what he's saying. I'm more surprised than I was at Miriam's unexpected gift—surprised, and disappointed. Even after all we've been through lately, I believed Aaron knew me better than that.

He thinks I like to teach.

I consider telling him the truth. Teaching pales beside the hunt. It's mind-work, not Sense-work: confined, not free. It requires patience I don't possess to keep quiet while a novice stutters out something I've Sensed at once. What's more, watching Miriam open herself to the Ecosystem reminds me how much I long to return to the field, how precarious the chances are that I will. Teaching is my penance, not my pride.

But I don't tell Aaron that, and his next words show me the wisdom of holding my tongue. "Perhaps," he says, "it is you who should inform the Sensorship of these promising developments."

"Master?"

"You have observed the girl, and know her talents best," he says. "The council will be pleased to have you join us. We have missed you at our gatherings."

"If my words may be of use to the council," I say, bowing slightly to hide the smile spreading across my face.

Aaron holds out a hand for me to help him rise. "At first light tomorrow, then."

He says nothing more, only pats my arm before hobbling away. I watch him go, my heart thumping so wildly it's a mercy I'm not in the Ecosystem at this moment.

That night, I lie in my bed of stone, mind racing, I

see myself standing before the Sensorship, reformed but unbowed. I'll report on Miriam and the children, prove I'm capable and contrite. Trustworthy. I rise to pace my three-paces-wide room, gaze out the window at a stone vista silvered by moonlight. I yearn to touch the far greater world that lies beyond, but while the night lasts, I can't.

Tomorrow, I tell myself. Tomorrow is the day I return. The day I win back everything I've lost.

I DUCK INVOLUNTARILY as I enter the Sensorium. It's been just over a week since my first fatal assembly, even less since I was banished from their ranks. It's been years, though, since I first spoke to the circle of Sensors, and that under circumstances little better than this. I keep my eyes lowered and my hands in my lap until I'm called on to speak.

At Aaron's behest, I take the central circle. My elders, I struggle to convince myself, regard me probingly but not maliciously. My gaze lingers on Esther, who saved me at the cost of losing her former apprentice, Samuel. If the crescents beneath her eyes are darker than a week before, she must know, she *must* know, that it was the Ecosystem, not I, that cut them so deep.

I deliver my report, and they listen in silence. Miriam I praise more than the children, but not, I think, unduly. I try to highlight my role in replenishing the Sensorship without calling attention to the fact that I was the one who depleted it. Nathan glares, but the others seem amenable to my version of events. I can only hope it's so.

"I humbly invite your questions," I conclude, bowing deeply.

Into the formal silence that follows, Nathan speaks. "The girl Miriam," he says. "You are sure of her?"

"That she possesses the Sense," I say, "I'm sure."

"And that she will complete the training?"

I look to Aaron, but his gaze is elsewhere. "My charge, as I understood it," I say, "was to select the most promising candidates in as short a time as possible. This I have done."

"Many have begun the training," Nathan presses, "only to falter along the way."

"She's gifted, and her intentions serious," I say. "If she falters, it will not be for lack of dedication."

That brings out a snort from my questioner. "And how long before she is ready for the hunt?"

I'm taken aback by this turn. I swallow, cast about for words. None are forthcoming.

"I warned you about this, Aaron," Nathan says. "You thought us so reduced as to require novices to prepare novices. But the way of the Sensors has never called us to place our trust in such"—he waves a hand at me—"doubtful experiments."

Aaron clears his throat in the ensuing silence, a cavernous silence from which I fear all possibility has fled. "Sarah is one of us," he says.

"As was Barnabas," Nathan answers. "And Samuel."

I look everywhere for help, but there's none to be found.

"I will train the girl," Esther says. Though I should

feel grateful, I can't help interpreting this as another rebuke. "What of the children?"

All eyes turn to Nathan, but he meets the unspoken request with a fixed stare.

"I will train the boy," Ezra says, "if indeed he can be trained."

"And I the girl-child," says Judah. "If the council approves."

I know these moves make sense. Of the remaining Sensors, only Adam cannot take on any new responsibilities, as he has volunteered to train Samuel's former apprentice, Rachel, in addition to his own, Jarrod. But Nathan's refusal to take a new apprentice can't be reconciled, unless he's too furious with me to fulfill what's expected of him. *I didn't ask for this charge*, I say to myself, willing them to believe.

"Thank you, Sarah," Aaron says from behind me, and I bow mechanically to the room. "I would ask you to withdraw while the senior Sensors discuss this matter."

I do, noting the term: *senior Sensors*. I've never heard him say that before, though I've thought it many times myself.

The morning breathes an omen of thunderstorm: air sweltering, sky greenish with cloud. Fingers of wind rustle the canopy, too high to touch my skin. I close my eyes and let my Sense take over. It's as sure as ever, untroubled by the turmoil in my mind. *Each life unites with all others*, I hear Aaron's voice speaking to me from a distant past. *To the common eye a chaos of random events, to the one who owns the Sense an intricate, seamless tapestry, ever changing, ever new. And never beyond one's grasp.* Half his words were foreign to me then, but I harbored in the stillness of my soul the rhythm of it, the order. The Sense.

And now here is Aaron, his staff sliding across stone with a sound like the coming of rain: *hush, shush, hush.* I can't tell from his stooped posture what news he brings. His eyes lift to my face, and I set my jaw to prevent the tremor from showing through.

"This is not permanent," he says, as convincingly as he can. "It is merely another delay. The council felt, for your sake, that further time was needed for the wounds to mend."

He doesn't say the vote was unanimous. But it always is.

"Esther, Judah, and Ezra will require your assistance in the training of the new ones," he goes on. "With our numbers so low, all will be preoccupied with the hunt. I foresee that Miriam and the children will be yours for as long as you wish to have them."

I nod, numb.

"It is an honorable charge, Sarah," he says. "The training of the young. It is what keeps our order alive." Then, with a gentleness I can hardly bear: "It is what gave me my two Sarahs. It is what gave me this."

His long, bony fingers unfold. In their grip, I see the thing I should have received more than a week ago, the thing he gave to her and was to have given to me: a diamond-shaped shard of polished tooth, its thickness twice that of his nail, its minute surface carved with a design of nested diamonds dyed in blue like a branching of veins. It has passed through more hands than his, more than hers, more than I can count. It was to be mine on the day I became a Sensor. It is mine now, on the day I see that dream slip away.

"You never speak her name," I say.

"Not true," he says as he closes my hand around the token. "I speak it every day to you."

I study the charm, feel its cool hard shape like an imprint on my flesh. I grip it in my palm and bring it to my lips. "It passes from master to apprentice," I say, my throat tightening. "There won't be anyone to receive it."

"If that is how it is meant to be," he says, "then let it end here. With Sarah, the brave and strong."

Sarah, the brave and strong. Sarah, the Sensor. Sarah, who wanted only to stand in the lost one's place, to follow her fading spirit through the forest.

I bow my head and hear him pronounce the words of the investiture, but they have lost all meaning.

A NEW AND endless penance stretches before me. I meet it because I must, not because I have any hope of release. Each night, I dream the edict has been lifted, my former master greeting me at my doorway with knife and kill pouch. Each morning, I wake bereaved, and return to my thankless work.

I rise at dawn, meet Miriam and the children on the village terrace, return them to their masters' homes before nightfall. In the day's black gloaming, I walk to the shoreline of the stone island and halt within inches of the charred circle, my legs straining to take another step, my toes curling for the feel of grabgrass and living earth. From my lonely vigil at the pavilion's edge, I Sense the life that blooms in the Ecosystem's dark belly, hear it calling to me. But I can no longer answer, and so I stand like stone until the night falls around me.

Days pass. The Conservator taught of a time, long ago, when high summer fell to something called winter, months of bare boughs and water you could walk on. But that season comes no more. The heat of each day never lessens; leaves fall only to bud again. With nothing but time before me, I develop a routine: drills in the morning, a quick break for lunch, practice in the heat of the westering sun before we end for the day. Occasionally, I'll ask the children a question to keep them occupied, but my focus is Miriam. I describe her progress to Aaron, who nods distractedly. Even without his approval, I know it's her I'm meant to cultivate. She's the one I'm training to join the others in the field. The one I'm training to replace me.

I can't prevent this from happening. If I refuse to work with her, one of the other Sensors will, and I'll have forfeited my last connection to the Sensorship, losing in the process what little contact I have with Aaron. Maybe, if I'm successful with my first pupil, I'll be kept on in this halfway position: not a Sensor, but not a commoner either. I might become a permanent trainer. If so, I can try to make my students what I would have been. What Aaron tried to make me.

But it's hard. Not only to accept my drastically reduced role, but to shape Miriam. She's all bones and sharp edges, like shards of pottery poorly stuck together. She frightens easily, and when my impulse turns to anger, she shrinks. How to sculpt her ungainly body for the hunt is a puzzle I worry I can't solve. I'm convinced I have to toughen her, but to do so, it seems I have to coddle her. When I think of this brittle girl taking my place, the hurt grows so great I have to walk away. But there's nowhere to go, and so I always return, and the lessons resume.

Our first month is spent measuring her Sense, gauging its strengths and weaknesses. Every Sensor has bad habits, and these can't be allowed to calcify. For me, the issue was airborne objects, which I had a tendency to duck—a bad idea, since ducking is a fear response, and fear rouses the Ecosystem. Aaron cured me of my skittishness one very long week when he made me stand stock still while he rained small and (relatively) painless pebbles on my four-year-old head. With Miriam, the faults are harder to pinpoint, but by week three, I've concluded that she has difficulty Sensing lifeforms beneath a certain threshold of persistence. At first, I think it's a concentration problem, but it's more than that: it's as if traces of her family's censure speak to her, drowning out the phantom voice of the forest. I rack my brain for ways to heighten her Sensitivity, and finally I have an inspiration. I show up the next morning with a small clay pot, reach inside to work the greasy white stuff onto my fingertips. When I approach her, she shies away.

"What's that?" she says, eyes wide.

"It's tallow," I say. "For your ears."

"Ick," she says, flinching.

"*Ick*?" I repeat. "Sensors don't say *ick*."

"Sarah," she says, "I don't—"

"Hold still," I say, and she does, though I can feel her straining away from my sticky fingers. I'm careful not to touch her directly, and I'm confident that with the tallow as a medium between us, I'm not violating any taboos. Her ears fill quickly.

"I don't see how this is going to help," she says. "You

told me it's not really my ears that hear the Ecosystem anyway, so...."

She stops. Her face softens, her body stills. I send out my own Sense, detect the sharpening of hers. In deafness, she's found her inner ear.

"You see?" I say.

She lip-reads, nods. Our day's lesson continues without distraction. I'm thankful it worked. I consider telling her to bind her unmanageable hair to stop it from getting stuck in her ears, but I'm not up to that struggle.

By week six, a more serious issue arises: her inability to channel the chaos of Sensations that bombard her. At any moment, an infinity of life-signals strikes the novice's Sense: wings and heartbeats, roots drawing water, insects tunneling beneath bark, scent-trails plumbing the forest for mates or victims. All of them distinct, all of them twined, but not all of them equally necessary to the Sensor's attention. Before we tackled Miriam's Sensitivity problem, those signals formed a mere background, a hum against which the occasional impression leaped out in stark relief. Now, she experiences everything in a frenzied rush, a buzzing or boiling that never stops. She's drowning in it. I remember those early days of constant jitters, flinching at the slightest provocation, falling into bed exhausted by the roar but unable to sleep while its echoes rocked me through the night. If she fails to master the Sensory input, she'll go mad.

"Easy," I say to her on the morning she stands at the pavilion's brink, her eyes squeezed shut, her fists clenched at her cheeks. I want her to focus on the flight of the bloodbirds, but she's gotten them hopelessly tangled with everything else. "Find the strand and unravel it. Run it out like a thread between your fingers. Feel its texture. What does it feel like?"

"Rough," she gasps. "Like it's pinching me. Piercing me."

"Smooth it out," I say, trying to match my voice to my words. "Float, don't squeeze. Run your fingertips lightly over the thread, like you'd run your fingers through your hair."

Bad comparison. A fell-cat's claws couldn't untangle that thicket of hers.

"It hurts," she whimpers. "Sarah, it hurts."

Rebecca and Esau watch helplessly, their eyes like saucers.

"You are in control," I say, though it's plain from her contorted face that she won't be for long. I reach out with my own Sense, detect the barbs digging into her palms. "Remember who you are. Master it. Don't let it take over."

"I'm…trying," she chokes.

"Not so hard," I say. "Smooth. Smooth."

Her breathing quickens.

I'm about to intervene, distract her; I'm even ready to lay hands on her to vent some of the pressure through my own Sense. But just when I think she's lost, her face relaxes, her brow unfolds. I tilt my head and Sense the steadier flow that bathes her body. The Ecosystem has settled, as it does when one finds one's place in it.

She opens her eyes. They're the one striking thing about her, so black they're practically purple. For the moment, they're clear of pain and fretfulness.

"Better," I say.

She smiles for the first time in the six weeks I've known her. I'm almost tempted to smile back.

"Take a rest," I tell her. "Then we'll try again."

"Why don't you let me try?" a male voice calls from the village behind us. At the sound of it, the serenity vanishes from Miriam's face, and her shoulders hunch as if she's about to receive a scolding. I turn, expecting to confront a father or uncle, but that's not who I see.

The teenage boy who approaches is taller than I am, shaggy-haired, and stripped to the waist in the manner of the thresher crews. He crosses the pavilion with an easy, loping stride. I know his face, but can't place his name. He missed my investiture, I'm pretty sure. I've seen him at the pavilion's edge, his long arms swinging a stone scythe with the same careless sweep I hear in his voice.

"I'm here for the tryouts," he says, planting his fists on his hips and regarding me with an impudent stare. The muscles of his flat stomach jump in a way I'm sure is supposed to be some kind of demonstration.

"The tryouts were weeks ago," I say.

"But they're obviously still going on," he says, aiming a grin at Miriam. She goggles back at him, her eyes larger and more timorous than a killdeer's.

"We're training," I say. "Or were."

"Right," he says. "The old Sensory-channeling

stunt. It works better at dawn, you know. When there's less life to deal with."

"And you learned this how?"

He shrugs. "Watching, listening. Peeking into your bag of tricks."

The smirk on his face is good-natured, but it's a smirk nonetheless.

"The Ecosystem," I say, "doesn't play tricks."

"You sure about that, Sarah?" he says, and sticks out his hand.

I recoil. On the rare occasion I've passed threshers in the lanes, they've given me the widest berth possible; strut as they may, they seem to know the rules. I wish I could slap his hand away, but that's exactly what I can't do.

"This is no place for you," I say.

His hand hangs in the air for a moment before dropping to his side, accompanied by another grin and shrug. "Sorry," he says, not sounding it. "What about my name? Am I allowed to tell you that?"

"We're training," I repeat. "Privately."

"Sorry," he says again. "Guess I picked a bad time."

He turns to go. The words on my tongue remain unspoken.

But then he stops and says over his shoulder, "The name's Isaac, by the way. See you around."

He tosses a salute at the children and saunters off. As he crosses the pavilion, I watch not him but Miriam, whose eyes linger on his retreating back, her lips trembling. I realize today's lesson in control is about to take a turn. And I can't say it makes me unhappy to break the news to her.

"If he tries to touch you," I say, "I'll feed him to the forest."

FOR THE NEXT several days, the morning lessons have no sooner begun than I discover our stalker lurking around the training site. He keeps his distance, watching coolly from the shadows of the stone houses. But he's no less disruptive there, for Miriam's mind takes flight the instant he arrives. I glare at him, and at her, but he only smiles and waves, she only fidgets and falls apart. Her blind spots return with a vengeance, snares as large as sickenmore trees escaping her notice. When I command her to focus, she stammers like a ninny. She complains no more of pain, but that's only because she's too distracted to attend to anything. How strange, I think, that a girl determined to become a Sensor can become such a scatterbrain in a boy's presence. He renders her speechless. More important, he renders her Senseless.

I consider resorting to Aaron, but it irks me that I can't handle this nuisance on my own. Lessons turn to lectures, of a kind I heard only once—and that when I was a child of three—before I heeded them.

"Would you be a Sensor?" I berate her.

She nods, but her concentration is elsewhere. The

strands of the Ecosystem she was meant to handle lie untouched.

"Then forget him," I say. "Forget all that the village holds: friends, family, lover." Her eyes nearly pop from her head. *That* she heard. "The Ecosystem will flay you alive if you set foot in it with divided mind."

Her gaze drifts. I'm getting nowhere.

"You have to make a choice, Miriam," I say. "Would you always go hungry?"

"I didn't know," she murmurs.

"Didn't know what?"

She stares at me mutely. I can't imagine who this boy is who holds such power over her, and I don't really care. All I know is that if I don't do something to break his hold, my quest to recover some of what I've lost will come to an abrupt and undignified end.

"You!" I bark at Isaac, who lounges on the stone, watching. "Get over here!"

He clambers to his feet and lopes toward us, bare-chested as always, cocky and self-absorbed. Maybe, coming within a stone's throw of the forest day by day without disaster befalling him, he's forgotten his place in the order of things. His skin will never prickle at the Sense of what lies beyond his prison of stone, and he'll know nothing save the Ecosystem's spoils, its terrors burned or boiled away. But I'll show him what true power is.

"Couldn't keep me away, could you?" Isaac says as he draws abreast of us. Miriam shies from him. For a girl in love, if that's what she is, she certainly acts like a dolt. Maybe all such girls do.

"We need your help with an exercise," I say. "Something we can't manage on our own."

"I was wondering when you'd ask." He does the thing with his stomach, muscles rolling like a wave, and I realize I'm going to enjoy this.

"Come with me," I say, and he follows, Miriam and the children trailing behind.

"Sensor stuff," he says to the little ones. "Watch and learn."

I'm *really* going to enjoy this.

We walk to the edge of the pavilion. The life of the forest booms beyond, but with Miriam in such a state, I'm the only one who can Sense it.

"Why do we need the Ecosystem?" I ask Isaac.

He shrugs. "It's the source of our food. Among other things."

"Yet it kills our people."

"I don't know about all that."

"It's killed two in the past weeks," I say. "Or didn't you notice?"

"Well," he says, "we've *lost* two Sensors, if that's what you mean. As for it actually *killing* them, that's something else." He's ready with a smile to meet the disbelief in my eyes. "What, is this some kind of test?"

"It is," I say. "Miriam, can you stand beside Isaac?"

A hobbled warhog would move more gracefully than this collection of tics and hiccups, but she does as I ask.

"Perfect," I say. "Now, Isaac, can you do something for me?"

"Sure thing," he says. "What do you need me to do?"

"This," I say, and step aside as the attack comes.

It comes from the cicatrix, the ones I Sensed swarming before I led these two into the insects' flight path. That's the thing with cicatrix: they don't attack Sensors. They're unique in that regard. But when our shield is down, they can do some very nasty things.

The leader of the swarm aims for Isaac, razor-sharp wings whining. Miriam shrieks and falls to the stone, but he must think there's something he's supposed to do, because he doesn't react until the leader's wings slice his cheek. When I first detected the swarm, I Sensed that they were merely passing through, buzzing the village on their way to their next meal in the trees. But now that there's blood on the table, the entire swarm wheels as one and streams toward Isaac's face.

He yelps, his swagger deteriorating into a windmill of spastic swipes as the cicatrix cloud him. They're in his hair, sinking the spurs at the end of their six segmented legs down to the roots. He tries to bat them away, but they cling to his hands, and he falls, his head a seething mass of olive-colored bugs. Their mandibles clutch his scalp in fifty different places, and they'll peel it clean if I let them.

I consider it. But I don't.

I step to the fallen boy's side, grip the swarm leader between thumb and forefinger, stroke its carapace with the index finger of my other hand. It calms, and I pluck it free. The others, leaderless, abandon their meal and fly off in as many directions as there are cicatrix. Their lazy drone vanishes into the trees.

Miriam and Isaac climb shakily to their feet. The roots of his hair seep bright red blood, but he'll live. The greater damage lies in his eyes, which are wide and teary and filled with a new thing: fear. He should consider it a favor that I taught it to him before he decided to raid his first bloodbird nest.

"This is a bug," I say, and hold the docile insect up for Miriam and Isaac to see. They flinch as if I'm about to hurl it in their faces. "You hear them every day, every night. They never stop singing. You know why?"

They're too rattled to respond, but I take their silence as a no.

"They're breeding," I say. "Eons ago, it used to be seasonal, but not any more. The males sing for mates, and the females lay their eggs, and the grubs gestate in the ground before climbing up the trees and mutating under their shells. Then the shells split and the newborn cicatrix crawl out to mate some more. It never stops. There are trillions of them. Trillions upon trillions. The only reason they don't take over the entire planet is that some things like to eat them almost as much as they like to eat us."

I open my fingers, and the cicatrix hovers indecisively at waist level. To my immense satisfaction, it divebombs Isaac's face once more before wandering off to reassemble its squadron in the forest.

"We're bugs to the Ecosystem," I say. "Tiny, edible bugs. So far as it's concerned, the only difference between us and the cicatrix is that we don't reproduce very fast. And some predators find them bitter. Nothing finds us bitter."

Miriam looks at me as if she's never seen me before.

"Make your choice," I say to her. "Be a Sensor. Or bring him back here tomorrow for the next swarm to find." When they say nothing, I snap: "Class dismissed."

And I leave them, the children tagging behind, the cicatrix song climbing steadily in the trees.

UNBELIEVABLY, ISAAC SHOWS up the next day. Not at the training site. At my home.

Such as it is. Sensors don't live in luxury; in fact, our dwellings are smaller than the norm, since they house no more than two people. They're just as bare, with bed, table, chair, firewell. They cluster on the eastern fringe of the village, at some remove from the commoners' dwellings. Mine belonged to Malachi, Aaron's predecessor as Chief Sensor, who died a natural death after many years in the field. My less than two months' residence in his hut have done nothing to erase the mustiness of his half century.

Isaac waits at the doorway when I exit. I startle, almost collide with him. He pulls a long grin.

"Payback," he says. "For that trick with the bugs."

If I dared touch him, I'd flatten him.

"Sorry," he says. He's had the decency to put on a vest, though its neck is deep enough to reveal the muscles of his stomach. "A strategy. Or—what do you call it?"

"A snare," I say. And I keep moving.

He tails along. "A snare," he muses, as if I invented the word. "You make it sound like the Ecosystem's *trying* to trap us."

"It is." If nothing else, this fool gives me insight into the commoner's mind. Who'd have thought, despite the Conservator's speeches, despite all the evidence around us, that anyone could fail to grasp such a basic truth? "When you're out with your threshing crew," I say, "you never wondered why a Sensor stands guard?"

Again, the grin: carefree, irreverent. "I know we have to be careful out there, but—"

"Careful doesn't begin to describe it," I say. "Every time you come near the village border, you're an inch from death. From the cicatrix, or worse."

"But they didn't touch you."

"I'm a Sensor, Isaac," I say. And think: *was.* "The cicatrix leave the village alone because of us. If we were to vanish, you'd be swarmed in a week."

"And we couldn't stop them?"

"Fire might work at first," I say. "But pretty soon you'd run out of fuel. And where would you go for more?"

He's silent for a long time, as if he's turning it over in his head: the village drowning in cicatrix, ten million bugs scuttling over every stone in the pavilion, blanketing every sleeper in their beds. It's a vision I've grown accustomed to, but apparently, it's never dawned on him.

"That stinks," he says at last.

I sniff at the understatement. "It is what it is."

"Doesn't seem like much of a life, though. Sitting around waiting to be bug chow."

"That's why you need the Sensorship," I say. "People who don't sit around waiting for it."

He scratches his head. It seems an innocent enough

gesture, but I can tell the scalp's bothering him. "What about farther out? Nothing but gobbling monster bugs everywhere?"

"I wouldn't know," I say. "There's a reason we don't go that far."

"Which is?"

"We'd be dead before we got there."

He's silent again, seemingly at a loss for a smart response. We turn into the lane that leads to the training site. He shuffle-steps to keep up with me.

"So," he says. "You're teaching Mimi to be like you?"

"Mimi?"

"Miriam," he says, and has the grace to look embarrassed. "That's what we used to call her when we were little."

An unfamiliar tingle, one that doesn't come from my Sense, tells me he wants me to pursue the topic. I resist, keep my voice flat and matter-of-fact. "I trained for fourteen years to become a Sensor. Miriam has just begun."

"But she'll keep training with you until she's a Sensor?"

"With me, or with one of the masters." I have neither the time nor the stomach to explain. "She'll work with us until she's ready to go out on the hunt. Unless, that is," and I throw him a sidelong glance, "something gets in her way."

Once more, he's quiet. Not, it seems, taking my hint. Simply reflective.

We've nearly reached the pavilion when he speaks again. "What's it feel like? The Sense?"

"You wouldn't understand."

"Try me."

I stop. Look at him. The grin is gone, the swagger. No commoner has asked me this before. I feel the tingle again, the warning, but decide to try.

"All right," I say. "Breathe."

"Seriously?" But he takes a deep breath, lets it out. He repeats the act a couple of times and looks at me expectantly, as if waiting for me to congratulate him.

"Fine," I say. "Now, stop breathing."

At first, he seems uncertain what to do. Then he takes a deeper breath, holds it, holds my eye. His face remains calm at first, his expression haughty, as if he thinks he can beat this test. But gradually, I see the pressure building in him, the desire to draw breath. His eyes take on a panicked look, as if I'm the one keeping him from filling his lungs. He holds out far longer than I expected, even though by now he has to see my point. Finally, he gives up and lets the air out in a whoosh.

"My Sense is my breath," I say. "I don't know where it came from. I can't remember a time I didn't have it. But I can't stop it, or—"

"You'd die?" he pants.

I nod. And die a little more, admitting it.

"And Mimi," he says. "Miriam. She has it too?"

"She's passed the first tests. We have reason to believe she's ready for greater trials."

He says nothing. I watch his eyes, which remain intense, the sleepy arrogance of a few days past long gone. I wish I knew what this boy was to Miriam, and she to him. Am I warning a prankster away from his sport?

Or advising a suitor to give up his hopes? I have no idea which pull is the strongest, home or forest. That, too, was taken from me.

"Isaac," I say. "Are you courting Miriam?"

"Mimi?" His laugh is brash but unconvincing. "I grew up with her, but...no way. Uh-uh."

"You seem awfully interested in her training."

"I heard about it," he says evasively.

"From her?"

He avoids my eyes. "I knew you were training new Sensors. I couldn't believe it when I found out about Miriam."

"That she was our top pick?" Now I'm on firmer ground. "Why shouldn't she be?"

He laughs, shakes his head. "Mimi's no hunter. There was this one time we snuck into Daniel's house, and she got her foot caught on the windowsill, and, well, let's just say it wasn't pretty." He laughs again, superior. "So I thought, if she can do it.... I mean, I thought I could help out, teach her a thing or two."

Whatever goodwill he's earned is gone. He's jealous, simply jealous of the clumsy playmate who's surpassed him.

"If *Mimi* completes the training," I say, "you won't recognize her. Her steps will be sure, her hands lethal weapons. Her every nerve will be attuned to a world you can't begin to imagine. And when she crosses your path, there'll be no more awkward, admiring glances. She'll pity you, the way she'd pity a baby incapable of feeding itself."

He stares at me, aghast. So far as I'm concerned, the

interview is over. But when I try to march past him, he blocks my way.

"What about me?" he says. "Could you teach me?"

Now it's my turn to laugh. "You don't have the Sense. What could I possibly teach you?"

"Anything," he pleads. "I'll do anything."

"You'd be wasting your time," I say. "And mine. If you truly care about Miriam, the best thing you can do is leave her alone. Go back to playing your little games with the threshers, and let her learn how to put food on your table."

He places his hands on his hips, refusing to move.

"So that's it?" he says. "My only choice is to walk away and let Miriam become a heartless monster like you?"

For a moment, I'm too stunned to speak. If I dared touch him I could break his neck, but he seems to know by now I don't dare.

"Get out of my way," I say.

He doesn't budge. I wait for an opening and slip past. He doesn't try to stop me, but he does call out after me, barbed words that sink deep into my skin.

"I don't pity babies that need to be fed," he yells. "But I do pity anyone who feeds them with no love in their heart."

WITH ISAAC GONE, I expect Miriam to recover her focus. Instead, she collapses entirely.

Her eyes seek the village lanes, where he no longer appears. Her head swivels to the sound of the threshers, where he may well be. She arrives late the day after learning he's gone, later the next, still later the third. On the fourth day, I wait with Rebecca and Esau till the sun touches the stone, but she doesn't show. I enter Esther's hut to find her in bed, arms crossed over her chest, eyes fixed on the stone ceiling. She rises like a vapor and shadows me to our training site, but she might as well have stayed home. Nervelessly she fumbles the Ecosystem's signals, listlessly she scans the skies for bloodbirds and, finding one, shrugs her bone-thin shoulders when I ask her to project its path. The buzzing that nearly drove her mad a week ago makes no more of a dent on her than my commands. I consider another cicatrix snare to jar her into wakefulness, but in her nearly catatonic state, I fear they'd eat her alive.

"Miriam," I say. "The village needs you to complete the training. *You* need to complete it."

She looks straight through me.

"He's a commoner," I say. "You could be a Sensor. You could be…free."

Her eyes sharpen, and I shudder like an apprentice caught under her master's gaze. It's as if she's finally discovered what *I* need from her.

"Without your Sense, what are you?" I try. "You're nothing."

Unexpectedly, she laughs. Actually laughs. The harshness of the sound makes me flinch away.

"Go," I say, dismissing her with a backhand wave. "Tomorrow we'll try again. And you will mind me."

She smiles, but it's a smile of condescension. Her shoulders no longer droop as she walks off, and I note that her hair has been wrestled into a braid. Scooting the children away, I head for the Sensors' quarters to seek Aaron.

I find him in his humble home, the home I left only weeks ago. He's been spending most of his time here, since the deaths of Barnabas and Samuel. With no apprentice to train and his legions desperately busy, I suppose there's little for him to do. Still, it pains me to find him huddled on the edge of his stone bed, his hands clutching his staff and his long gray locks dangling by his wasted cheeks. I see in his lonely vigil the fate that awaits us all after our days in the forest are over. For me, those days may already have come and gone.

He looks up when my shadow falls through his doorway. "Sarah," he says. "Is the training done so early today?"

"The training may be done for good," I say, and

he gestures for me to take a seat in the chair across from him.

I tell him everything, or almost everything. The only things I leave out are Isaac's final words and Miriam's arrogant demeanor. Technically, I should be reporting any bumps in the training to Esther, but she's been so preoccupied with the hunt, she hasn't noticed Miriam's deterioration. And in all honesty, if I'm to admit failure, I'd rather admit it to a sympathetic ear.

Aaron listens without interruption, nodding thoughtfully. He smiles only once, when I mention the cicatrix trap.

"Have you a plan for proceeding?" he asks when I'm through.

"None," I say. "I didn't think I'd encounter so much resistance in a trainee."

"It is rare," he says. "Though not unheard of. I remember a day when my own apprentice was less than enchanted with her lessons."

I remember that day, too. It was in the first year of my apprenticeship, when I was a girl of three. A Sensor's memory matures early, but even so, my recall of that year is uncommonly sharp, of the day even sharper.

"It is a hard life," Aaron broods. "I have wondered, over the years, if it might be too hard. That thought has recurred to me in recent days, as I have watched over you."

"Master?"

He sighs deeply. "The Conservator would not

approve of what I am about to tell you. But it seems to me now is the time you were told."

I brace for his words.

"As you know, you were identified for the Sensorship shortly before you turned three," Aaron says. "And confirmed within a year of that time. But have you never wondered why your training began so young?"

I answer automatically. "It takes years to complete the training."

"To complete the training, yes," he says. "But not to elicit the skills. Miriam has made great strides in the few short weeks you have worked with her. So there must be another answer."

"I trained for fourteen years," I say. "And you've told me I was a fast learner."

"Faster than you know," he says. "I reported the completion of your essential training to the council on the day you turned five."

"*Five?*" Two years. A mere two years from the time I began.

He smiles. "You see now what a fine student you were. But of course, we did not send you on the hunt then. We do not dispatch children to face the Ecosystem."

This is all news to me, and I scramble to understand. "Then what have the past twelve years been for?"

"Your natural gifts have been honed, and your body has grown tall and strong," Aaron says. "But you miss my point. It is not what you have gained in that time, but what you have avoided. We identify Sensors young,

Sarah, because otherwise we might have no Sensors at all."

At first, I flounder for his meaning. But then, under the probing of his eyes, it comes to me.

"Miriam will never be a Sensor," I say. "For she loves Isaac more than she hates the Ecosystem."

"Say rather that she loves him more than she loves the hunt," Aaron says. "Had she begun the training at the age of three as you did, she might never have discovered her love for this boy. Frankly, I was surprised when one her age appeared for the trials. Most by that time have given themselves to another. But it may be that she did not fully know her own heart."

"Why wasn't I told this?" I ask. "I might have trained a younger, a better prospect. Why was I chosen for failure?"

"We did not know," Aaron says in a soothing tone. "You spoke highly of the girl, and her promise was evident to all. The children would not have been physically ready for years. We took a chance, and it seems we were deceived."

I stand. Anger and frustration make my voice tremble. "The only one who was deceived was me. I thought I was chosen as your apprentice because I possessed a particular gift. Not that I was chosen so I would know no other choice."

"It has been the same for all of us," he says. "We cannot live two lives, that of the village and that of the field. Even among those chosen young, there are some who find the sacrifice too demanding. Some like—"

"Barnabas," I say in sudden insight.

He nods. "His investiture was delayed time and again while he struggled to find his way. Nathan had given up on him, but the council considered the years devoted to his training too precious to cast aside. Our numbers at that time were perilously low. In retrospect," he says sadly, "it would have been far better if we had let him return to the life he could not bring himself to renounce."

I think of Barnabas, tall and bashful, forsaken by the council that stole his youth and abandoned by them to die a hideous death. And I think of another Sensor lost to the Ecosystem, another Sarah whom the man before me trained for the field even though her heart longed for the village. It seems to me, as I study the face of my former master and hers, that I've always known what happens to Sensors who give themselves to love. How could I not? For I myself am living proof.

"Miriam will complete the training," I say. "I won't have my life thrown away to gratify her vain dream. She'll give up this boy, and if she won't, then I'll take her place, as I should have from the beginning."

"That remains for the council to decide," Aaron says, meeting my eye. "And do not be too sure of yourself, Sarah. Miriam will fight to defend her love. She may die to defend it."

I've never wished to strike that face, the first face I can remember, the last face I would expect to seal itself in a lie. I don't wish to strike it now. But I don't wish to see it, either.

"Then she'll die another fool," I say, and my anger makes me add something I couldn't have dreamed. "Like your precious Sarah."

Before he can respond with word or look, I leave his home to seek the girl who'll die for love, or for the want of it.

I FIND HER mooning about the pavilion, her head cocked as if in expectation. But her ears, I know, seek not the living hum of the Ecosystem but the homely sweep of the threshers. In my absence, her air of superiority has melted back into the lovelorn look of the silly girl she is, the girl who'd choose husband and babies over the far greater world she's begun to fathom. If I'd known this about her, I'd have let the cicatrix swarm.

"You're coming with me," I say, and clutch her arm, far too furious to heed the taboo. Her flesh is soft yet sharp, layers of baby fat over a birdlike frame. The muscles she might have won through training remain thready and thin, and they can't resist me as I drag her toward the pavilion's edge.

"Where are we going?" she manages, her voice as tremulous as a child's.

"Into the forest," I say. "The deep, dark forest."

Her eyes widen, one of the few signs I've seen since Isaac's departure that she's aware of what's going on around her. "I'm not ready."

"Then you'd better learn fast," I say, and take the first step I've taken in weeks onto the charred circle.

The cinders crunch beneath my feet, the bracing fragrance of moistness and roasted soil rising to my nose. Miriam fights me for the first few steps, pulling weakly against my hand. But she soon gives up, not so much in defeat as in acceptance, as if she doesn't care where she goes now that I've torn her from him. I have no master plan, no surprise lying in wait for her. I simply want her to see what I've seen, even if this is the first and final time she'll see it. Even if, for that matter, it's the final time for me as well.

At the edge of the circle I pause, my eyes taking in the muted green of the towering trees. I sniff, and the gingery rosin of sap flirts with my nostrils; lick my lips, and taste the venom that powders the air. But it's my Sense that truly comes to life, my Sense that shows me what's out there beyond the capacity of my five poor senses. If Miriam could see the world as I do, see it before she's prepared to evade its power, she'd fly for shelter. The Ecosystem is a parade of horrors, and anyone who forgets that is asking for her own death.

But this is my world. I didn't choose it, and now that we're here, I'm not sure I want to share it. I certainly don't love it. I just don't want to let it go.

"Why did you start the training," I say, while she quails before me, "if you knew you were going to fail?"

"I didn't know," she whispers, and tears well in her lovely eyes.

"You knew," I say. "You've always known. Did you think this was a game? Do you have any idea what I've given up for you?"

"I didn't know," she insists. "If I'd known he…."

"Say it," I snarl.

She shakes her head, eyes closed, tears trapped on thick lashes.

"Say it!" I command, and squeeze her arm so hard I know it hurts.

"If I'd known he still loves me," she chokes.

Now that the words are out, I can breathe again. "So you decided you'd become a Sensor to forget him. Poor little ugly trickling, you thought you could drown your sorrows in the forest. Or make him jealous. And then win him back."

She flinches, and I know I'm right.

"But the Ecosystem doesn't drown our sorrows, Miriam," I say. "It only drinks our blood."

She bows her head and is silent.

"I'm going to show you what you were running from," I tell her. "If you're lucky, you might live."

I wrap my fingers around her wrist, squeeze as if I'm gripping the handle of a blade. Dragging her behind me, I step onto the sward.

The Sensations of grass and earth rush through my soles, up my legs, before curling into a painfully tight ball in my chest. I drop Miriam's arm, close my eyes, and nearly sob with the relief of it, the grief of it. For a long, shaky moment, I feel like a novice again, battered by impressions beyond my control; my legs wobble with the overwhelming force of this monstrous life, so much greater than my own. But then, like a searing song blooming in my breast, mastery returns, and I'm alive once more, my body a receptor so fine its Sensibilities seem infinite. I'm attuned to the hidden life of the forest, the deadly creatures it shelters, the terrible secrets it holds. I drink in its anger as if it's truly the air I breathe. From afar, I touch the swamp where Barnabas's torment is only now coming to an end, the arachnard tree where Samuel's lifeblood has long since ceased to flow. I even see, or think I do, the footprints of the one who came long before, the woman who, in giving life to me, gave up her own.

This is the world Miriam thought to win when her dreams of love seemed to have shriveled. This is the world she'd lightly throw aside if she could make those dreams come true. I Sense it all, the world she nearly gained, the world I almost lost. And I Sense something more.

The Ecosystem shakes itself awake, kindles with anger. It feels the presence of an alien life. Not mine, for even in my near-swoon, I'm too well disguised to attract its notice. But it knows someone is here who hasn't learned to elude it.

Miriam.

I open my eyes and find her no longer at my side. At first, I think she's returned to the village. But then I see her tiptoeing toward the woods, arms outstretched as if in a trance. I Sense the snares fermenting ahead of her, the death-traps preparing for her to step in their way. She appears oblivious to them, or perhaps she doesn't care.

"Miriam!" I scream.

A stabbing nettle bush rears its head, projectile stingers aimed at the thoughtless girl who approaches. With a sound like the twang of a bowstring, it releases its darts. They fly with a speed I can only Sense, not see. I open my mouth to scream her name.

But she doesn't fall. She continues to wander toward the forest, and it takes my confused Sense a moment to realize what's happened.

The darts have embedded themselves harmlessly in the ground. They never touched her. She dodged them.

A poisonrose vine attacks next. It coils like a tongue, homing in on her ankles. But before it uncoils, she takes a sure step to the left, and its aim is spoiled, its barbs wrapping nothing but air. I can't tell if her eyes are open, but she moves languidly, her arms out like a sleepwalker's. She couldn't have seen it. She must have Sensed it.

By now I've reached her, and I grip her wrist. She makes no sign that she's aware of me. Her eyes are closed, her face so calm it's practically blank. Yet she's no longer the pliable, unresisting girl I dragged to this place. Her body's grown impossibly strong, as if she's being reeled in by the Ecosystem itself. I plant my feet and clutch her arm with both hands, but she yanks free and I sprawl on the turf.

"Miriam!" I call, but she doesn't respond.

Ahead, at the very edge of the forest, I Sense a hexlox tree coming out of its doze, and I make one last lunge at her retreating heels. A sharp blow to my chin staggers me in midair, and I land face first on the sward, I try to push myself upright, only to find my arms pinned to the ground. I struggle to free myself as Miriam steps into the shadowed forest and is gone.

A constricting power far greater than muscle drags me forward. The hexlox roots have snaked around my wrists, pulling me toward the tree's waiting trunk, where a pustule opens like a toothless mouth. With the remnants of my Sense, I clutch at the ground, seeking not a handhold but the only thing I can think of that might save me. My fingers find it, close around it, pull it free. A burning pain invades my palm, a sure sign of the numbness to follow.

The roots tighten like a serpent's coils, mash me against the animate tree's trunk. I'm thrust headfirst into the pustule, and though I gag on the slime and rotten pith, my hand releases the fistful of death's-cap mushrooms I gathered from the sward. The tree's gullet convulses, its roots letting go as I'm vomited out in a wave of pea-green sap. Before the roots can constrict again, I scramble to my feet, leap past the retching trunk, and plunge into the forest to search for Miriam.

But she's gone.

I reach out with my swimming Sense, try to determine what might have taken her, to locate the imprint of her feet on the forest floor. It's been only moments since she vanished, and there should be a trail, a succession of snares strong enough to be picked up by my Sense. I stand perfectly still, calm my heart, reach out for her. I Sense the life of the awakened Ecosystem swirling around me, but the one life-form I seek is as invisible as my own fate.

I lift my voice. Her name leaps from my throat and rebounds against the clustering trees. "Miriam!" There's no answer, unless it comes from the Ecosystem itself, which takes up the word with its million mocking voices.

Miriam Miriam Miriam Miriam Miriam

"Miriam," I say one last time, but I know she can't hear me.

Sticky from the tree's vomit and clutching my paralyzed arm against my side, I turn from the forest and retrace my steps to the village. To the Sensorium, where my judgment waits.

THEY'VE GATHERED AT the council-house, Jarrod and Rachel along with the Sensors. Only Saul and Levi, who must be with the threshers—with Isaac—are missing. Aaron, seated in his customary spot near the central circle, won't meet my eye, but the others glower at me as if I'm some noxious creature trespassing on their private party. I'm conscious of my bedraggled appearance, my hair slicked with hexlox sap, my numb arm crooked at my side. Their hostile gaze steers me toward the space I last occupied when I reported on Miriam's progress. I feel as if this spot was appointed for me, not today but on that day so long ago I can't remember it, the day when Aaron plucked me from the funeral and decreed that I should be the sacrifice to follow in the lost one's path.

To my surprise, it's not my former master who delivers my sentence. The one who rises to his feet, tall and broad and commanding, is Nathan.

"We are assembled not by consent but by compulsion," he announces. "Our elder brother, who has stood in the post of Chief Sensor these past five years, has stepped aside in recognition of his unfitness for further service. A time will come to honor all he has done for our order. But now is the time to take up the matter he has proved powerless to address: the matter of his willful apprentice, the Sensor known as Sarah."

I glance at Aaron, who stares dumbly into space, his withered frame buried beneath his furs, his palsied hands clutching his staff. The staff's a mark of authority no longer. It's only a broken old man's cane.

"Daughter of Sarah," Nathan says, and my ears burn at the ugliness with which her name falls from his lips, "the apprentices Jarrod and Rachel have witnessed you journeying into the Ecosystem with the trainee Miriam, against her will and in violation of the Sensorship's ruling. How do you respond to their charge?"

"She's gone," I say. "It took her."

"The charge," Nathan repeats. "How do you answer the charge?"

"What does it matter?" I say. "She's gone."

"It matters much to you," he replies. "And you will give answer to us."

"I don't need to answer to you," I say. "Not anymore."

"Take care, child," Esther speaks from her position at the lodge's periphery. "We hold your fate in our hands."

"You've always held my fate in your hands," I say. "Since I was three years old, you've told me what I could do and be, what I couldn't hope or dream. You've bred me like one of the Ecosystem's creatures, reared me for a single purpose. And you wonder why I hate it so."

The bare room echoes my voice before falling into

silence. I risk another glance at Aaron, but find him shrunken in his furs as if my words have further cowed him. No one speaks until Esther, her voice a trifle softer than the stone, asks, "And you accept no responsibility for what you've become?"

"I'm a Sensor," I say. "A killer, like all of you. I've killed so many times in my dreams, I wake each morning expecting to find my hands dripping with blood. Release me from this room, arm me to set foot in the Ecosystem, and I'll kill again and again. If you're any different, tell me why you're not out there searching for Miriam."

"The girl has no training," Nathan says. "She's as good as dead."

"We're Sensors," I say. "We're all as good as dead."

Silence consumes us once again, but it's a silence too cold for me to believe they've heard what I said. If I could find it in me, I might pity them, for they're all like me: stolen from their cradles to live as I've lived, to be brought fully alive only in the face of the thing that kills us. Aaron called ours a hard life. What he should have said is that it's no life at all.

"You are a Sensor no longer," Nathan's voice breaks my thoughts. "You have disgraced our order and endangered our standing in the village, and the Sensorship unanimously votes to expel you from our ranks."

Hearing the ruling is no more awful than I'd imagined. "What about Aaron?"

"Our elder brother has left the council," Nathan says. "He has no vote to cast."

For the first moment since I entered the Sensorium, my heart rallies at the thought that Aaron chose to forsake the order rather than vote against me. But when I try to catch his eye, I find him unchanged. He might truly be dead, if the wobble of his long gray locks didn't tell me he lives.

"Leave us now," Nathan says. "Let the name of Sarah be forgotten, as it should have been with the whore who begot you."

At the sound of these words, the crushing shame I'd expected to feel presses down on me, met by a hot anger not even the Ecosystem can kindle. I muster the presence of mind to bow, and not, I think, either cringingly or contemptuously. No one returns my gesture, not even the apprentices. The silence is total as I leave the circle and, holding myself as erect as I can, exit the room for the last time.

Only when I'm safely away from the Sensorium, out on the village stone with the stifling air of the Ecosystem all around me and the hardened sap of the hexlox tree encasing me in a sickly shell, do I realize my heart's pounding and my throat too dry for anger or grief. Numbly, I remove the token from the pouch sewn into my uniform and dab its glossy surface, thankful they didn't demand its return. Probably they never knew it had passed to me. I picture my life ten years from now, my body swaddled in clumsy furs, my days spent hemmed in by suffocating stone and even more suffocating companions, everything I've been taught to dread having become my daily fare. In time, my stunted

Sense will wither to a husk like my useless body, a dead rattle inside a hollow frame. What will they name me, now that Sarah is dead? Who will there be to follow?

This is what I've lost.

I'VE BARELY BEGUN the walk to a home that's mine no longer when Isaac comes charging across the cobbles, scythe in hand. I shy from him, though I can't say whether it's his safety or mine I'm concerned about. He hooks the scythe roughly over his shoulder and glares at me.

"Is it true?" he says. "Miriam's gone?"

"You threshers hear everything."

"And you Sensors wreck everything."

"I'm a Sensor no more," I say. "But yes, Miriam's gone. The Ecosystem has her."

I don't know whether I expect anguish or despair, but I get neither. "Bring her back," he says.

"You'll have to talk to the others," I say. "There's nothing more I can tell you."

"You could tell me you're sorry. You could tell me where to find her."

I turn to leave him, but his hand lashes out and traps my wrist. I try to pull away, only to realize he's stronger than I thought. Stronger, maybe, than I am, at least now that I have nothing to fight for. I focus on the tightness of his fingers on my skin, the pounding of his pulse against mine. It's almost, I think, like Sensation, the keenness of it, the urgency and danger. Aaron's hands were always so gentle. As if in a vision, I see Isaac's face before me, though it's a face filled not with anger but with an emotion I can't name. Then I blink and the anger returns.

"Let me go," I say, and he does. The mark of his fingers shows against my skin. I'm pretty sure it'll bruise.

"I hope you don't touch her that way," I say. "If I get her back for you, you have to promise me you'll never touch her that way."

He looks at me, puzzled, then his face lights with understanding. "I'm coming with you."

"Don't be ridiculous," I say. "You don't have the Sense."

"Maybe not," he says. "But I've got something better."

"Love," I say archly. His face falls, and for the first time I can remember, I'm tempted to touch a commoner. Tempted, and swayed. My fingertips brush his arm, where I feel, beneath a surprisingly downy covering of hair, the hardness of his laborer's strength. It's only a moment before my hand withdraws.

"Love won't save you out there," I say. "The Ecosystem has no heart."

"I can't lose her," he says.

"No," I say, as gently as I'm capable of. "But if you want me to find her, you can't come with me."

He hangs his head, and I wonder how to explain. If I were still a Sensor, I'd tell him it's impossible for commoners to travel in the Ecosystem. That he'd slow me down, get in my way. Every inch of the place is booby-trapped, I'd tell him, designed to ensnare people who lack the Sense. The cicatrix are just the beginning. Other things, bigger things, eat first and ask questions later. In my mind's eye, I picture him stumbling through the woods, forcing me to attend so carefully to his safety that my Sense of the dangers surrounding us is fatally dulled. You want to help a Sensor? I would say to him. Then keep out of her way.

But I don't say that to him. I'm suddenly so nice. I tell him that someone needs to wait behind in case I don't return. Someone needs to be there to organize a rescue party if I'm cut off. If he comes with me, there'll be no one left in the village who cares enough about Miriam to try to bring her back.

I don't know if he believes me. He nods once, but his face sets in the expression of concentrated fury I know I carry myself, the one I've carried for years. The one that's always scared off boys like him. And I think, if I don't come back, what a shame it is that I never saw this side of him. Maybe there was nothing to see until now. Maybe it's the loss of the girl he loves that's made him into the man before me.

This one, I think, hates the Ecosystem almost as much as I do. This one I could have learned to like.

WHEN ISAAC HAS finally returned to his post among the threshers, I make my way to the spot where I last saw Miriam alive. I listen for the sound of his scythe, but in vain. The Ecosystem will make inroads today.

My body tingles not with Sensitivity but with anxiety. I have no fear for my own life, but I dread learning Miriam's fate, discovering she's beyond my reach. There are so many things that can kill her out there. If I'd been more honest with Isaac, I'd have told him what our newly elected Chief Sensor told me: chances are she's already dead, and if I venture out in an attempt to retrieve her body, I won't be coming back either. But I'm glad I didn't tell him. Let him have hope. It won't make a difference in the end, but I suppose it's better than having nothing.

Two sets of footprints remain visible in the charred ground, twin dusty trails leading to the spot where I lost her. At the circle's edge, I kneel on the cinders and take a deep breath. My arm's numb from the mushrooms, but the hairs quiver with awakening Sensitivity. I test the air briefly for bloodbirds, venom, anything that might kill me quickly while I'm focused on the search.

Finding nothing, I fall forward, palms on the sward, and let my Sense soak up the will of the Ecosystem.

It's unlike anything I've experienced before. Throughout my training, I've been taught to shield myself, to lay hands on the Ecosystem only with the lightest of touches. Now, I make no attempt to hide. I open myself to it, let it strip me bare as a branch in a tempest, urge my body to seep into its every pore. I sink my hands into the hot, loamy soil, turn my fingers to roots that trace the windings of its buried will. If it had a heart, that heart would beat wildly. If it had a heart, I'd find it, as it would find mine.

My head snaps up in shock, and a gasp escapes me.

I'd no idea there was so *much* of it.

Direct contact with the Ecosystem expands my Sensitivity so fast it beggars my ability to process the signals, and I'm sent careening across the globe like a wayward comet. In less time than it takes to blink, I'm hurled past the point I could travel in a day's journey, to a place where forest slopes downward into swamp, the same marsh where the bones of Barnabas lie, even now being picked clean by watermites. Then deeper still, into desert territory with twisted trees my Sense names though I've never seen them, gash trees whose tangled roots grow upward and whose crowns are spiked with thorns, roosting-places not for bloodbirds but for great croaking crows with a nose for the jugular and teeth that bristle like mouthfuls of burrs. Raveners, my Sense names them as it zooms through, scattering the atrocities in a flurry of black feathers. The ground swerves upward to far distant mountains our village must once have known, for they've been preserved in fairytales, though what I remember of those tales as a child comes nowhere near the reality: soaring piles of earth carpeted with berserkflowers and pain trees, ominous precipices from which terror wolves and chimaerae launch themselves onto their prey. I press on, rushing ever outward, until I feel as if I've Sensed the planetary scope of the Ecosystem, flung my soul across its surface and circled back to the spot where I kneel, hands clenched in the dirt, mouth dry. As I come back to myself, I realize the one I seek is no longer hidden from me.

I've found her.

She's far, far away, not so far as the mountains but far enough that she might as well be on the moon. Even now, bald evils with wings gleaming like tar transport her to the spot the Ecosystem has chosen. I perceive their destination, hopelessly deep in the Ecosystem's bosom, where it plans to leave her for me to claim if I can.

Alive.

Alive, and unharmed. She can't free herself, can't find her way back if she could. But not a strand of her hair has been crinkled, not a mark has been left on her bony arms. The Ecosystem shows her to me in every detail: every shudder of her shoulders, every flutter of her lashes over wide purple eyes. Through the vibrating strings of my arms, I feel the ripple of its deep, inhuman laughter. If it had a heart, it wouldn't toy with me so. If it had a heart, that heart would be her.

But it has no heart, and so it shows her to me. It shows me life, and death, and it dares me to choose between them. And I know why it shows me these things.

It doesn't want her. It wants me.

IN THE DYING light of day, I set my feet on the swARD and lope into the forest. I've taken the time to rinse the hexlox stink from me, not because I care how I smell but because I need to be as sharp as can be to face what I'm about to. I know exactly where I'm going, can trace the steps as plainly as a trail of phosphorescent mushrooms gleaming in the moonlight. Though the trail will fade in time, vanishing not from the ground— for it was never there to begin with—but from the place where the Ecosystem etched it in my mind, I have to believe I can follow it before it dies. It's a long way I have to travel, to the edge of the forest and beyond, but I suspect the Ecosystem will let me live until I get there. Still, I'm taking no chances, so I reach out as far as I can to Sense the snares that come alive with the night. Masking myself after such prolonged and intimate contact will be practically impossible, but I vow to elude it as long as I can. I wonder if the other Sarah made the same vow when she set out on her final journey, and if, in the end, that was what doomed her.

I considered returning to the Sensorium to visit Aaron before I left. But I knew that if I saw in his eyes what I saw in Nathan's, I'd lose my nerve. So I leave him behind like everything else, the village that was never mine, the life that was never really mine either. All that remains to me now is the thing I hate.

The Ecosystem is where I belong. I think I've always known it's the only place for me, the only thing that understands me. The only being on earth that matches my thirst for blood. It's been calling me my entire life. Now's its chance.

COME AND GET me.

Book Two: Scarred

Generally speaking, a howling wilderness
does not howl: it is the imagination of
the traveler that does the howling.

—Henry David Thoreau,
"Chesuncook" (1858)

THE HOUSE WHERE I grew up was small and spare and full of shadows. The man crept about the stones with a delicacy that belied his massive hands and broad shoulders; his movements were those of a person who worries he'll upset something that isn't his. Memory began for me in this place. For the first few days I spent there, I shied from him, not for fear of anything he might do to me but lest I interfere with whatever uneasy truce existed between him and the house. At night, when I'd lie on the woven pallet he'd prepared for me at the foot of his great stone bed, I'd feel the floor vibrating with a guttural sound as if the rock beneath me were about to split in two. And I'd clutch the animal hide blanket tight to my chin, and recite in my mind the only nursery rhyme I knew.

> Through the forest, dark and drear
> Lonely hunter, home is near

The words comforted me, but also troubled me. The one word I didn't know, *drear*, made me shiver, though I couldn't say why. It had that shivery kind of sound. When the man brought me to this house, he'd said to me, in a kindly voice that reminded me of

other voices I couldn't place: "Your home is here now."
So for me, home wasn't *near* as it was in the rhyme;
it was *here*. Maybe, when the lonely hunter found his
home as I had, the forest wouldn't seem *drear* anymore;
maybe it would seem like another word I did know, the
word *dear*. Sometimes, in my mind, I recited the words
that way:

> Through the forest, dark and dear
> Lonely hunter, home is here

And even though I couldn't convince myself that
that was the way the rhyme went, because when I said
the words in my head I always heard not only my voice
but another voice, saying the words the other way, I
told myself I liked my way better. And I wondered if,
some day, I might tell the man my rhyme and discover
if he liked it too.

In the morning, when I'd wake to find home still
here and the floor solid as anything beneath my cheek,
the man would lift me from my bed and splash cold
water from a stone basin on my face and set me on a
chair at his table, one of only two chairs in the house,
both of them so big my legs dangled far short of the
floor and I had to jump down after breakfast was done.
While I ate, scooping cold meat and roasted nuts into
my mouth with my fingers, the man stood by, never
joining in the meal, never speaking, only reaching out
from time to time to redirect a crumb of food onto
my earthenware platter. I would smile at him, shyly
at first, then with increasing boldness as I saw that he
returned my smile, though I also saw with the keenness

of my three years that though his face smiled, his eyes remained elsewhere. The second voice in my rhyme wasn't his, it was only as like to his as it was to mine, but I wondered if the rhyme was about him, if he was the lonely hunter in the forest, dark and drear. But that was silly, I told myself, because this was his home, even though it was mine as well.

After too many days had passed for me to count, I got together the courage to tell him: "I like this home."

He startled, and one of the shadows flew across his face. Then he smiled, with everything except his eyes.

"I'm glad you like this home," he said, his voice deep and powerful yet tinged with the reticence of his movements, as if he fretted that his words might tip something balanced precariously on one of the stone shelves. "It's your home now too, you know."

"I know." I looked down, not sure if I should say the next thing I intended to say, but wanting very much to say it. It was a word I knew, though I couldn't remember when I'd heard it, and it seemed the right thing to say to someone as big and old as him. "I like you too, Grandpa."

He smiled and gently corrected me.

"My name is Aaron," he said. "But you must call me *Master*." And though I didn't know that word, I quickly adopted it as the only fitting one for him. I practiced it right away.

"What are we going to do today, Master?"

"Let's take a walk," he said, holding out his hands to help me hop down from my chair. He swung me a little as I did so, and I felt myself settle to earth in a slow spiral. I liked that too, and I laughed.

His big fingers fiddled with a rawhide tie with which he meant to pull back my shoulder-length hair. I waited patiently, holding my breath and standing perfectly still. Eventually, he got most of it to stay in place, though a few curls hung before my eyes.

"That will do for now," he said, more to himself than me. Then, to me: "Are you ready, Sarah?"

Something about that name made my stomach twist. But I decided that if he could be called *Master*, I could be called *Sarah*, even if it didn't sound like the right word either.

"I'm ready," I said. "Master." And because I didn't know otherwise and vaguely recalled that this was what one did with people his size, I reached up and gripped his hand.

His fingers closed on mine, squeezed lightly. Then he dropped my hand and knelt beside me.

"Sarah," he said. "I am your master, and you must learn to do as I say. There will be many things I tell you that might seem strange, even cruel. But you must obey me, and not question my commands. Do you understand?"

"Yes, Master."

He smiled again, but I thought I saw a pinch of pain in his eyes. "One of the first things you must learn is not to touch me without permission. And you must not let anyone touch you. I've been careless so far," he said softly, and again I had the feeling he was not talking to me. "But we must be more vigilant in the future. This is one of the first lessons you must learn if you are to become a Sensor."

My lips burned to ask why, but remembering his injunction, I refrained. "What is a Sensor, Master?"

"That," he said, rising to his full height and seeming to fill the small house, "is what you are going to be. We begin the trials today." And without saying another word, he strode out of the house, with me at his heels.

We walked along the lane that led past the queer cottages on the village's far side, then turned and passed under a gate that opened into another, wider lane. My master kept a steady pace, a grown-up's pace, and I struggled to make my legs move as fast as his. He didn't look at me, just strode along with his eyes fixed straight ahead and his jaw set behind his long dark hair. Smoke threaded through the lanes and weighed on the rooftops, and in the distance, I heard a rhythmic sound like a whisk broom ending in a solid *chunk*. Then the lane we were walking ended, and in front of me was a bare, level expanse of gray stone stretching all the way to the black circle. Beyond, the forest lay in sunshine, not a bit dark and drear. My mouth opened at the sight of it, and I took an unsteady step forward as if tugged by an invisible hand. My master observed me for long moments before speaking.

"We will begin the trials in this place," he said at last. "You must attend carefully to everything I say, and try to do exactly as I ask. Do you understand?"

"Yes, Master."

He smiled. "Then let us begin."

And we did. Though he called them my *trials*, or sometimes my *lessons*, the things we did that day seemed like nothing but play to me. We circled the stone yard, pausing often to listen to the whispers coming off the forest or to watch graceful birdshapes wheel and dive above the trees. We lay down on the stone and spread our arms and closed our eyes, waiting until I told my master I felt the familiar tickle in my skin that he said meant I was going to be a Sensor, then we'd jump up and move to a new spot and repeat the process. We stayed through the morning, stopped for a midday lunch-and-privy break, then continued throughout the day before retiring to my new home in time for supper. Each day we returned, and each day we added new activities to the routine. Some days, he'd tell me to turn my back to the forest and clap my hands once when I felt one bloodbird gliding from the trees, twice when I felt two, three times when I felt three. Other days, he'd leave me by myself at the edge of the village stone and retreat to the end of the lane, though he'd always remind me not to take the farther step onto the black circle that he said was forbidden to me until I learned the many things he had to teach. That was hard, because the pull of the forest teased and tempted me. But standing there alone was like a game too, because when he'd hide in the shadows and I'd lift my head to the rolling crowns of the woodland trees, I'd have to shout out to him the names of the forms that streamed through my mind, names of things I'd never heard of before but that seemed to flow from my mouth like notes plucked from the string of my tongue. And when he'd return to the spot where I stood, my unshod feet obediently rooted to the sun-warmed patio within throwing distance of the place that strummed me so, he'd smile and tell me I had done well, and I'd be so thrilled to have won my master's game, I'd nearly forget his warning and move closer as if to fit myself against his waist. And sometimes, he would seem to forget too, and we'd walk a few steps home hand in hand, me and my master, my tall-as-the-house playmate, the only person in my life.

I saw other people from time to time. Most of them were grown-ups like him, and they would either smile benignly at me or ignore me altogether when they crossed our path in the broad lane. Occasionally, I'd see a child my size or somewhat larger, the only difference being that they wore heavy furs that were more like jackets or cloaks, while I wore a tight but comfortable undershirt and shorts of prowler monkey hide. (I knew that's what it was the instant I ran my fingers over the bristly fur, because the feeling was the same as that of the living monkeys I'd stroked in my imagination on the village stone.) The children, unlike the adults, never came close enough either to smile at me or to ignore me, but I'd hear their screams and giggles as they darted between houses and down branching lanes. Once, when my master had gone to stand in the shadows so I could play the naming game, and I had done what he always told me to do, close my eyes and let my mind reach out to the forest until I felt its itch and tickle, I heard a snatch of verse from one of the children and was brought immediately back to the world of smoke and stone:

> Rock-a-baby, have no fear
> Daddy's home and Mommy's here

The magical word *home* thrummed through me like the chords of the forest. Though most of the other words of the rhyme were unlike my version, the cadence was precisely the same as the one from my nighttime incantations—which, by the way, I'd never told my master about, as I'd felt less and less of a need for them as the house at night settled and finally silenced. I faced the village and saw a girl about my size sitting alone by one of the stone houses, holding something I couldn't make out. I took a couple of hesitant steps toward her, and saw that what she held was a miniature duplicate of herself: a creation of sticks and dead grass that would have been a person except, I was most sure, it lacked the ability to move on its own. The girl cuddled and cradled it, chattered and sang to it, made it stand upright and dance and swing as if it were alive, and I found myself drawn toward her and her mannequin, a tiny twin for which, unlike the invisible things of the forest, I had no name.

I'd taken no more than three steps from the edge of the terrace when the huge dark form of my master rose before me and, for the first time I could remember, I was afraid of him. Breaking his own rule, he snatched my arm and, not painfully, pulled me away from the girl and her imaginary double. When we came to a stop, I saw that his sudden entrance had scared the girl as well, and the village was silent and empty once more.

He let go of my arm. "Are you hurt, Sarah?"

"No, Master."

"Do you know why I caught you just now?"

"No, Master." My eyes betrayed me, as they drifted from his stern face to seek the child who had vanished down the lane.

"Sarah."

"Yes, Master?"

"You must not allow the village to entice you," he said in a tone far more cross than usual, and though I had no fear that he would hurt me, I trembled at his words. "You must heed the forest's voice alone, do you understand?"

"I'm sorry, Master," I said, though I wasn't sure what I'd done wrong. My eyes pinched with unshed tears, and I bit my lip so hard I could taste my own blood.

"The Ecosystem calls to you, Sarah," he said more gently. It was the first time he'd used the forest's proper name, but I knew at once what he meant. "Yet its voice may be muted by other calls that beckon to us. There is danger in straying from your appointed path."

"Danger?" *Through the forest, dark and drear.*

"Risk," he said. "Distraction. And in distraction, death."

"Death, Master?"

"Everything dies, Sarah," he said. "Death is the end of life. But it is the beginning of life as well, for in the Ecosystem, that which dies serves that which lives. What feeds upon the cicatrix?"

"The bloodbirds," I said without thought. "And the preying mantis. And many other creatures besides."

"And what feeds upon those creatures?"

"Other creatures," I said. "The prowler monkey is taken by the arachnard, and the ghosthawk is brought down by the Great Horned Howl." I rattled off the names as if I'd been drilled on them for weeks, yet the majority of the words that poured from my mouth had never been heard before by my ears. "All things in the Ecosystem feast upon other things. Even the things that are too big for anything to eat are eaten in time by things that are too small to see." It startled me to hear myself say that, but as soon as I heard my own words, I knew them to be true. "Is this what you mean by death?"

"It is."

"And if I heed the voice of the village, I will be eaten, too?"

His eyes widened for a moment, then he laughed. It was a rich, rolling sound, and it made relief surge through my chest.

"Let us return to the naming," he said, and though he didn't touch me, he held out a hand to guide me. "We will talk more of these things another time."

We went back to our places and commenced the naming game again, and I did my best to listen to the silent song that flowed from the forest and to ignore the broken shape of the miniature girl that the regular-size girl in her haste had left behind.

In the weeks and months that followed, I learned all there was to know of death. My master showed me the remains of once-living creatures, the spiny shells of hollowed-out insects, the desiccated fibers of plants that had once towered above his head as well as mine. He let me touch and caress his hexlox staff, explaining to me the process by which he'd severed it from its owner, scorched it thoroughly but without consuming its pith to draw out any living mite or toxin that lingered in the wood, then polished it daily with a leathern strap until its surface was smooth as bone and gleamed like sunset edged upon cloud. He spoke to me of human deaths as well, of injury and sickness and old age, of villagers who'd closed their eyes at night and risen no more from their stone beds. From him, I learned that though all things die and are consumed, it was only against human beings that the Ecosystem harbored an unwavering grudge, for we were of another order, different and distinct. And so upon our deaths, once the healers were done arraying our bodies for burial, we were consumed not by earth but by fire: fire that cleansed, that lifted our essence to the sky while preventing the corruption of the flesh from attracting any unwelcome visitors from beyond our walls. I learned from him, too, that the death of a Sensor was of even graver significance than the death of a village commoner, for it was the Sensors alone who could walk in the Ecosystem without fear, reading its thought and shielding themselves from its probing intelligence. Thus when the body of a Sensor was burned, all of the villagers were assembled to witness his release from the world and to honor his service to our race.

Yet it was not solely of death that my master taught me, but of life. As my trial period came to a close and my Sense, confirmed beyond all doubt, bloomed in the years that followed, I learned everything there was to know of the beating, pulsing, crawling, climbing, dozing, droning, soaring, roaring life that lurked in the forest beyond the village stone. I hadn't so much as set foot on the sward, my feet remaining anchored to the invisible barrier just shy of the charred circle, yet I came to believe in those years that nothing could stay hidden from my Sense, that the densely tangled life of the Ecosystem was an open tablet for me to read with effortless ease—far more effortless, in fact, than the clay tablets on which the Chief Warden recorded village business, which I couldn't read at all. As the years quickened and my age gave me freedom to roam beyond my master's eye, I glimpsed from afar the village threshers, the firestarters, the Chief Warden and his retinue of clerks and busybodies, and I saw how their attitude toward the Ecosystem differed from mine: to them it truly was dark and drear, a place to be ignored whenever possible, avoided at all cost. I saw the Sensors glide out into the field and return with game, water, and wood, lofty figures dressed in clothes like mine who moved with an ethereal confidence I had not yet learned to emulate, and I understood what my master had said of our order.

He had warned me not to be proud, not to forget that our powers were given to us for the good of our people, but for a child of three, then five, then nine, it was easy to forget that part of the lesson. I remembered the little girl of years past, the girl who had played with what I'd learned was called a *doll*, and I asked my master, not mentioning her memory, how he had determined that I and not one of the other village children was to be his apprentice and learn the Ecosystem's ways.

"Ah," he said. "There was no choice in the matter. It was meant to be."

And he told me for the first time the story of how he suspected I possessed the Sense, the story of my nighttime encounter with the mystery of the forest in the year before my third birthday. That story made many things come clear, made me appreciate why he had opened his home to a girl as young as I, devoted day after day to her training. It made me understand why the forest called me so strongly, why even in the first days of my training, it had seemed not a place of dread but a place full of wonder, where unseen animals rustled in the undergrowth, bracing winds tingled on my skin, and thrilling nightsounds urged me to come and explore. My master's words made me realize that I had been chosen for the Sensorship not by chance, not even by him, but by my very blood.

Yet there were some things he didn't tell me then, at the age of nine. He didn't tell me how it was that he'd found me that night, unaccompanied, a child not turned three, so near the Ecosystem. He didn't tell me why girls played with dolls and sang to them and rocked them. Isolated though I was from the commoners, my awakening to the Ecosystem had taught me how new lives came to be, how buds blossomed and larval cicatrix emerged and blood-red bloodbird eggs hatched. Nor was I so completely isolated that I didn't see women from time to time holding and rocking and singing to their own doll-like companions, other women plodding through the lanes with distended abdomens one day, flat bellies and mewling lap-mates the next. Many times I longed to ask my master whose stomach had disgorged me, many times the words twitched on the end of my tongue, but as he never raised the subject, I assumed there must be some reason for his silence. In the absence of answers from him, I made up my own: I was an orphan, a foundling, even—though I didn't believe this myself—a spontaneous product of the soil. Whatever I was, I knew I was no doll. Whatever I was, I knew I was something else.

He didn't tell me what I was then. I didn't find out until much later, in the twelfth year of my life, the ninth year of my training. That was when I first heard the story of Sarah.

MY MASTER HAD left me for much of that day, explaining only that he and the other Sensors had business to conduct. I was accustomed by that time to his absences, which lasted sometimes as long as a day but no longer, for once I turned five and could be trusted on my own, he had resumed dedicating a portion of his time to the hunt. There was no doubt he was slowing down, a man more than twice as old as the younger Sensors. But I respected him for participating in the hunt, something Chief Sensor Malachi had ceased to do many years before, and when my master returned home, no matter what small kill he brought, I made sure to show him through word and look, never through touch, my admiration.

He came home at the end of this day with an unusually exhausted expression on his face, though I knew he'd done no hunting. While he slumped in his chair and I prepared his meal, I asked him what was the matter.

"The Sensorship requests a trial," he said wearily. "A test."

"Of what, Master?"

"Of you. Do not fear," he said, seeing my face. "They wish only to measure your progress, and will ask you to show nothing you are not well prepared to show."

"But why," I began.

He waved a hand, refusing to meet my eye. "I am tired tonight, Sarah. We will rest now. All will be well."

That night, for the first time in years, I felt the floor shake as it had in my early days living in his home, but I had outgrown the lullaby and so lay awake listening to the stone rumble beneath my back.

My master walked me to the Sensor meeting-house the following morning. Panic flared in me when I realized he was leaving me at the door, but he only smiled and, as gently as the kiss of the wind, laid his strong hand on my cheek.

"All will be well," he said as he had the night before. "Remember who you are: Sarah, the brave and strong."

It was the first time he'd called me that, and it was enough to get me through the door.

The Sensorium seemed full of gloom when I entered, leaving behind a day that was bright and clear. I knew all of the Sensors by name, but had never addressed or been addressed individually by any: Chief Sensor Malachi, the Conservator Nathan, then Hanna, Esther, Samuel, Adam, Judah, and Ezra. They perched on benches as if their bodies had been carved from the stone, stiff torsos sprouting from haunches of granite. I didn't know whether to sit or stand, and if so, where. But no one said a word to me, all seeming content to stare at my discomfort with eyes I could barely see in their shadowed faces.

At last, the Chief Sensor spoke. His voice was a wheeze through his snow-white beard. "The child has grown."

"As children will," said Esther, in a way I could not determine to be teasing or not.

"But has she learned?" the Conservator joined the conversation. Along with the other apprentices, I had attended history lessons at his home, but his manner today gave me no confidence he remembered which one I was.

"Her master swears it," I heard the tiny, piping voice of Hanna, whom we would lose to the Ecosystem within a year of that day.

"It is not her master's judgment we seek," Nathan countered. "For he has been mistaken before."

Hearing those words brought unexpected anger to my chest. "My master has never—"

"Hush, child," Malachi said. "Nathan, we are here to judge the apprentice, not the master."

Nathan settled into a brooding silence. The others leaned forward on their benches and studied me for a long empty time without saying another word.

Finally, it was too much for me to bear. "I can do many things," I said. "I can Sense the will of the Ecosystem, and I can anticipate its snares. I know the ways of life and death. I have seen the bloodbirds circling in the skies, and I can Sense their hunger. I know—"

"That is not at issue," Malachi interrupted. He

turned from me and addressed his fellows. "The child is bold."

"Too bold," Nathan said in a sulky voice I'd never heard from a grown-up.

"Too like," Esther said, and I couldn't tell whether she was agreeing with Nathan or not. "Master Malachi, you know I have questioned the wisdom of this from the start." She looked at me once more, and said something so strange I had no idea how to respond. "Child, do you know who you are?"

"I'm…Sarah," I stammered out at last. *Sarah, the brave and strong*. "Apprentice of Master Aaron. Training to be a Sensor."

Esther's eyes bored into me, as if she could see something I'd either refused or been forbidden to say. "The child does not know," she told the others.

At this, the stone figures came to life in a confused hubbub, issuing exclamations of surprise, bewilderment, outrage. Nathan didn't participate in the general chatter, but crossed his arms smugly on his chest. Not knowing what I didn't know, I could make nothing of their reaction. So I asked, avoiding Nathan's eye, using the form of address in which my master had instructed me, "Please, Mistress Esther, I don't understand."

"Go back to your master," Malachi cut in. Of those assembled, he alone seemed not at all flummoxed by Esther's pronouncement. "Ask him what he knows of the name of Sarah."

"That's my name," I said, offended.

"So it is," Malachi said. "But there is more you

should know of the name you bear. And it is fitting that you learn these truths from your master's lips."

With that he dismissed me, and I left the Sensorium benumbed, too shaken by what Esther and Malachi had said to wonder why I had not been asked to demonstrate my skills as my master had led me to believe.

We danced around each other the rest of the day, neither of us willing to ask the other what needed to be asked. Whether he knew the purpose of the meeting and had withheld it from me, or had been misled by the Sensorship himself, I couldn't tell from his cagey, hesitant eyes. When, after a day of terse and unproductive instruction, we returned to the home we shared, I felt once again what I'd felt as a child: there were things in the house I could neither see nor name, and this time both my master and I picked our way around them. In the midst of dinner, a platter from which I was serving him his meal slipped from my hands and shattered on the floor, spilling its contents of meat and greens. I knelt to pick up the pieces, and saw how badly my hands shook.

He knelt beside me and, avoiding my eyes and hands, helped me collect the remains of the meal. When we rose to stack the shards of pottery on the table, his fingers touched mine, and we both flinched as if we'd been bitten.

"Master," I said. "Who is Sarah?"

"Why," he said as if in surprise, "she's you."

"No." My throat grew tight. "There is another.

Or," the thought occurred to me for the first time, "there was."

"Oh, Sarah," he said. "What have they said to you?"

And he told me. Long before he was done, long before the shadows grew deep in the room and the whispered will of the Ecosystem stirred in the forest dark and drear, I found myself huddled on his chair, my bare feet now touching the floor but my body feeling as if it belonged to the little girl who had entered his house nine years ago. When it grew too dark to see, he struck a flint to the litter of twigs and branches in the stone hearth, and the flames drew his long nose and sharp cheekbones from the quivering gray curtain of his hair.

"She was the finest of our order," he told me. "Tall and slim like you, yet strong as any of the others, Nathan included. I have seen her returning from the field laden with catch that would have staggered a lesser hunter, yet she never stumbled, her steps remaining straight and true. Her hair grew long like yours, and it streamed behind her when she ran. She never wore it bound, not once she became a Sensor. Wisdom might have taught her differently, but her wisdom was of another sort."

As he spoke of this other Sarah, her figure rose before me, a long, lean woman sprinting through the forest, arms pumping easily, loose hair flying. Without memory of her, when I looked at the vision's face, I saw my own.

"She began her training as you did, at the age of three. And she progressed, as you have, with wondrous speed. She took to the field at the age of sixteen, one of the youngest Sensors to join the hunt. Malachi and Nathan were doubtful, but she performed beyond even my expectations, making forays deeper into the Ecosystem than any of us dared, always returning with a kill that put all others to shame. Her hunts often lasted till dusk, when the rest had long since returned, even if they returned empty-handed. But she refused to give up the day's hunt without something to show for her efforts. There were times I would wait at the forest's edge, watching the Ecosystem grow dark, the fires of the village start to glow in the twilight, and doubt and fear would gnaw at me. But always she returned." He shook his head sadly. "She was brave, Sarah. Braver than all the rest. Braver than her old master, of that you can be sure."

"They told me I was too bold," I said.

"That is what the timid call the brave," he returned. "They said the same of her. They could not see that she was a new kind of Sensor, one who did not simply evade the Ecosystem but confronted it, met it face to face. Not that she was proud. There was no boastfulness in her, no scorn for others. She did not hunt for greed or glory. She simply was what she was. She could not have imagined being anything less."

"But she died," I said.

"Yes," he said, and the firelight showed me his cheeks, lined with tears. "After more than ten years in the field, there came a time when I waited for her, and she did not return."

"How did she die?"

"Is it not enough to know that the Ecosystem killed her?" he cried. "There are many ways, and all are cruel."

"But she," I chose my words carefully, "you brought her back."

"I brought back her body," he said, his hands held before him as if he were still bearing her dead form. "Her body only, from which her spirit had long since flown. We burned it, as we burn all who die, and released her mortal frame to the wind. And then I went in search of the one she had left behind. The child some months shy of her third year who, I saw that night, had inherited her mother's gift, and who after long persuasion I convinced the Sensorship should inherit her mother's name. The one who sits before me now."

"My name," I said. "What was it?"

"It was Ruth," he said. "But it is Sarah now, as it was meant to be."

Ruth. A name long forgotten, it stirred something in me like the touch of the Ecosystem's fingers. I tried to remember that girl, but I could no more picture her than I could her mother.

My master told me of his efforts on my behalf, his difficulties convincing the others to allow him to train Sarah's daughter. They were not so much skeptical that I had received the gift as distrustful of the woman from whom I had received it. Especially Nathan. He believed, and many of the others were swayed by his arguments, that it was my mother's recklessness that had doomed her in the Ecosystem. So for the first several months after her death, I lived among the healers, until Malachi's will prevailed over Nathan's and the council approved my transfer to my master's keeping. Sensors, my master explained to me that night in terms he had not allowed himself when I was a young child, are forbidden to love another human being lest their connection to the Ecosystem be diverted. Love, he told me, leads to marriage, and marriage to children, and the love of a parent for a child is so all-consuming, no one who felt such love could remain in full possession of the faculties needed to survive in the field. But my mother would not deny herself this right, and though forbidden to marry, she had given herself to love, and to the child who came of it. When her pregnancy was discovered, the Sensorship cast her from the order, her former master alone abstaining from the vote. But she persisted in the hunt after her child was born, and no plea of his could deter her. In Nathan's eyes, it was only fitting that, less than three years later, the Ecosystem took its revenge.

"She continued to bring back the food the village needed," my master and hers told me. "Though I managed to convince the others that it was my own. We would meet in the forest beyond anyone's eyesight, and she would pass to me what she had killed. Then she would slip into the village empty-handed, and I, some time later, would arrive with our combined catch."

"You helped her."

"The village's need was great," he said. "As was hers. I could not let the person she was die. Afterward, when it happened, I blamed myself for not stopping her. She was my apprentice, and I should have taught her better. Made her wise." His eyes, mournful in the fire's dying light, were turned inward, and I knew at last what he'd been seeing all those years ago when his thought lay elsewhere. "But I could not make her less than she was. She was born for the Ecosystem, as wild and hungry as the thing she hunted. I could not take that from her, even though it cost her her life."

"And why do you tell me only now?" I asked. "Why have you kept this from me?"

"You would not have understood," he said. "You would have felt only grief, and anger, with no comprehension of what she sacrificed, what she suffered. Your anger would have turned against her, or against it. And, Sarah, you cannot allow that to happen. Anger will draw the Ecosystem to you, bring you squarely before its roving eye. Had I told you all this as a child, you could not have prevented the seed of anger from taking root and growing."

I nodded, and met his eye, and hid from him the seed I felt sink deep into my bosom. "Who was my father?"

"Another of our order," he said, "by the name of Abraham. I believe, and Malachi supports me, that your lineage explains the unusual strength of your gift. So far as we are aware, you are the first Sensor to be born of two parents of the same order."

"And what became of him?"

"When his part in this was discovered, he fled the

village," my master said. "None has tried to seek him out, but he must have died by now."

To my surprise, I felt not sadness at the loss of the man who had fathered me, but satisfaction. It was he who had taken the other Sarah from me, who had exposed her to the Ecosystem's wrath. In giving me a mother, he had stolen her away. Let his bones rot on the forest floor, food for things both large and too small to see.

"Your mother's death changed my position within the Sensorship," my master said, and I wrenched myself back to listen to his words. "I was once thought to be Malachi's natural successor, but the loss of my apprentice made the matter more tenuous. And when they learned today that I had not told you the story of your ancestry...." He shook his head, smiling ruefully. "But I have made my choice," he resumed. "And I do not regret it. Let them try to deter me. Sarah's daughter was meant to be a Sensor, and a Sensor she shall be."

"When will I be ready?"

"It will not be long," he replied. "Six years at most."

"Six years!"

"We must proceed with caution," he said. "The Sensorship will doubt my judgment if I present you too early, and that may delay your investiture indefinitely. We cannot hope for success before the end of your seventeenth year. Be patient. I promise you, your time will come."

I believed his promise, as I believed all things that came from him. Yet the time to come was long. In that same year we lost Hanna, and though I mourned with the others for the end of her unoffending life, I felt a secret pleasure that the Ecosystem had taken her, a woman as unlike the Sarah of my master's story as could be, a Sensor who would sooner have handled a fell-cat than a baby. The apprentice named Barnabas joined the Sensorship shortly thereafter, and I attended his investiture, followed the observances, hearkened to the Conservator's lessons, intent all the while on showing any who doubted me that the daughter of Sarah would be her mother's very image in all ways but one. In dinnertime conversation with my master, I learned of his mending of fences with Nathan's faction, and when Malachi died later in the year, the vote was cast as my master had anticipated, his gleaming hexlox staff becoming the emblem of his office. As my teen years swelled, I worked my body harder than ever before, carving away all traces of baby fat, honing my frame into the physical avatar of the woman I carried in my mind. In those years, too, I watched my master's advancing age take its toll at last, his strong hands grow veined and bony, his back bend until it was I, not he, who looked down on the other. He told me then to call him Aaron, and I complied. The rule he had imposed so many years ago he now seemed to forget, and his hands sought my arm for support or comfort, whether his own or mine. But in all that time, it never occurred to me to seek a companion closer to my age, to look with interest at another of my order, much less at one of the villagers among whom I now walked aloof and alone. My monthly blood came in my fourteenth year, and I reported it to Aaron as I would have reported a broken finger or a deep flesh wound, but it meant nothing to me. To the mysteries of the heart I was as closed as stone, and I knew no desire but one. I was determined to be who my mother would have been, should have been, had she resisted the lure of the village.

And ever during those long years, I stood at the edge of the pavilion staring out into the Ecosystem, longing for the day I could match my strength against its own. *I will eat its heart at last*, I thought. *Eat the heart of the forest, dark and drear. Someday soon, I will eat its heart, as it has eaten mine.*

Book Three: Sworn

Most of us walk unseeing through the world, unaware alike of its beauties, its wonders, and the strange and sometimes terrible intensity of the lives that are being lived about us.

—Rachel Carson,
Silent Spring (1962)

IT'S DARK IN the Ecosystem at night. I've always known this, of course: I've sat outside Aaron's hut when the vault above my head was so black I couldn't see the treetops tossing in the breeze, could only hear their branches making a sound like showers of sand sifting through giant fingers. Yet even on those nights, the darkness wasn't total, for there was always some spark from the outskirts of the village, some lamp or firewell kept burning to give eyes to the threshers and ward off the things of the wild. In the field, Sensors return before nightfall and never carry torches, which attract the Ecosystem's ire. Only my mother, if Aaron spoke the truth, was bold enough to test the outer limits of custom and safety by remaining in the Ecosystem while twilight fell.

The fathomless darkness of true night awes me, but doesn't trouble my Sense. In fact, when the boles of ache and hexlox and sickenmore fade to dusky pillars and the dense canopy blocks the last purple light of the sky, my Sensitivity is heightened, its golden filaments glowing brighter than ever before. If I make it out of this and return to the Sensorship—or, better, do as my mother did and hunt without their leave—I might decide to walk the Ecosystem blindfolded from now on.

Making it out of this, however, is no sure bet. I don't need to see, but I do need to sleep. And I've no idea if my Sense will guard me while my senses lie dormant.

I can do without sleep for a night, two at most. But Miriam is farther away than I can cover in two days and nights, and if I don't let myself sleep, I'll be edgy and unfocused, inclined to hallucinate. Not an ideal condition for someone hoping to evade the Ecosystem. So far, I've Sensed no evidence that it knows I'm here, but considering how long I probed it for Miriam, that won't last. I wish I could trust my initial impression that it plans to kill me only when I reach her prison, but I'm not the trusting type.

No, I'll have to sleep. And I'll have to find some place where the Ecosystem can't detect me while I do.

I reach out with my Sense for a likely place to spend the night. The trees are out of the question: tempting though the image is of nesting high above the night-hunters on the ground, my experience with the arach-nard reminds me of the other things that nest in tree-tops. Besides, even if I could locate a tree not bent on killing me, I have no way to secure myself to a branch while I sleep. I've taken no supplies, not even my kill pouch and knife, which I assume are in the Sensorship's keeping. All I've retained of my former profession are the clothes I wear and my mother's token, tucked within the lining of my shirt. If I last through this night, I can devise a weapon out of wood or stone, kill something to transform into useful materials like water bladder and kill pouch. But until then, it's essential I spend my time on the ground.

My Sense ripples farther outward, flowing into the nooks and crannies of this invisible world. I review my options. The less contact I make with the Ecosystem's sensezones the better, so bushes, tall grasses, or other areas of leafy vegetation are out. There's unstable ground in the vicinity too, bogsand and sinkholes, a tracery like veins in the earth's flesh. Sleeping there will ensure I won't wake up tomorrow morning. And there's animal life aplenty, dozing arachnards and vigilant ghosthawks swooping through the forest with eyesight as keen as my Sense and talons far sharper than any blade. If I sleep in the open, predators will find me. If I sleep under cover, the Ecosystem will smother me and drag me down.

What I need, I decide, is a rocky area, something inorganic. Something that can't see me but that might shield me. Such a spot will show up as a hole in my Sense, a space not there, since I can't Sense what's not alive. I detected a few such holes when I searched for Miriam, one of them quite large, but all of them too far away to be useful to me now. Finding an oasis close by in the middle of the raging forest will be hard, but not impossible. The Ecosystem's old, but it's nowhere near as old as the earth's crust. And it's big, but it hasn't managed to cover every inch of the planet's surface. Not yet.

I cast the feelers of my Sense as far as I can, silence my thoughts, wait for a response. It's a long time coming, but finally, at the outer edge of Sensation, I find it: a blank, a vacancy in the teeming soup of the forest. It dips sharply away from the life that surrounds it, so it must be a hillside or depression in the ground. My Sense tells me it's ringed by young growth, saplings and vines, so the dead spot likely suffered fire from a lightning strike and the Ecosystem hasn't had time to fill it back in. A couple of days from now, it'll be all but gone. For my purposes, though, it's perfect: large enough to hold my body and sufficiently shielded by a nearby copse of ache trees to minimize the chance of something carnivorous stumbling across me in the night. It'll be rough and rocky, but that shouldn't present a problem for one accustomed to a bed of stone. If I can mask my scent while I sleep, all the better.

I head for the sanctuary. While I walk, I recite a mental mantra I make up on the spot. *Stay alert. Stay invisible. Keep hidden, even in sleep. Lower heart rate, silence breathing. Be there and not there, present yet absent. Let the mind of the Ecosystem forget, let its thought pass by like wind upon water.* I've managed all of these feats a thousand times while I'm awake, but I have no real reason to believe I can accomplish any of them while I'm asleep. None, that is, except for the fact that I'm Sarah's daughter. I hope that'll be enough.

The chosen spot nears. The deepening dark has brought out a host of flameflies, their yellow-green tails bobbing and twirling as they emerge from the ground and spin around me. They're burning hot to the touch, but I avoid them all, slipping through their dance with a surety I hope will last the night. The males attract the females, which flame so brilliantly during the mating ritual they consume their partners. Every so often, I see the brief ball of green fire and smell the faint whiff of scorched chitin that tells me another new life and new death have been achieved.

At last, my destination appears before me, a ten-foot-square patch of rocky soil visible in the flameflies' pulsing glow. It's on higher ground than I realized from afar, where all I could tell was its relationship to the life around it. Now I see that it lies above the stand of ache trees, with deadened stumps at the peak of a slope that drops into blackness beyond. It's not completely dead; organisms too small to see have swarmed to consume the trees that burned, while young vines have started to knit a tapestry around the edge. But none of these things would bother me if not for another, nastier surprise, one the dead zone must have blocked from my Sense.

"Curse it," I mutter into the night.

Tunneled into the far side of the slope is a nest of the creatures some Sensors call horrornets, others braindigger wasps. Either term is appropriate: the adults carry stingers capable of piercing bone, while the nymphs feed on the still-living tyrantulas and unicorn beetles their parents drag to the nest. The hive is dormant for now, adults and brood sleeping peacefully with a synchronized buzz. At first light of morning, though, the workers will be abroad in quest of food for the young. I'm far too big for them to bother with, but all the same, I don't want to be caught sleeping if one or a dozen or a hundred of the little monsters decide to poke the giant two-legged creature that's lain down near their home.

I pause, undecided. Now that I'm here, I realize how tired I've grown, the flamefly lights flickering in odd patterns my muddy mind has started to interpret as omens. I cast my Sense wide in hopes of finding another dead zone, but there's nothing remotely as perfect as the spot that lies at my feet. I'm fairly confident I can wake before the horrornets do; in fact, I doubt I'll sleep half as soundly as they. Did I expect the Ecosystem to prepare a nice comfy bed for me? This is the best I'm going to get.

I make my decision. I step onto the hillside.

And instantly regret it. No sooner does the ground receive my weight than it collapses, the rock I'd thought solid revealing itself to be the brittleness of shale. I scramble for my footing, succeed only in turning the slide into a rockfall. I flip onto my stomach as my legs go out from under me, land heavily enough on the downslope to knock the wind from my lungs. My hands sink into loose soil and find sufficient purchase to halt my slide, but when I try to pull myself up, the earth crumbles between my fingers and I'm slipping downward again. By the time I stop struggling and come to rest, I'm several feet down the slope, not so much hanging onto anything as simply hanging. The ridge where I've fallen is steep, the soil so drained of life it's like chalk in my hands. As delicately as I can, I try to wriggle upward, but the entire hillside feels as if it's about to disintegrate, and all I can do is lie still.

I Sense movement below me, the horrornets stirring uneasily as falling rock troubles their waspy dreams. I'm not panicked—yet—but I'm not sure how I'm going to get out of this. If I slide into the nest, its denizens will swarm, paralyze me with their stingers, and present a much larger meal to their brood than they've ever imagined. If I stay where I am, they'll wake in the morning and do pretty much the same thing.

Moving my head even a fraction of an inch makes the soil shift, so I reach out with my Sense, hoping to find something solid to hold. There's not much. The still-living roots of burned stumps dangle tantalizingly a couple of feet above me, but I fear they're all that's preventing the whole hillside from coming loose. Some immature virago creepers have twined up a slope to my right, so the ground must be healthier there. But I'll have to push off to get at them, and pushing off the desiccated soil is exactly what I can't do. If only I'd thought to bring a snare, something I could lasso over one of the stumps. But I didn't. I tested the Ecosystem unprotected, and I lost.

Only my effort to hold still keeps me from laughing. The forest didn't need to lift a finger to kill me. All it had to do was sit back and watch me kill myself.

The buzzing of the horrornets swells. The slope shifts with my tense breaths. The creepers have become aware of me, and they poke their immature snouts in my direction, trying to decide whether I'm solid enough to wrap themselves around. The hovering lights of flameflies cluster into a single, brighter orange globe, as if they've come together to witness my end.

I have one chance. I close my eyes and leap. The hillside vanishes the instant I do, and I fall.

But I don't fall far. Something grips my wrist, hauls me onto solid ground. I open my eyes to a light so blinding it's as if every flamefly in the world has decided to immolate itself in a mass suicide pact. I feel the creepers nosing hopefully at my fingers, realize I've been pulled onto the adjacent hillside. When I lower my eyes from the light, I see the bare feet of a Sensor, flickering in the orange glow.

Aaron, I think. He's followed me. Forgiven me. Saved me.

But once the pain in my eyes subsides and I can bear to look at my rescuer in the light of the torch he carries, I see it isn't Aaron. It isn't even a Sensor.

It's Isaac.

HIS FACE IS smug, his grin an invitation for me to fall to my knees and praise him to the skies. That must be why he looks so shocked when I disentangle myself from the creepers and shove him in the chest, sending him sprawling.

"Idiot!" I scream. "You could have gotten yourself killed!"

That's when I see he's not alone. The light of his fallen torch shows me his companion: Rachel, Samuel's apprentice before his death. The youngest and least experienced of the apprentices, not to mention one of my accusers this past day. Her small frame looks ghostly, floating in the dark behind him.

"You brought her into this?" I shout as Isaac climbs to his feet. "It's not bad enough I have to babysit you, now I have to deal with her as well?"

"A simple thank you would suffice," he says.

"For what?" I'm not in control of my voice, much less my Sense. The horrornets or something worse could be on their way to gobble us while I berate him. "For charming more dimwit girls? Delivering the Ecosystem another sacrificial victim?"

"For saving your life," he says. "For being smart enough to test the ground before I threw myself after you."

His words sting. I almost hope I don't survive this trip, lest the story of how I was outdone by a commoner makes the rounds of the village.

"I didn't need saving," I say, and try to convince myself I would have caught the creepers on my own. "Now I've got to waste another day dragging the two of you out of here instead of searching for the girl you claim to care about."

"We're not leaving," he says. "We're coming with you."

The utter stupidity of his pronouncement forces a laugh from my throat. "We've gone over this, Isaac. Three can't travel safely in the Ecosystem. Three Sensors couldn't do it, much less one Sensor, one apprentice, and one commoner."

"Is that what you call us?" he says. "Commoners?"

I'm momentarily embarrassed, but not enough to let myself be distracted. "It doesn't matter what I call you. Three traveling together are sure to attract the Ecosystem's notice. I'm surprised it hasn't attacked us already."

"And you were doing so well by yourself," he says.

"That's not the point," I say, my face warming with renewed embarrassment. "If I travel alone, I might survive. If I travel with you, we're sure to die. Rachel's got no experience in the field, and you don't have the Sense."

"I had enough sense to know you were in trouble,"

he says. "To know that if I didn't help you, the brain-diggers would sting you and leave you for their brood to eat."

My retort is stopped cold by his words. "What did you say?"

He looks as surprised as I am. I turn on Rachel.

"Did you tell him about the wasps?" I demand. "Have you been giving him lessons?"

The girl's eyes are so wide she barely has any face left. Numbly, she shakes her head.

"Hey," Isaac says, reaching out as if to stop me from throttling her. "She didn't have anything to do with it. What, are braindiggers some sort of secret?"

I round on him, and he pulls back. Which, given my mood, is exactly the right thing for him to do.

"Commoners," I begin, then take a breath and start over, "villagers don't know about things like braindigger wasps. Only Sensors do. Who told you about them?"

"No one," he insists. "It just came to me. When I grabbed your hand."

My Sense is fully alive again, buzzing as loudly as any horrornet nest. But at the same time, it's reeling, and I don't know whether to believe him or not.

"Isaac," I say. "When you were with Miriam. Did you ever touch her?"

"What's that got to do with anything?"

"I need to know," I say. "You've touched me now, twice. And I've touched you. Did you ever touch her?"

"I guess," he says. "I mean, sure, we held hands, and

once...." The shock that crosses his face can't be greater than mine. "You think I got the Sense from her?"

"I don't think you have the Sense at all," I say, but my mind is working feverishly to grasp this new idea.

The Conservator always insisted that the Sense was innate, something you either had at birth or didn't. Commoners, he told the apprentices, could no more acquire our power than learn to fly. If we were forbidden to touch them, I'd believed that was for our own protection, to prevent us from suffering the fate that befell my mother. But what if there was another reason?

"Hold still," I say. Then, not knowing if my words are true: "This won't hurt." And carefully, hands trembling, I place my palms against Isaac's cheeks.

They're warm, and smooth, but beneath their smoothness I feel the pits and bumps of a recent shave. He doesn't flinch, but a slight quivering, perhaps the effect of his breath, seems to animate his face, though his eyes remain steady and unblinking. I feel my own cheeks warm, but I don't let go. I close my eyes and try to reach out as I do in the Ecosystem, to plumb beyond what I can see to what I can only Sense. An inner world, as broad and deep as the one outside. As broad, as deep, and far more mysterious.

It starts at my fingertips as it always does, the slight tingling that warns me of danger, of another life form heading my way. Yet it's different this time. The tingle spreads up my arms, to my chest, where I feel the thumping of my own heart. And then something wholly unexpected happens: across my mind's eye, there flashes an image of a plump-faced baby, its toothless mouth split in a desperate scream. The image changes, and I see a child of five running across the pavestones, lean and lithe, eager for fun. The child becomes a boy of twelve hoisting a scythe, lounging and laughing with his fellow threshers. Next a youth of sixteen, crouched by himself at village's edge, peering intently at the ground while shielding something with cupped hands. Finally the vision yields to the Isaac I know, yet in a different place and time: sitting outside a stone cottage at night, neither laughing nor alone, holding hands and looking earnestly into the almost-purple eyes of the girl I seek. The tingling in my fingers is so intense it's as if he's gripping my hands, not hers.

Then I feel him grip my hands for real, forcefully moving them back to my sides. I open my eyes and am startled by how close his face appears.

"I think that's enough," he says.

I nod, and my throat catches, and I've nothing to say.

"Did you feel anything?" Rachel asks me or Isaac, maybe both. I'd forgotten she was there.

"Nothing," we say as one.

THERE'S NO CHANCE of anyone sleeping now, so we sit on the ground by the ruined hillside while Isaac and Rachel tell me their story. But first, Isaac does something so painfully simple, I'm mortified no Sensor has thought of it. Tearing dead branches from the tree stumps, he plants a sort of fence around us and lights each stake with his torch. It's crude, and I Sense the Ecosystem regarding it with frustrated fury, but the flames will probably keep the creatures of the forest from encroaching on our island for the night.

"I thought you were a thresher," I say.

"And I thought I was a commoner," he responds.

I stiffen, but then catch his teasing tone. "No, seriously."

"I'm full of surprises," he says with a grin.

He does most of the talking, while Rachel sits at his feet, watching him, occasionally adding something he's too embarrassed or—I'd never have thought it—modest to mention. The branches crackle and smoke and sputter, but he's always ready to relight them. When his torch burns down, he gathers more twigs, binds them with bits of feebly protesting creeper, and uses the smoldering stub of the old torch to light the new. He seems comfortable leaving the circle of fire, handling the vines, and though I can't Sense whether that's a result of his contact with me, I can't help admiring his courage. It's his first time off the village grounds, and he should be quaking in his boots, if he were wearing any. Instead, he's sitting easily in his open-necked vest, telling his story, his face in the firelight alternating between seriousness and humor.

"After you left, Rachel found me and told me what happened in the Sensorium," he says. "She told me what they said to you, what they said about your—"

"Mother?" I finish. "The whore?"

"What they said was shameful," Rachel chips in, her voice as tiny as her body. The Sensorship keeps waiting for her to grow. "Jarrod and I never thought they would—"

"Spit on me? After you told them about me and Miriam?"

She cringes as if she fears I'll strike her.

"We did as we were told," she says almost inaudibly. "As we were taught was right. We didn't mean to hurt you, Sarah."

I take a deep breath, let it out. I find it in me to smile at her.

"It's okay," I say. "I had it coming."

There's an uncomfortable silence, during which the juvenile creepers nose at us curiously, too tender to do any real damage, requiring only the occasional swat to mind their own business. Finally, Isaac resumes his narrative.

"Rachel told me your next move would be to Sense where Miriam was, to locate her through your connection to the Ecosystem. She told me you wouldn't bother looking for tracks...."

"Because there wouldn't be any," she adds.

"And so you'd follow her Sense-trail instead," he says. "She told me how that works, and she said you're one of the best at doing it." He drops his eyes and flicks away a creeper that's exploring the pouch at his side.

"You two seem to know an awful lot about me all of a sudden," I say. "How did you know I wasn't using this whole rescue mission as an excuse to avoid public humiliation?"

"I don't believe that," he says. "You're not the kind to give up. You wouldn't have left the village if you didn't think you had a pretty good chance of finding her."

"I'm flattered," I say facetiously, but the truth is, I am. Also more than a bit surprised. Am I that easy to read? "So you two had a lengthy discussion of my enviable personality traits, and then...."

"It wasn't that lengthy," he says. "I already knew you could use a little work in the, uh, feminine graces."

"I was raised by a man."

"But not by a warhog," he shoots back. "So we might expect a little more polish in the area of people skills."

He smiles, and when I say nothing, he clears his throat and continues.

"So anyway, I asked Rachel if we could follow you

like you followed Miriam. And after she gave me the whole speech about how I'd get my head whacked off the instant I set foot in the forest, she agreed."

"Wait," I say to Rachel. "You searched the Ecosystem for me?"

"Not that way," she says. "Samuel never taught me how, and after he died...oh." Her eyes fall, but she charges ahead. "Your trail was fresh enough for me to Sense where you'd gone. By following the snares you avoided. We got a little lost."

"She was amazing," Isaac says. "I was the one who slowed us down."

"By refusing to wear shoes," Rachel says with a smile, and the two of them share a private moment.

It's not private for long. "Shoes?" I ask.

"I told him to wear moccasins," she says. "To deaden his impression. But he insisted on going barefoot."

"And stepped right on the biggest thorn in creation," he says, laughing. "Which didn't help in the speed-and-mobility department."

The biggest thorn in creation, I don't bother telling him, is big enough to impale his entire body. "Show me the foot," I say.

"It's fine," he protests.

"I don't give up, remember? Now show me the foot."

He looks grouchy, but he extends a lanky leg toward me. Sure enough, there's a puncture wound where the big toe of his left foot meets the ball. A clean wound to all appearances, but I'm taking no chances. I lay two fingers on the small, slightly red hole and Sense instantly that its maker was another immature creeper like the ones that keep trying to pick our pockets, with no venom or parasites to speak of. I remove my fingers before they have a chance to tingle, but in the moment before I break contact, I receive a mental picture of Isaac flinching when the thorn went in. I'm baffled by this new connection, and I wonder why, in all the times I've made contact with Aaron, his life was never revealed to me as Isaac's is now. But I chase the questions away and say to him, "Why didn't you listen to Rachel?"

"Have we met?"

"It's not a joke, Isaac. You might be developing the Sense for all I know. But Rachel and I were born with it. So was Miriam. If you're going to insist on spending time with us, you're going to have to stop being such a jackalass and follow our orders."

That brings everything to a screeching halt: Isaac's smile, Rachel's delicate glances of admiration. Only the torches aren't shut down by my words, and their crackling and popping fills the silence that follows.

"People skills," Isaac mutters at last.

"People skills can go to rot," I say. "The Ecosystem isn't a person."

"You think that's why it killed your mom?"

"I know that's why it did. And as soon as *I* can kill something, we're wrapping your feet."

Isaac glares at me, then leaves the circle to attend to the torches. I notice for the first time that he's hobbling ever so slightly. I'm left with Rachel, who sits with her hands in her lap, eyes downcast. I try to think of something to say to her, but all I can think of is that I have nothing to say to her. I listen to Isaac gathering wood in the darkness, watch as he reenters the ring of protection. He drops his load of branches and gets to work relighting the stakes.

When he's done, he sits facing me. "So we can stay?"

"I can't very well make you leave without attracting every predator in the Ecosystem," I answer. "But you're going to have to do it my way from now on. The longer we delay, the colder Miriam's trail grows. Understood?"

He nods slowly. His eyes flicker in the torchlight. "Can I ask you one thing?"

"Make it snappy."

"All right," he says. "If you had a chance to live for one day like your mom did, would you take it? Even knowing you'd die, I mean."

I open my mouth, but no sound emerges. Apparently, my mother has been quite the subject of conversation in the village.

Isaac stretches out on the ground as if to sleep, but it turns out he has one more thing to say. "You tell me the Ecosystem wants us to die because we're human. If that's true, shouldn't we want to live like we are?"

He doesn't wait to hear my answer, not that I have an answer to give. Throwing Rachel a friendly smile, he crosses his hands behind his head and lies back, his eyes lifted to the pitchy vortex where the sparks from his impromptu candles twist into nothingness.

AT FIRST LIGHT of dawn, we're up and moving. I've slept not a wink, and I suspect that Isaac, relaxed as he's trying to appear, hasn't either. The Ecosystem has to be a creepy place for him, especially at night: the whirring of cicatrix and flapping of vampire bees, the gold-green glow of curious eyes just beyond the range of our torches, even the touch of the night wind must be disconcerting for someone who's spent his nights ensconced in stone. But in that respect, I'm no different. For the first time in my life, I long for the protective walls of a home I no longer have, and I stay rigidly awake, jumping up to relight the torches the moment they flicker. I keep my Sense on a hair-trigger, but nothing threatens to breach our defensive perimeter except the fluttering of wind on flame. When dawn shows me the pale green underbellies of the ache leaves, I'm first to stand and rouse the others.

I have three objectives for this morning: getting away from the horrornets, diverting the Ecosystem's consciousness, and fashioning a blade to kill larger game. The first of these goals is easy; the second will be nearly impossible, so I skip it and focus on the third. I survived the past day on a sip of water from a clear-running stream and a handful of chokeberries—which, unlike blueberries and blackberries and lots of other berries, don't actually choke you, though they do rot your stomach if you eat too many. But we're all going to need a more substantial meal to keep going, plus I'm determined to wrap Isaac's feet and add to our stock of supplies. At some point, I'm going to have to show my traveling companions how to eliminate what they've eaten without attracting the Ecosystem's attention. But I'm nowhere near ready for that lesson, so I stick with the more pressing need: finding a weapon.

I scan what's left of the dead zone for a fragment of rock I can shape into a blade, but there's nothing suitable, only the soft, chalky soil that nearly sent me tumbling into the horrornets' nest. I'll need something tough, sandstone or chert, and that means time spent on blind searching: I can't Sense stone. Silently, I curse myself for not raiding the Sensorium before I departed the village. I long to wrap my fingers around the knife that was so briefly mine, a solid piece of flint, haft and blade, that fit my palm as if the two had been made for each other. For all I know, maybe they were. Aaron presented the weapon to me solemnly but without fanfare on the morning of my first hunt, and I was too nervous to ask him if it had once belonged to my mother.

Isaac stretches long arms above his head, hops from the creepers to the forest carpet. He's definitely favoring the injured foot, though he's trying not to show it. "What's our plan, boss?"

"I need a knife," I say. "For food, and for something

to take care of that foot. In a pinch, I could set a snare instead." I don't tell him that's not my strong suit. I'm at my best when it's just me, my weapon, and my kill.

"Would this work?" From a sheath at his belt, he pulls out a long, curved blade. He holds it awkwardly, point up, as if that's his idea of how to stab a forest creature. I stifle a smile.

"Hand it over," I say, and he does.

I weigh the stone blade in my palm. It's much heavier than my knife, built for slicing grass, not flesh. Even if I manage to plunge it into a moving target without losing my grip, it's too broad, the tip too blunt, for me to pinpoint the spot I need to make a sure kill. I want this hunt to be as impressive as possible: a clean thrust, a dropped body. I don't want him to see me miss.

"It'll have to do for now," I say. "Until I can find something better."

He throws me an offended look, but keeps his mouth shut. Wordlessly, he strips the sheath from his side and hands it to me, and I strap the blade to my hip. The hum of the horrornets shaking off their hive-sleep fills the air as we leave our first night's camp.

We walk in single file: me in front, Rachel bringing up the rear, Isaac sandwiched in between. No torches; I refuse to give the Ecosystem any more reason to hate us than it already has. The forest wakes, bloodbirds croaking from high perches, the carpeting of animate vines and mosses sniffing for the patina of prey. Rachel I barely pay any mind: she's experienced enough to Sense and avoid snares, though as a hunting partner, she's quite useless. Isaac is another story. With the spreading of the light, I Sense the Ecosystem's interest in him perking up. It's figured out that he's the one responsible for last night's torches, and it must have figured out as well that he doesn't know how to disguise his presence. If it hadn't been for the horrornets, I'd have insisted he stay at our camp until I found something to cover his feet. But even that, I fear, won't be enough to hide him from its hunger.

I decide to test him. If he's truly beginning to manifest the Sense, he'll need practice and encouragement to draw it out. The lunacy of training a thresher in the middle of the forest flashes through my mind, but I give it a try.

"What's the name of that tree?" I ask, keeping my voice low. Not that it matters—the Ecosystem doesn't need to hear us to snare us—but there's no point in advertising our presence.

"An ache," he says, matching his volume to mine. "Everyone knows that."

"And that one?"

"It's a…a hexlox," he says haltingly. "It's—hold on—it's animate." I glance over my shoulder to see the shock that fills his face. "Really? The trees can move?"

"Some of them," I say. "Very few are ambulatory, but lots can manipulate their roots and limbs. Hexlox draw their prey into pustules," and I point to the growth on its side, "using root structures that telescope in response to body heat. Once inside, their victims are consumed by digestive juices."

"Juices?" he says. "You mean, like sap?"

"Something like that." I have no idea if any of this will make sense to him, but he listens in silence and apparent absorption. "That's one of the things about the Ecosystem. Lots of plants are more like animals in the ways they move and the things they eat."

"What about ache trees?" he asks. "Are they predatory?"

"Listen to them," I say, "and see if you can figure it out yourself."

He's silent for such a long time, I think he's lost interest or admitted defeat. But then he says, in a voice pocked with hesitation, "They don't…I mean, they don't eat anything. They're just trees. With leaves and stuff."

"It's the leaves you have to worry about," I say. "Ache leaves produce nausea and disorientation on contact with exposed skin, which makes you more vulnerable to true predators. There's no such thing in the Ecosystem as 'just trees.'"

"But if they can't move…."

"Not all predatory trees need to move," I say. "Pain trees exude a resin that attracts game. It's easy to recognize, even without the Sense. Very sharp and sweet, like…." I try to think of something within his experience it might be like. "Like the smell of cut grass after rain. Except once you're close enough to identify the smell, you're already hooked. You'll walk right up to the tree and take a face full of venomous needles without batting an eye."

"Is there a cure?"

I frown. Sensors don't talk about *cures*. "The venom paralyzes the lungs. I suppose, if there were a way to bleed or burn out the poison, you might live. But you'd never think to try, because the tree would have you under its spell. You'd sit by the trunk with a big smile on your face while you slowly suffocated. And then the roots would feed on your flesh as your body decomposes."

He shudders, actually shudders. "So what do you do if you encounter one?"

I turn my back to him so he can't see my expression. "That's the trouble, Isaac. It's not like a snare you can physically avoid. You have to Sense the tree from a safe distance, then mask yourself so it doesn't know you're there. Disappear while you plot a course around it. Which means you need to make it think you're just another part of the Ecosystem."

In the ensuing quiet, I hear his footsteps behind me, one heavier than the other. "Can I learn to do that?" he says at last. Doubtfully.

"It's not something you learn," I say. "It's something you *do*."

"But Sensors are trained."

"Only to heighten capacities we already possess. You didn't need to learn about the braindiggers, right? Their name just came to you."

"Out of thin air," he says, as if that proves his uniqueness.

"That's a basic skill," I burst his bubble. "Rachel and I were subjected to naming drills when we were three or four years old. Probably we could've done it earlier, except we didn't have the language to say what our Sense told us. If you lack the ability to mask yourself, anything I tell you about it would be completely useless."

"Could Miriam do it?"

Not well enough, I think. "She was…capable," I say carefully. "But inexperienced. She'd spent her entire life walking without awareness before the Ecosystem's eye. When the time came to blind it, the Ecosystem was too much for her."

The sound of his footsteps ceases. I turn to find him standing with his weight on his right leg, Rachel hesitating behind. I Sense the Ecosystem holding its breath, almost as if it's waiting to see what he'll do. Its mind has sharpened to a point upon him, but I get the Sense it's more inquisitive than hostile.

"I should go back," he says.

"What?"

"I'm holding you up. You'd be following Miriam's trail if you didn't need to hunt for my booties." He laughs harshly. "Rachel can take me, or I can find my own way. I'm sorry I came. I should have listened to you."

His miserable expression stops me from uttering the obvious response. "But you're here now."

"By mistake," he says. "And against every bone in your body. If it were up to you, I wouldn't be here at all."

He's right, and yet for some reason, I can't say it. "If you want to stay…."

"Not exactly a ringing endorsement," he says with another laugh. "What's the quickest way back?"

I'm about to say something, having no idea what, when my Sense lights up like a burning meadow and

Isaac's blade springs to my hand. "Get behind me!" I shout at him and Rachel, but she's already Sensed it and is tugging his arm. A moment later, the crashing in the underbrush is audible to everyone, and Isaac's eyes widen. Just before the thing comes hurtling into view, he and Rachel spin out of the way, and I'm left to confront it alone.

It's an adult male warhog, two hundred pounds of explosive muscle propelling a snout decorated with leathery knobs and spiny protrusions. Fiercely territorial, and always angry as a result. I leap to the side, avoiding its charge but moving too hurriedly to plant my blade. The warhog stops in a spray of dirt and leaf mold, tosses its ugly head, and with shocking agility reverses course for another charge. I try to spear it as it roars past, but my aim is spoiled by its speed, and my blow glances off its armored hide. Shockwaves travel up my arm, and I barely manage to keep a grip on the blade.

The warhog wheels again, charges straight at me. I'm thinking too much, trying to stay out of its path. I need to do what I just told Isaac: melt into the forest, plunge my blade into its back through the invisible slit in the cloak I draw around me. If only I'd Sensed it earlier, if only I hadn't been distracted by....

"Isaac!"

From the corner of my eye, I see him streaking toward the monster, his injured foot seemingly forgotten. The pig, its rage doubled at the sight of this second intruder, lowers its head and gallops toward him. I Sense what's in its mind: tusks ripping through flesh, head flinging his body like a ragdoll. The vision's so sharp, I nearly choke on the scent of Isaac's blood.

Just in time, I collide with him, and we tumble out of the creature's path, landing with arms wrapped around each other and Isaac's borrowed blade dangerously close to his spine. I throw myself free and spin to face the enraged warhog, which has renewed its charge at the sight of bodies down. Its head is lowered, its tusks jutting, and in a frenzied burst of Sensation, I realize I won't be able to dodge it.

I have no time to think. I do the only thing I can.

I launch myself over its head as it thunders toward me. My leap isn't perfect, and a dizzying flash of pain tells me one of its tusks has opened the inside of my thigh. I ignore the rush of blood as I land on the creature's back, straddling it between sharp spinal plates, sinking my knees into its flanks to hold on. My perch is slippery with blood and the creature's maddened bucking, but I have just enough time to drive Isaac's blade deep into the hump of muscle at the base of its skull. Then I'm flying through space, spraying blood as I twirl out of control. I hit the ground heavily, roll to a stop and stand to face the creature's next charge. But I'm hobbled and empty-handed, and the Ecosystem is a howling fury in which there's nowhere to hide.

The skewered warhog stumbles, rams its head into the bole of an ache tree, falls to its knees. Its hindquarters lift as if to get its weight under it, but its front legs are limp beneath its heavy head. With a final spasm, it crumples at the base of the tree, twitching feebly for a moment before it lies still. An inch of Isaac's stone blade protrudes from its neck, showing me where the point must have found its brain.

In a blur, I see Isaac and Rachel running toward me as I collapse, my hands groping for my thigh. I'm too sick and lightheaded to look at the wound, but I know that if the artery's been sliced, I'll die. I lie back, hoist the leg, watch blood seep between my fingers. I turn to Isaac and Rachel, who've squatted by my side. His vest is off, and I feel his hands touch mine.

"I'm sorry," I say. "Isaac, I'm so sorry."

His head is down, intent on his work. "Shut up," he says gruffly. "And hold still."

"Take Rachel with you," I say. "Find Miriam. Leave me here."

"Don't you ever shut up?" he says.

I open my mouth to speak again, but his hand moves to my forehead, and in the moment it meets my skin, a calm comes over me that closes both my lips and my eyes. I see flashes of his life, too brief for me to remember from one moment to the next. Mostly it's his eyes I see, and his smile. But those are fading too, into a gentle night sprinkled with stars.

SARAH RUNS THROUGH the forest. She has my long legs and neck, my shoulder-length hair, my high forehead and hard chin. In my eyes, she's beautiful, though in the glimpses I've caught of my face in pond or puddle, I've never seen myself as beautiful. She stares straight ahead as she runs, head held high, muscles a fluid blur against the Ecosystem's green.

Then she winces as if a blade has sliced her, and I see the shaft of an arrow protruding from the back of her thigh. She runs on, but another arrow strikes home, this one in her calf. The missiles fly all around her, some embedding themselves in trees, others in the earth, by far the greater number in her shoulders, arms, legs. Still she runs on, blood streaming, feathers adorning her. Only when the final arrow plunges into her back does she fall.

I cry out and reach for her, but my body lies heavy and useless. I feel the blades of grass against my legs and spine, sharper than ever before. My hands wander to my chest, where the point of the arrow, red-tipped, smears its gore on my fingers. I stare at the sky as the bloodbirds circle.

IT'S RACHEL'S VOICE I hear first. "Is she awake?"

"Shouldn't be," Isaac answers. "I put her under pretty deep."

I'm lying on my back against soft ground. My leg throbs, but the stickiness is gone, and the wound's been wrapped with something just short of tight. I test my eyelids, which flutter at my command, letting in a crack of firelight. I could open them, but I don't. I lie still and listen.

"How did you do that?" Rachel asks.

I hear his soft laugh. "I trained as a healer. But there's more of a need for threshers, so I don't get to use it much."

"Could you teach me?"

"Don't see why not. It's all about where you touch, energy currents and pressure points. Kind of like the Sense, I guess. Except with people instead of the Ecosystem."

Someone moves, probably him. There's quiet, then a nervous giggle from her. "Like this?"

"More like this." Her giggle dies, and the silence resumes.

At last, I feel too guilty to eavesdrop any more. Not quite sure what I'll find, I open my eyes.

There's not much to see. The two are sitting cross-legged facing each other, Rachel resting the tips of her fingers against Isaac's forehead. Daylight has faded from the forest, and a small fire burns in a pit they've dug. He's bare-chested, which makes sense, since my leg's bound with strips torn from his vest. Other than that, it's as innocent as two kids playing patty-cake.

Nonetheless, they jump apart the moment I sit up. Nonetheless, a tight, angry ball forms in my chest at the sight of them.

"Feeling better?" Isaac asks. Rachel climbs to her feet and noisily collects sticks.

"You really are full of surprises," I say to him. He nods slightly, then tosses me a small object, which lands at my feet.

I bring it close to study it in the poor light: an intricately carved ornament of polished wood as long as my pinky finger, in the shape of a serpent twined around a staff. The design is beautiful, though its meaning is lost on me. Whatever it is, I'm surprised he'd share it so casually. My own token remains within my breast pocket despite my acrobatics, and I have no plan to let any other see it.

I pitch the snake-and-staff thing back at him. He lets it lie where it falls. "Very pretty," I say. "Any other hidden talents you want to warn me about?"

"Afraid not." Seeing me fingering my leg, he adds,

"I'd leave that wrapped. At least until the thread's ready to come out."

"You sewed my leg?"

"Had to. It was a pretty deep cut. It's going to leave a scar."

This doesn't surprise me. "So you knock me out, then you sew me up while I'm asleep…."

"You were thrashing around so bad, I had to put you out. Plus I thought I was doing you a favor." He holds up a long, curved needle, one that came from a spiny anteater. The pointed end is blackened with fire. "It hurts like hex."

This doesn't surprise me either. I rock forward, get my legs under me. Isaac and Rachel rush forward, but I brush them aside. The injured leg feels sound, no wobble and minimal pain when I take a step, though whether I can run on it remains to be seen. The two of them watch with hushed concern as I walk the grassy clearing where the warhog lies. I reach for the creature's back, only to discover the blade's gone, a blood-crusted hole marking the spot where it went in.

"Where's the knife?" I say, turning to Isaac.

He holds it out. "I needed to cut strips for the dressing."

"And I suppose Rachel kept her Sense sharp while I was napping?"

"I was going to—" she begins, before I cut her off.

"No warhogs or other lethal quadrupeds in the vicinity? Or were you too busy with your healer lessons to notice?"

Rachel shakes her head, watching me with wide and careful eyes.

"I guess you two are doing fine without me," I say. "Maybe I should be on my way and leave you to fend off the Ecosystem with needles and love taps."

"Cut it out, Sarah," Isaac says.

"Excuse me?"

With a swift, jerky motion, he drives his blade into the trunk of the nearest tree. Luckily for him, it's not one that can fight back. "It wouldn't kill you to admit you're grateful. For once in your life."

"I beg your pardon," I say, "if I didn't thank you properly for jabbing a white-hot needle in my thigh."

"You prefer to bleed to death?"

"I prefer," I begin, and I don't know what I prefer, "to be left alone. Don't they teach you commoners anything?"

He flinches as if I'm the one who jabbed *him*. "Fine," he mutters. I wait for him to say something more, and I realize that no matter what he says, I'm determined to throw it back in his face.

But I never get the chance. Isaac retrieves the blade from the tree, yanking it out with an effort and handing it silently to me. He returns to the spot where he'd been sitting and collects his healer supplies, the ornament, the needle and thread, stuffing them all in the small pouch that hangs at his hip. When he walks off to gather more wood for the fire, I see that his limp has returned.

Rachel looks anxiously between the two of us.

Finally, she decides to tend the fire, dropping twigs into the pit and nudging them with a forked stick, breathing life into the embers. I watch her cheeks light with their ruddy glow, then I kneel by the warhog and begin the work of slaughtering.

THE FOLLOWING MORNING, with Isaac's feet wrapped in stiff sandals of warhog hide and a ragged cape of the same material knotted at his throat, we're on the road again. The cape was my idea. The more of him that's covered with dead things, the better. I'd have pressed for a hat, too, if we were talking. The thick gray cloak hangs down his back like the corpse it is.

He's not said a word to me since last night. Not while I butchered the pig, not while he built up the fire and helped me skewer the meat, not while we gobbled thick, bubbling cuts of warhog bacon. After, I led the two of them to a stream where they could wash away their traces, then I went back to the campsite. While I did my best to cure the hide over the fire, he retreated with Rachel for a continuation of their private lessons, then went to sleep. I passed another restless night, most of it spent staring at his motionless form. When I approached with his sandals this morning, he snatched them from me and tugged them over his feet without so much as a wisecrack or a grimace. And when I said, "Time to move out," he rose without a sound, kicked dirt over the smoldering fire, and followed.

In all the ways that should matter, I'm feeling more confident about this expedition than ever before. True, my bandaged leg is stiff and sore from the sewing, which pinches my skin and warns me against sudden movement. But we're well fed, well stocked, and well-armed, Isaac's blade having proven handier than expected. Warhog aside, the Ecosystem has made no extraordinary effort to kill us, and I Sense our fires have scared it off for the time being. Miriam's trail is as sharp as ever, a fixed needle pointing me toward the place where she's being kept. For three people who've strayed deeper into the Ecosystem than anyone before—only one of the three in complete possession of her Sense—we could be doing a lot worse.

And yet, the silence in my wake is killing me.

My Sense is on the forest, but my mind is on him. Now that the heat of our fight has cooled, I'm left wondering why I was so angry in the first place. The image of Rachel's childish hand resting on his brow is imprinted in my memory, and I can't shake it loose. For as long as I've known him, it's his intrusiveness, his lack of respect for the taboo, that's most infuriated me. Now that we've shared so many illicit touches—his hand gripping my wrist, my palms on his cheeks, a roll on the turf before a charging warhog, a brush on the forehead that sent me spiraling into sleep, and, by far the worst, his fingers probing my thigh while I dozed—I should be thrilled to have him at a distance. I've finally driven him off, and yet all I can think of is how to get him back.

If, by some miracle, we succeed in our quest,

he'll return home with Miriam, who'll retire from the Sensorship so the two of them can live out their lives in the commoner's way. He'll thank me, probably; wish me well, maybe—and those will be the last words I'll hear from him. They'll settle into their cottage in the village of stone, raise children, grow old, while the Ecosystem fades into the back of their minds. The horrornets, the cicatrix, the pig, the scar, the steps we take right now won't trouble his memory, becoming topics for dinner-time or thresher-time or bedtime banter at most. And I, meanwhile, will....

Will what?

I can't go back, I know that. Can't become one of them. I can't face Isaac and Miriam and the life they make together. Now that I've discovered it's possible to survive in the Ecosystem, I suppose I could abandon myself to the forest, live day to day for as long as I can. But when I contemplate such a life, I'm shocked to discover it no longer feels like freedom. Every touch I've traded with Isaac is a violation of everything I've been trained to believe, yet every one of those touches has elicited something new, a peek into a life other than my own. It's as if I've glimpsed a new Sense I never knew existed, and I can't stand the thought that it might have opened so briefly only to close for good.

His words from two nights ago return to me: *If you had a chance to live for one day like your mom did, would you take it? You tell me the Ecosystem wants us to die because we're human. If that's true, shouldn't we want to live like we are?*

I feel as if I'm ready to answer, or at least to try. But the boy who asked me is no longer interested in what I have to say. He plods two steps to my back, the only sound he makes the crackling of his feet on dead branches. The words I might have offered him stick like thorns in my throat.

By evening, we've covered five leagues or more, enough distance for the forest to become unfamiliar to my eyes, though not to my Sense. The voice that speaks constantly in my inner ear tells me the names of the predominant trees in these parts, *maul* and *shredder* and *juggernut*, each with its own special way of maiming us if we come too close. Isaac has slowed us down considerably, not only with his limping pace but with his frequent stops to gather wood for the evening's fire. Each time he bends to pick up a stick, he asks Rachel if the wood is safe, and each time he asks her instead of me, I do my best to ignore him. It works, I guess. He doesn't approach me. When I announce that it's time to bed down for the night, he says not a word.

I scan the area for a suitable sleeping place, and this time I'm luckier than on previous nights: close at hand, I find a clearing where a collection of juggernut branches has fallen, probably from storm. Decomposition hasn't set in yet, so we needn't fear these offerings from the trees. We can build a lean-to from the thickly scaled branches, a wall of non-life to shield us from the forest. I explain my plan to Isaac and Rachel, and both seem agreeable, though neither speaks. He unties his cloak and lifts branches into a tipi, their tangled ends knotting to hold the structure firm. Then he stacks his load of kindling outside the shelter and strikes a flint to the pile. The blood-sweet fragrance of burning wood fills our campsite.

I eye him as he rises to roast strips of warhog. He's trying to conceal it, but his limp is definitely worse, and I'm pretty sure I know why. Back in the village, we have ways to soften the skins of the things we kill. But those methods take time, and my quick-cured hide must have stiffened to a punishing degree. Knowing Isaac, he'd never admit how much it's hurting him, certainly not after last night. I gnaw at tough warhog flesh, look for an opening. When at last he sits, legs stretched out and ending in their ridiculous boots, I swallow the last bite of pig and ask, "Feet hurting?"

He says nothing, only reaches for a cut of meat. Rachel sits by his side, nibbling her own delicacy, but her eyes travel to the clumsy bundles wrapped around his feet. I try to think of something to say to remove her from the conversation, but *get lost* doesn't seem to strike the right tone. So I simply say her name: "Rachel."

It's enough. She leaps up and busies herself with the fire.

"We still have a long way to go," I say to Isaac.

"So?" he responds, his first word to me since last night.

"So if your feet are bothering you, that'll slow us down. Which will mean more time before we reach Miriam."

"Like you care."

I draw a deep breath. "Can I take a look? Warhog isn't exactly the footwear of choice," I joke, and risk a smile.

He looks away, glowering. His tongue works bits of meat from under his lip.

"Isaac." I can't believe I'm begging him. "Maybe I can fix the sandals, make them more comfortable. I want this trip to be over as much as you do. I want to find…."

I can't finish. I can't bear his distance any longer. I reach out as if to touch him, then rise and walk away.

"Here," he says.

The sandals make a crinkling sound as he removes the bands of warhog hair that hold them in place. I turn, not sure what I'll see, not sure what I want to.

It's far worse than I imagined. The cured hide sticks to his soles, and when he tears the wrapping free, I see where the material has chafed his skin horribly. The original puncture wound is barely visible in the mess of cuts that cover his left foot. Strangely, though, it's his other foot that's more swollen and puffy, the sole yellowish beneath the blood. My Sense prickles uneasily as I drop to the ground by his feet.

He makes no effort to move away. A sickly smell rises from his right foot, assaulting my nose and my Sense at the same time. "Histeria," I whisper.

"So that's what you call it," he says. "It must've happened when I went for that cursed pig."

I stare, bile rising in my throat, dismay in my mind.

"It's worse than the other one, huh?" he says.

"It's…." Hesitantly, I lay my fingertips on the suppurating wound where the histeria barb struck. His flesh recoils from my touch, quivering flaccidly as if there's no muscle beneath it. An image of gritted teeth and red, rolling eyes momentarily mars my vision. I roll up the leg of his pants and see the same puffy flesh ascending midway up his calf, shot through with veins of the deepest purple. He smiles ruefully.

"I really put my foot in it this time, didn't I?" he says.

"Why didn't you tell me?"

"I thought you knew."

"Histeria is insidious. But once it's had a day or two to work…."

"I've heard the stories," he says. "All the healers have. I guess I should have listened."

"Isaac," I say, and my voice trembles in a way that isn't mine. "If you'd told me, I could have sucked out the poison. Why did you insist on going barefoot?"

He doesn't answer. For the first time since yesterday, when his eyes meet mine, I don't feel wounded by what I see there. He lays a hand on my arm. My skin shivers at the Sense of the poison working its way inward.

"There are medicines," he says softly. "In the forest. At least, that's what the healers say. No Sensor will talk about them. I've been looking for them since we left camp."

"Medicines?" It's not a word I know.

"Treatments," he says. "To heal wounds and things.

From plants, mainly. People used to know about them, ages and ages ago."

I rack my brain for a plant that will treat a histeria sting, but I know I've never heard of it. More importantly, I've never Sensed it. My stomach sickens on its recent meal. "There's nothing like that, Isaac. Nothing."

"Then I'll have to keep looking by myself."

He tries to push himself up, but pain lances him, and he falls back. I stare at his ruined foot, then put my hands on his shoulders to ease him to the ground. In the moment before I let go, I Sense his body blazing with venom.

"I forbid you to take another step," I say, as firmly as my voice will allow. "You're no good to...to anyone like this. I'll tie you down if I have to." Blade in hand, I approach the boundary of our campsite.

"Where are you going?" he calls out.

"To find the thing you need," I say. "To find... medicine."

I'M BLIND IN the Ecosystem for the first time in my life. I don't know what I'm searching for, what I'm trying to Sense. Isaac has given me a list of names, plants he claims once existed, though he has no idea what they look like. *Goldenseal, aloe, jewelweed.* The healers, it seems, have lots of dusty lore, little firsthand knowledge. Even if he described these supposed remedies minutely, I'd hesitate. In all my years, I've Sensed only things that are malevolent, to varying degrees. Things that can trick you, cut you, kill you. Nothing that can cure you.

Full dark has descended, and I'm left to my doubting Sense. Guilt eats me for failing to detect the histeria when the warhog attacked, to check Isaac's condition once the fight was over. I have no excuse except that my concentration was focused on the more pressing threat beforehand, my own injury after. And then, the next morning, when he refused to let me wrap his feet.... Why didn't I see that he was hiding something, why didn't I Sense the sickness working its way into his blood? Histeria is furtive, but it's not imperceptible.

Sensing the things that kill us is what I'm supposed to do.

But it's also all I do. I'm no healer. I know how to avoid what tries to kill us, not how to stop it once it starts.

Fighting the panic that will only reveal my presence and spoil my instincts, I reach out into the night-singing forest and touch with ambient nerves the life that lurks in the darkness. I Sense bat-winged insects, nettle and poisonrose bushes, a lone Great Horned Howl caught in the act of spearing a late-bedding killdeer. I breathe in the rank smell of wildlife torn by a shredder tree, finger the crowns of a hundred mushrooms that could kill me in a hundred different ways if I touched them with actual fingers. This is the Ecosystem I know, a garden of endless, inexhaustible death. The idea that I might find anything in this toxic desert to combat the poison creeping up Isaac's leg squeezes a laugh that's closer to a wail from my throat.

He's survived more than a day with a histeria sting. The blood vessels in his lower extremities have constricted, forcing the venom upward. By daybreak if not sooner, the hot poison swirling through his veins will drive him mad. Under its influence, he'll hiss, spit, bite at anything that comes near. His flesh will peel and putrefy, and he'll tear at it with his own teeth. Soon after, he'll lapse into a coma from which he won't awaken. That's the slender mercy of histeria. He won't be conscious when the toxin sears the last ounce of strength from his limbs and the last shred of sanity from his mind.

I tear at plants that numb my flesh, knowing they're useless to me. A scream rends the night, and my Sense is instantly shattered. I realize at once what I should have before.

Rachel.

I turn in utter darkness and race back to the campsite. In my fear and haste, I crash against trees, mindless if they're predatory or not. I blunder through bushes that could be as deadly as the one that impaled Isaac. My injured leg throbs, blood from the opened stitchwork slicking my skin. I hear the shriek of cicatrix directly in my ear, and I realize the shield that protects me has fallen. I'm a commoner alone in the Ecosystem at night, and I cover my head with my hands, surrendering to its power and terror as the cicatrix descend upon me.

Then I stop. And breathe.

And fall to my knees. The spark of our campfire shines in the distance, but that's not what brought me to a halt. It's the smell. An unfamiliar smell that pierces my fogged mind like my very last chance.

I locate its source. My hands, unguided by sight or Sense, gather the aromatic leaves clustered at the base of what I guess to be an ache tree. If by accident I should touch a fallen ache leaf, I'll become so dizzy I'll never find my way back to camp. But I ignore the risk and tear the smelly stuff at the tree's feet. I don't know how much to collect, what to do with it once I'm done. I don't know if it's the thing Isaac called *medicine*. All I know is that it's the one new thing I've discovered in the dark, the one new thing, it seems to me at this moment, I've discovered in my entire life. I ball the leaves in my fist and sprint in the direction of the glowing campsite.

I burst through the trees to find Rachel pinned against the lean-to, fending off Isaac with bare hands. I'm not sure which of them screamed. She's stronger than she looks, or in his delirium he's weaker, because he staggers at her blows. But she's trapped and panicked, and she can't fight him off for long. His face streams with sweat, his eyes glow sheer as a fell-cat's in the firelight. If he bites her and works the saliva or a deliquescing tooth into the wound, she'll be next to die.

With a single charge, I bring him down, try at the same time to catch him as he falls. We land just as the lean-to drowns our bodies in spiky branches. I roll free, ready to strike again, but his eyes are raised to the darkness and his body thrashes without purpose. For a moment, I see him as another creature felled by my bloodlust, and my heart bursts within me. I turn to Rachel.

"Did he bite you?"

She shakes her head, eyes riveted on Isaac's slack face.

"Hold him still," I say, dropping to my knees beside him. She places her hands tentatively on his arms. "Harder!" I snap as he fights me. "Hold his head! Harder, curse you!" Her hands fuss uselessly beside his ears before they find his hair and grip. I try to ram the wad of leaves between his teeth, but I can't pry them apart. He snarls at me, nearly bites.

"You need to mix it with water," Rachel says quietly. "Like a potion."

I have no time to ask how she knows this, why she didn't tell me before. I reach for the makeshift canteen I fashioned from the warhog's stomach, crumple the leaves into the water and shake violently, then tip Isaac's head back and pinch his nose. He gasps spasmodically, and I pour the concoction down his throat. He coughs, tries to spit it back up, but I clamp my hand over his mouth until he reflexively swallows. I fall back, Rachel landing in my lap, the two of us watching him in an agony of suspense.

His limbs continue to flail, his head whipping so wildly I fear he'll bash his skull. I shove Rachel to the ground and crawl toward him, wondering if I've done more harm than good. I'm about to grab his arms when Rachel speaks again from behind me.

"You have to apply it topically."

"What?"

"The medicine. It has to be put directly on the wound. As well as given by mouth."

Again, I don't bother to ask how she knows so much. I unwrap a section of my own bandage, paying no attention to the bloody, half-open wound. I tip the canteen until the bandage is soaked, then press it to the sole of Isaac's ravaged foot. He flinches, kicks, but I grab the foot with my other hand and hold firm. The heady aroma of the leaves penetrates my senses, though it says nothing to my Sense.

Through my skin, I feel the stutter of his racing heart, the wild yawing of his fevered mind. I see his poisoned dreams: dreams of his lost love drowning in a lake of blood, her body consumed by creatures far greater than cicatrix. It's as if I'm in his dreams with him, lost in lurid fantasies. With the corner of consciousness that remains my own, I force my hands to press harder on the bandage, while with the strength of my will, I command his anguished body to calm.

Heartbeats pass, or days. At last, his chest heaves a huge, wracking sigh, and when he exhales, his body sinks to the ground in a posture resembling natural sleep. It's hard to tell in the campfire's light, but I think some of the sickly color has drained from his face. Through the point where our flesh meets, I feel his pulse settle, his mind grow restful. I don't know if I Sense or dream, if the thoughts that pass between us are his or mine. But none of that matters. I've healed him, and the relief that pours through me draws a sob from my chest.

His eyelids flutter, his lips move soundlessly. I lean close to hear.

"Mimi," he whispers.

I fall back, bury my face in my hands, and gulp air until my breath is my own. Beside me, Isaac snores deeply, floating with his beloved in sweet-scented sleep.

IN THE PALE light of morning I see his face, the hue of death no longer clinging to his cheeks. His eyes open, and he smiles weakly.

"Now we're even," he says.

He reaches for the cloak he took off the night before, wraps it around himself like a blanket. I rise, shake sleep from my legs. Rachel stirs the embers of our fire with a stick. She must have stayed up all night while the two of us slept.

"How are you feeling?" I ask Isaac.

"Like hex," he says with a grin. "How do I look?"

"Like hex," I say, but I can't help smiling back. The truth is, he looks like a miracle to me: the gauntness of his face and the circles under his eyes are nothing compared to the wonder of his smile. "Are you hungry?"

"Not for warhog, thanks," he says, grimacing. "Got anything else?"

"I'll see what I can find." Last night, I Sensed choke-berries in the vicinity, plus I'm confident I can snag something flightless. The thought of diversifying our diet is appealing, as is that of absenting myself from his eyes for a time. "Be right back." And I'm off.

I return in a trice, snap-necked tricky vulture slung over my shoulder. Isaac's out of bed, taking delicate steps around camp. The sight of him on his feet makes my heart sing. I can't stop smiling when I look at him, and I can't stop looking at him. I suspect he knows it, too.

He sits nearby while I pluck the bird and Rachel builds up the fire. Even when it starts to blaze, he hugs the cloak around himself with both hands. I pass him the pig-bladder canteen, its contents redolent of the leaf that saved him. "You need to keep your fluids up."

"Look who's the healer now," he teases, but he tips his head back and takes a long, satisfying swig. When he hands the canteen to me, our fingers touch, and even that fleeting contact is enough to make images dance through my mind.

"How did you know I'd find it?" I ask.

He shrugs. "Lucky guess."

"But which one was it? Goldenseal, aloe? My Sense couldn't name it."

"None of the above," he says. "It was witch hazel."

I'm confused. "Then why'd you tell me about the other things? If it was witch hazel you needed?"

"Does it matter?" Beneath his playfulness, I see he's hiding something. "Maybe it wasn't about looking for a particular thing, but just about looking."

I remember the feeling I had the night before. When I Sense something new in the Ecosystem, it already feels old: it was there for me to name long before I encountered it. When I chanced upon the witch hazel, it was as if I'd found myself in a genuinely new world, one where the

Ecosystem, if only for a moment, had faded to nothing. I don't say this to Isaac, though. If I did, I'm afraid of what else I might say.

"But witch hazel *was* what you needed, wasn't it?" I say instead. "The only thing that could have healed you."

"It has a reputation," he says evasively. "But I think you're the first to prove the rumors true."

I take this in. Finding the witch hazel was strange enough. Finding that it was what I was supposed to find is even stranger. But now, watching him, I realize something stranger still: finding it wasn't chance. I can practically see the medicine flowing through his bloodstream, smell it in the breath between us. When my hands fell on the strange herb in the forest, they told me this was what would heal him. They didn't guess. They knew.

As if reading my thoughts, he says quietly, "If you think that's crazy, go get my pouch. I've got something that'll really throw you for a loop."

I lay the half-plucked bird down and retrieve his healer's pouch. He releases the drawstring and shakes something onto his palm, holds it out to me. The familiar, life-giving scent envelops me before I see the oval green leaf in his hand.

I look at him, startled. "Where did you get that?"

"Witch hazel's really abundant out here," he says. "Much more so than near the village. I collected a bunch yesterday."

"But you told me...." My stomach tightens as if preparing to take a jump. "You said you didn't know what those medicine plants looked like."

He smiles sheepishly. "I guess I lied."

"But then," I say, "you could have healed yourself all along."

"Yeah, I guess so," he says, as if the thought just dawned on him. "But if I had, you wouldn't have had a chance to do it."

I fling myself to my feet as my insides continue their downward plummet. The fragile health of his body washes over me, and I feel myself swept along with it. I'm shaking so badly, I can barely choke out the words. "You risked your life to…to prove to me that I could find it? I almost didn't!" I finish incoherently. "Isaac, I almost didn't!"

"But you did," he says. "And if you hadn't, Rachel could have used what I'd already gathered. I told her how. So it wasn't that big of a risk."

My mind presents me the image from last night: Isaac raving, Rachel backed against the lean-to. The tears I've tried so hard not to shed burn on my eyes' threshold. "Why?"

"There's more to you than you think, Sarah," he says. "More to *it*, too." He gestures sweepingly at the forest. "The Sensors have told you all your life to fear the Ecosystem. Daniel doesn't see it that way."

"Daniel?" I picture the seed in the Chief Warden's hand, remember his talk of a new day dawning.

"Daniel believes there are avenues we haven't explored," Isaac says. "Possibilities for reconciliation between us and the Ecosystem. He's been training the healers to examine those possibilities."

"The Sensorship would never permit that."

He throws me a wry grin. "The Sensorship doesn't know. We've been growing things secretly, in the village. Things like witch hazel. We've been trying to learn what we can about how the Ecosystem works. To learn it in a way the council won't allow."

"You've been growing things?" I falter. "In the village?"

"We've got quite a little garden going," he says. "A lot of little gardens, actually. Scattered throughout the healers' houses."

The thought of wild things blooming in the village twists my stomach anew. How could I, how could Aaron and the others, not have Sensed the Ecosystem's presence in our own village? But then it comes to me: these medicine plants must be dead to our Sense. Whatever awakened me to witch hazel in the wild was slumbering when I left home. And that makes these hidden gardens deadlier than the deadliest of snares. "How long have you been doing this?" I ask.

"It started years ago," he answers. "Before you and I were born."

"But how...." Something isn't right about what he's saying, something doesn't fit. At last, I realize what it is. "How have you been gathering plants from the forest? You'd need a Sensor to do that."

For the first time since our conversation began, he looks away. "Yeah. Well, we did. A long time ago. Someone who went deep into the forest, and who was attuned to things the rest of the Sensors couldn't detect."

A hand clutches my chest. "Who was it?" When he doesn't answer, I raise my voice. "Isaac, who was it?"

He turns back to me, his smile at once beautiful and sad. "It was your mother."

LATER THAT MORNING, while Isaac takes a rest and Rachel prepares our gear for the next leg of the journey, I slip out of camp alone. To hunt, I tell her. But I'm not here to hunt. Right now, I feel as if I'll never hunt again.

The forest shimmers golden-green in the morning light. To a traveler who knows nothing of the Ecosystem, the woods this far from the village might seem serene, even beautiful: white-skinned breaches are the commonest tree, their yellow leaves pirouetting to the ground like glints of sunshine. Across the glade, a cardivore hops from branch to branch, head cocked, amber eyes peering through black bandit's mask. Commoners call them cardinulls, a name out of some dim memory. But stretch your hand to the woodland visitor and the bird will swoop, the razor edge of its beak lop your wrist as cleanly as an axe. Only fools and dreamers forget.

And my mother was one of them.

From the moment I learned her history, I've seen her as I wanted to see myself: Sensor, hunter, killer to the core. I've yearned to follow her, to be who she would have been had the Ecosystem not struck her down. I've even tried to forgive her for birthing me. I wonder if it was another like Isaac, a boy with the lure of a new life in his smile, who duped my mother all those years ago, persuaded her to misspend her gift in adorning the homes of the healers. I have no memory of her face, but I think I see it now, alight with her lover's lies as she rushes through the forest to fulfill his errand. Is that what killed her? Had she grown so drunk on promises she was overtaken at last by the Ecosystem's one true law?

Through patchy sunbeams, I spy a bright yellow spot approaching on the air—spy it, and Sense it as well. It's a butterfly, with long wings trailing in golden curves, a smattering of black dots sprinkled across their lazily flapping span. We call them swallowtales, and frequently see them flitting over the sward within reach of the village. Birds avoid them, as do cicatrix. Toddlers playing on the village stone clap their hands at the sight of them, entranced by their cheery colors and dancing flight. When their elders' vigilance fails, children have swallowed them, learning too late that the only tale they tell is death.

The creature finds the palm of my hand. I raise it to my face, observe its proboscis curling daintily. To my Sense, its slender body radiates venom like waves of heat. I close my fingers and watch it crumple.

When I return to camp, Isaac lies awake, warhog cloak tied at his throat, hands crossed behind his head. I don't allow him to speak.

"Daniel set you up to this, didn't he?" I say. "On the day you first talked to me and Miriam."

"Why would he do that?"

"So you could test me. See if I'd inherited my mother's...." *Weakness*, I think. "Ability."

He makes no answer. He doesn't need to.

"Well, his little experiment is over," I say. "He's meddled in the Sensorship's affairs for the last time."

"Is that a threat?"

"It's a fact," I say. "I'm going after Miriam. You can come if you want. If the star-cursed lovers bit wasn't part of the show."

"It wasn't," he says levelly.

I don't care if he's lying or not. I refuse to believe he's done any of this for me. "Suit yourself. But your next accident is your last."

"You need to stop making threats," he says as I walk away.

I spin, pull his blade from my belt and whip it at him. He flinches as it embeds itself in the earth between his legs.

"I suggest you learn to use that," I say before tossing the sheath at his feet. "Where we're going, you're going to need it."

THE FOREST SEEMS endless. Ranks of pillar-like trees crowd the horizon, blocking my view of what lies beyond. The day sets in hot and steamy, trails of vapor drifting from the canopy to be swallowed by the sky's slate blue. Shod in more forgiving slippers of tricky vulture wattles, Isaac shuffles behind me practicing thrusts with his blade, while Rachel follows, her tread almost noiseless, her eyes peeled for dead wood. She's collected quite a bundle, enough to fill her arms halfway to her chin. Weak as she looks, she doesn't utter a peep of protest. By midday, she'll need to double her burden. I don't expect to find any more after that.

The sun's climbed to its apex when we reach the deep defile that splits the forest in two. To our left, the ground rises in a long slope north, easy walking as far as the eye can see, though beyond, it gives way to tumbled boulders and the foothills of treacherous mountains. The southern arm drops downhill, gradually enough that none of us except Isaac risks losing our footing. The most worrisome feature of that route is the dense thicket of pain trees that gather in the lowlands to our right, so rife with seductive poison I can see the smoky haze hanging above the spires. We're too far away for the trees to ensnare us, but I keep alert for any change in the wind. We'll need to skirt the grove to follow the path I've charted, the only one that gives us a chance of speed. Safety I'm not thinking about. We never had that to begin with.

I call a halt and point south. "If anyone wants a break, now's the time."

Both of them look as if they could use a week's convalescence, but neither says a word. Isaac takes a sip of water and passes it to Rachel, who follows suit. When she offers it to me, I shake my head.

"Keep an eye out for snares," I tell her. "You too," I say to Isaac.

"I'll try."

"You'd better."

Plotting a course as far from the pain trees as possible, I start down the slope. The ground is soft beneath the leaf-fall, loamy, receiving our weight and holding for a beat before releasing. The air carries an alien scent, and not from the trees: the smell is rich, almost rank, my nose beginning to twitch at the deadly presence I Sensed long ago. It lies at the bottom of the hill, less than two leagues away, and I'd have reached it well before now if not for these two. But we can't avoid it, not without veering far from our errand. The Ecosystem knows this as well as I. Maybe it truly is toying with us—with me—letting me live so it can kill me when I reach my goal. Or maybe it plans to kill me today. Either way, I have no choice but to face the trap it's laid.

I've shaved a dead hexlox branch until it's as sharp as my Sense, tempered it in the campfire until it's as hard as my heart. I carry it before me, point at the ready. I'm no longer sure what I need to protect myself from.

The downhill stroll seems to have revived Isaac and Rachel's spirits, while the thing that lies at its base is too distant to trouble their minds. They chat openly behind me, their conversation broken only when she scurries to pick up a stick or he stumbles in his haste to avoid a minor snare. I could silence him at the point of my spear, but I let him talk. I'm done saving empty-headed girls from his questionable charms. I'm busy enough trying to save the one we've already lost.

"Think about it this way," he says. "If human beings developed along *with* the Ecosystem, how could it turn *against* us? That's impossible, right?"

"We grew beyond it," she answers. "And so it set its mind to our torment."

"Even if that's true," he says, "that was a long time ago. Can we really believe it's held a grudge since then? Are we so important it's spent every ounce of its energy trying to wipe us out?"

"The Ecosystem forgets nothing," Rachel responds. "You've seen so yourself. The pig, the wisteria, the braindiggers. You see how it hunts us."

I'm momentarily annoyed that she refers to the histeria by the term he's taught her, but I let it go with a sniff. Isaac pauses as if he's noticed, then presses on.

"It's hunting everything, Rachel. If you were a warhog and you got pricked by a wisteria thorn, you'd die, unless you were lucky enough to munch some witch hazel. Everything's trying to protect itself, and everything's developed defense mechanisms to do so. But that doesn't mean the Ecosystem has it out for us and us alone."

Rachel falls silent, as if mulling this over. The bundle of sticks shifts in her arms.

"Here's another way to think about it," he says. "If the Ecosystem's trying to kill us, why doesn't it send a plague into the village, something the Sensors couldn't detect, or couldn't fight if they did? If it wants us all to die, why does it rely on snares the Sensors *can* avoid?"

"It tempts us," Rachel answers, feebly. "It tricks us."

"But *why*?" he insists. "Why waste time on tricks if it could kill us outright?"

Again, she's mute.

"Here's what I think," Isaac says. "The Sensors assume that the Ecosystem developed snares to kill us. But couldn't it be that it's trying to protect itself *from* us? Wouldn't that explain why we had to travel beyond the Sensorship's normal hunting range before we found plants that aren't lethal, that are actually beneficial? To me, that makes it seem like the Ecosystem's built up a wall of defenses around the village because it fears us, not because it hates us."

At first, Rachel has no answer to that either. I mouth it silently, and though there's no way she hears me, the proper words spill from her lips.

"We Sense its mind," she says. "And its will. We Sense its hatred for us."

"Are you sure you're Sensing *it*?"

"What other mind could we be Sensing?"

"Daniel has a theory about that," Isaac says. "He thinks everyone has the capacity for the Sense, but it's dormant in most people. The ones who exhibit it are the ones who feel the threats most strongly. That would fit, right? If the goal is to keep the human race alive, the people who are most attuned to danger would develop the strongest Sense. If, that is, their village encouraged that particular brand of paranoia, and discouraged everyone and everything else. Which would mean you're not Sensing the Ecosystem's hatred so much as your own distrust."

My sniff is louder this time. Isaac ignores it.

"How else do you explain why things like witch hazel are invisible to you, but not to me?" he asks Rachel. "Your Sense alerts you to poisons, not cures. But all it took was for me to be out in the Ecosystem for a few days, and I'm spouting the names of things I never heard of. And avoiding snares on my own." As if to prove his point, he jumps clumsily, just in time to spare himself a nasty pinch from a wandering stab beetle. "Doesn't that prove I had the potential all along?"

I'm about to say something, but just as my mouth opens, I realize what my words would reveal: the connection, the images from his life that flow into my mind every time I touch him. The same connection that enabled me to save him last night. If he's stealing the Sense from me, can it be that I'm stealing the power of the healers from him? I'm trying to work out what that means when he speaks again.

"You've got to remember that humans are adaptable, Rachel. When the Ecosystem first rose, we might have needed the Sense for protection alone. But is that how we want to live forever? To cower in stone villages while five percent of the population bears the burden of survival? Wouldn't it be better to try to develop our Sense in a new way, a way that gives us all a shot at life?"

Rachel says nothing for long moments. When I glance behind me, I see her heart-shaped face harboring a small smile.

"Do you truly believe there's another way?" she says.

"I believe," Isaac says, "whoa."

His words are cut short as we top a rise and look out through the thinning trees. The aches and other forest giants have fallen away, yielding to a mixed stand with names like *leprous* and *fear* and *harm*. But even these have dwindled in number, and not twenty rods ahead of us, the only trees that remain are stunted outcasts, more like bare, shriveled stakes than trees. Beyond, a flattened heath of sedge grass and bushy copses stretches for a short distance before yielding to a solid sheet of green and gray swamp water, fringed along its southern border by a hedge of sawgrass and a smattering of the same half-dead trees. In the muddy terrain where the heathland ends, tall grasses called cat o' nine tails whip in the sharp-scented breeze, while the red-and-black shapes of the birds we name dreadwings dart in and out to tend hidden nests. Their raucous screams rise to a pitch of outrage as they become aware of us, but they won't attack unless we're foolish enough to plunge into the grass.

Far different are the dark, stubby trees that dwell in the swamp's shallows. These we call mangraves, and they send my Sense into a frenzy of warning as shrill as the call of the dreadwings. Animate trees with limbs like adders and minds to match, mangraves stew in the muddy waters of the swamp, held in place by a central bundle of roots but free to move their branches and secondary roots at will. They live for centuries, growing more cunning with every gulp of filth they swallow, every breath of fresh air they're denied. They've colonized this swamp in great numbers, choking it to a depth of ten feet. I recall the Conservator's lessons on the mangraves, which in days long past couldn't tolerate our climate and grew only much farther south. But now the Ecosystem creates its own climate, and deposits its creatures wherever they best suit its desires.

Isaac peers out over the swamp at the dragonflies that zip across its surface. Tiny gouts of flame trail behind them. "What's this?"

"A test," I say. "Of your theory."

"But it's…water?"

"Genius. Can you tell me what's in it?"

He squeezes his eyes shut, wincing as if in pain.

"Not so hard," I say. "I told you to Sense it, not pummel it into submission."

"Watermites," he gasps. "And something else.

Turtles, I think. And the trees...." His eyes fly open. "Are we supposed to *cross* this?"

"Not a chance," I say. "We're going around."

He presses his lips together as if he's about to argue, then lets out air in a sound of defeat. "Is this where Barnabas died?"

"They're not quite done with him," I say. "Watermites take a long, long time."

With Isaac and Rachel in tow, I warily approach the mudflats. The sickening odor pinches my nostrils, but it's the inhabitants I'm worried about. The dreadwings have flown to roost on the upper branches of the nearest mangraves, where they eye us suspiciously, ready to dive with rending beaks punier but no less sharp than a bloodbird's. The turf beneath our feet is short and spiny, though not as dangerous as the ranks of sawgrass that rise in an unbroken forest to our right, with edges sharp enough to open a vein. Mostly I'm focused on the mangraves. Their thoughts form in my mind, dark and muddy as the swamp's shallows. With relief, I Sense that they're not communing with each other, sending the underwater messages mangraves use to coordinate their attack. If I'm lucky, we'll be past them before that changes.

I halt Isaac and Rachel with a hand, point along the southern shore. "It'll be a day and a half before we reach the far side. Don't get any ideas about drinking the water. Rachel, keep alert for anything that might follow."

"Why are we going this way?" she asks in a low voice.

"Shortest route," I say. "The uplands to the north would take ten times as long, and the southern course...." I don't need to finish, for they can see the forest of pain trees that blocks passage to the right. "Any more questions?"

Neither says a word. Maybe they're learning.

"And, Isaac?" I say.

"Yeah?"

"This isn't the time to try to make friends with the Ecosystem. Clear?"

He nods. "Clear."

"All right," I say. "Then let's get moving."

WE MATCH STRIDES, Isaac and Rachel stepping in my footprints, breathing as silently as I do. She Senses, and he doesn't dispute, what I know: this place is deadly beyond reckoning. Mangraves are its chief but not sole evil. Grabgrass grows wild by the shoreline, interspersed with patches of bogsand—not true sand, which my Sense can't detect, but a subterranean plant whose spreading roots turn soil porous and unstable. These were among the first snares I learned to recognize, and I negotiate them with an ease bordering on carelessness. Other dangers demand greater caution. Snatching turtles lurk where mud turns to muck and muck to water, their gray-brown shells disguised in the slime and their bright pink tongues waggling an irresistible lure to frogs and fish. They're happy to lunge at larger prey, though: killdeer and warhogs that seek the water's edge by moonlight, shore-stalking great blue hellions that thrust their beaks deep into the mire. I know of no attacks on humans, but that's only because no humans willingly come here. The turtles aren't that picky. The big ones, several hundred years old, carry shells twice as long as I am tall. They'd have no objection to dragging one of us inside the cavity of that shell, where sharp beak and claws tear prey to chunks before spitting out the bones to bob on the swamp's turbid surface.

The narrow path we tread forces us close to the water's edge, the thicket of sawgrass blocking us on our right. I Sense the eyes of the swamp following as we advance, mostly lesser creatures roused by our presence, trollfrogs and water bugs and snakes that lack the strength or ferocity to kill. But I'm mindful of the dragonflies, a cloud of which could generate enough firepower to char hair and flesh. The mangraves remain somnolent, mucky water lapping their roots, their brooding power a goad to my edgy Sense. We're moving far too slowly for my liking. Despite my throbbing leg—I wouldn't let Isaac near the torn sewing, which dangles beneath the tattered remains of the bandage— I'd run if I were alone, trust my Sense to chart a safe course well in advance of my speed. But Isaac couldn't keep up with me while nursing his wounded foot, and he lacks the agility to dodge snares at a sprint. I don't know whether this strange hybrid, a commoner with dangerous beliefs and an equally dangerous confidence in his own budding abilities, can survive this place. He may be the first of a new breed. But that means he may also be the last.

The sun drags across the sky. The swamp stretches before us, stolid and unfathomable. Silence has descended on its waters, the dreadwings keeping quiet in their treetop roosts, even the dragonflies departing to buzz some distant cove. The stale air feels like a weight pressing me downward, whispering to me to lay myself in the muddy shallows until the small creatures at the swamp's edge lose their timidity and emerge to draw me out to deeper waters. What we'll do at nightfall I don't want to think; that a fire produced from Rachel's pitiful collection of sticks can hold off the mangraves seems too much to hope. I wish we could walk on through the night, but Isaac would never make it. The three of us haven't spoken a word since we began, and I wonder whether the oppressiveness of this place strikes the two of them with anything like the force it does me. Though I'm not eager to hear their voices, at least if one of them said something I could suppress my mounting urge to scream.

At what I judge to be suppertime, we stop briefly to drink, nibble a bite of tricky vulture, take a few moments' standing rest. Then we move on.

By dusk, I hear the two of them limping behind me, punished by the pace I've set. I've arrived at no solution to the falling of nighttime, found no break in the sawgrass, no patch of earth bare of life. So I push forward, thinking only to put as much distance behind us as I can before the two of them drop in their tracks. In the faded blue above our heads, I see the ghost of a half-moon rising, and I try to increase our pace before the image brightens.

All at once, the stifling air brings me the sound of Isaac's voice. I feel a fleeting sense of relief, a lightening of the load across my shoulders. But when I glance behind, I see he's muttering to himself, in words too low to hear. The sky dulls and the moon finds its nesting place, but his chant keeps up, a steady stream with a buried vehemence that puts me in mind of a curse. I raise a hand and turn to him.

"The Ecosystem's not deaf, you know," I whisper.

His brow is furrowed, his lips moving inaudibly. Though he pulled up short when I did, he seems unaware of me.

"Isaac," I say. In the dead air, my voice scratches like wind through sawgrass.

He shakes his head and meets my eyes. "Is it time for a break?"

"Not yet," I say. "Do you realize you've been babbling nonstop?"

"I have? What was I saying?"

I scrutinize his face. I've seen that look before, most recently on the face of the girl we're trying to save. "You really don't remember what you said?"

He shakes his head, but the distance and confusion never leave his eyes.

"You're Sensing," I say. "True Sensation is unconscious, and uninterrupted. It never stops."

I reach out with my own Sense, touch the strands of his. I don't know what's produced the change, but there's no doubt about it: the Sense has awakened in him for real. Whether he's crossed some invisible threshold on his own or the darkening swamp has triggered instincts within him, it's not his mind anymore that's doing it, not my hands that are drawing it out.

It's his whole body. It's him. He's Sensing the threat that hangs in the air.

"Do you believe me now?" I say quietly.

With an effort, he shakes his head. "They're just trees. They *can* kill us, but that doesn't mean they want to. Or that they're going to."

I'm in no mood to argue. "They *will* kill us if you don't hold it together. Listen to them."

I raise my hands, fingers spread to gather the undercurrent of the mangraves' minds. Isaac does the same. We stand in the sour night air, blot out everything that speaks to us of our humanity, let the waters of Sensation spill over us. Though he's weak and awkward as a child, there's no question he's tapped into it: the pulse, the ripple, the flow. He's Sensing it in its entirety. He's Sensing what I feared.

They've spotted him.

The swamp groans as the mangraves wrench themselves from the depths and stir the muddy waters. The dreadwings shriek, fling themselves into the indigo sky, but some are caught by the trees' unfolding limbs and dragged fluttering beneath the surface. The water roils and bubbles, spitting up all manner of foulness: snatching turtles with glassy eyes and immobile faces, water vipers that coil like strips of moonlight as they streak toward shore. In a flash, I recognize the trap the trees have laid, even as I see the horror in Isaac's eyes.

"They see you!" I yell. "They're using you to lock in on us!"

No sooner have the words left my throat than the

water bursts with the force of the mangraves' fury. A root twice as thick as Rachel's body curls around her legs, drags her from her feet. In the time it takes her small form to splash down, I realize the roots must have been inching to shore while Isaac and I talked. The one that holds Rachel lashes into the air, the wood she collected spraying in a wild arc before raining down on the swamp's surface. Her thin scream is answered by the call of the marsh, a hysterical chorus conducted by the trees. It all happens in an instant, and in another instant, Rachel's body vanishes beneath the turbulent waters.

In the instant that follows, Isaac strips off his cloak, dives into the swamp, and kicks for the spot where she went down. He takes no more than three strokes before another root clutches his chest and pulls him under.

"Isaac!"

My inexpert dive cuts the water mostly with my face. I've never had to swim before, but by flailing my hands and feet, I stay afloat. My Sense is a tendon strung so tight that even with the black water baffling my vision, I'm aware of the creatures that float up to greet me. A snatching turtle surfaces where it thinks I'm supposed to be, but I've already ducked beneath it, emerging on its other side. A cloud of watermites tries to surround me, but I squirt through a hole in the swirling colony before it closes on my ankle. While I swim, my Sense scans the swamp's living bottom, telling me when the water grows too deep for me to stand. Then I bob and scan the area around me, but all is still and silent. You'd never know that two bodies have gone down into the murky abyss beneath the placid surface.

The massive mangrave root registers in my Sense the moment before it strikes. I propel myself out of its path, the root glancing off my side with a force that knocks the breath from my lungs. Denied its kill, it folds back on itself to crush me. But it's not quite as fast on the surface as it was below, and I'm able to wrap my legs around it before it constricts. It lifts me from the mire as it did Rachel, slams me against the water so hard I feel as if I've run full-tilt into a wall. I struggle to keep a grip on consciousness, an even more tenuous grip on the root's slick surface. Having cast my spear aside at the water's edge, I can think of no plan but to ride it out and hope for an opening to launch myself beyond its grasp.

The tree, however, has other ideas. It thrashes me, a living whip, every thud against the water the concussion of a battering ram. I cling to it, fingernails broken and bleeding, face pressed into its rotten bark. When it discovers it can't crush me, it tries to drown me. I let go and fight to the surface, choke on stagnant water, clutch it again when it rises. How—or why—I hold on I don't know. Rachel and Isaac are gone, Miriam lost. Death by water, a true drowning death, is said to be among the easiest. I could let go for good, drop below the surface and take a deep breath, and all would be over.

Then I see them.

Half-blinded by the waves and my own streaming hair, I watch their moonlit forms float to the surface.

Their eyes are closed, their faces like amber. But the tree has let them go, and I understand why: the roots that held them are racing across the water. Coming for me.

I leap from my perch in a reckless dive, hit the water hard, come up gasping. With all my remaining strength, I strike out for Isaac and Rachel's slowly rotating bodies. I've reached them when roots wrap my ankles, one on each leg, their intention clearly being to tear me in two. But I'm armed with the blade I saw clutched in Isaac's hand, and I drive it deep into the nearest root, deep enough to tap the fluid that flows through its veins. The swamp bellows with the mangrave's fury. I strike again and feel the cutting edge slice through pulpy flesh. The roots retreat, sinking beneath the dark waters. I spin, ready for another attack, my Sense keener than the weapon I hold.

But no attack comes. The swamp has gone quiet, the water no longer bucking with the mangraves' wrath. I've learned something of value, and so have they. They're cowards, afraid to fight anyone who can fight back. A torrent of rage wells within me, and I give full vent to it.

"I'll kill you!" I scream, striking the water with the flat of the blade. "If you touch them again, I'll kill you!"

The trees can't understand my words, but they hear my voice, and they shrink back in terror.

I search for Isaac and Rachel, find that their bodies have descended. I dive blindly for the spot where I last saw them. Though the waters show me nothing, I'm directed by my Sense to their limbs, which wave like broken reeds. I bite down on Isaac's blade and circle their waists with my arms, then frog-kick to the surface. The water buoys their bodies as I head for shore, yet it feels as if I'm hauling twin corpses behind me.

At last, lungs bursting, muscles burning, I find the mucky bottom. It's all I can do to drag their limp bodies to land before I collapse beside them. Woozily, I regain my feet, take hold of each by an ankle, and pull. Without the assistance of the water, their flesh clings to the muddy shoreline. At last, with a sucking sound, they come free, and I'm able to draw them as near to the sawgrass as I dare.

I fall to my knees and scan the wreckage of their bodies. Rachel, I see at once, is dead, her insides crushed, her eyes and lips gaping. I listen for a pulse or a breath, but I know there's none to hear.

Isaac is another matter. Though his chest doesn't move, his body beneath its coating of slime appears sound, and the fact that he managed to retain his grip on the blade gives me hope. But I don't know what to do, have no idea how to bring him back. His healer's bag is gone, sunk to the bottom of the swamp, and even if I had it, I lack the skill to use it.

So I do the only thing I can think to do. I raise his torso in my arms, lower my head, and hold tight. I feel my own heart beating against his chest, my own lungs rising and falling, willing his to copy my movements. As I did on the night I healed him with the witch hazel, I try to reach inside him and find the spark of his life, if any remains. With that strange and fearful connection we share, I try to make medicine of my own body to restore him to me.

But this time, nothing answers my call. No images come to my mind. Though the warmth of his body lingers, he's truly gone.

Gently, I return him to the ground. Hesitantly, I stretch myself beside him. My fingers brush damp curls from his forehead, tuck slick strands behind his ears. An impulse takes me, and I press my lips against his cheek. His flesh is soft and warm, and though it tastes foul from the swamp's waters, I'm glad I did it. Glad I kissed him once, before the end.

The mangraves will come back. The lesser things of the swamp will find us, and the work of death will begin. Through my shoulder's contact with the wet earth, I Sense the Ecosystem's mind, and I'm surprised to hear no blare of victory, no mocking laugh. It merely nods as if satisfied, then turns its thought to other things. And I lose it in darkness and distance, as I hold Isaac's body close to mine.

I WAKE TO find him gone.

Rachel, too. The morning light shows the marks of their bodies in the slick bank, but neither of them is there. Isaac's cloak lies sopping and crumpled, yet his thresher's blade is nowhere to be found.

I spring to my feet. Every inch of me aches: muscles, lungs, head, heart. Bruises pepper my arms and legs and stomach, and the sewing in my thigh is so far gone it's a wonder I didn't bleed to death while I slept. I search the shoreline for mangrave tracks, thinking the roots might have dragged my companions away during the night. But there's nothing. Casting my Sense into the swamp, I discover that the tree I wounded has communicated my danger to the colony, and none dares approach me, even in sleep.

I squint into the daylight shimmering off the swamp's green surface. The air is absolutely quiet, not a puff of wind to shake the reeds or ruffle the water. High above, I see the soaring form of a bald evil, its pure white head and motionless black wings stark against dollops of pink and blue cloud. But strong as these birds are, a single one couldn't have removed two human bodies in the night, and I Sense nothing else nearby capable of the feat.

"Where is he?" I yell at the swamp. "What have you done with him?"

The mangraves shrink from me and sulk in silence.

It's when I turn from the water that I see a ragged opening in the skirt of sawgrass, as if something has gnawed the shafts to form a rough trail leading away from the shoreline. I reorient my Sense toward the gap, wondering what on earth could have produced it. No life form registers, and I don't waste further time wondering. I reach to the ground to scoop a protective layer of mud onto my shoulders, then plunge into the breach.

The trail zigzags through the field of sawgrass, just wide enough for me to squeeze between unbroken shafts. Whatever cut the grass did so at the base, leaving only the tiniest tips of sharp-edged stubble to irritate my feet. But that's enough to disguise the cutter's tracks in the wet ground, and I soon give up trying to find a clean print. I open myself to the Ecosystem, but there's no trace of a Sensory imprint on the grass, the earth, the air. It's as if a dream or a phantom passed through the field at night before vanishing at first light of day.

Abruptly, the trail in the sawgrass ends, and I find myself in a clearing, a roughly circular bowl ten or twelve feet across scooped from the closely packed stems. The first thing I see is Rachel's body, laid atop a sawgrass pile in the center of the glade. With the ranks of grass towering to a height of eight feet around her, she seems even smaller than she truly is, a girl as small as that first girl's doll. Her hair, still damp from the night, has been arranged so it seems to spill naturally down her shoulders, and most of the mud has been daubed from her cheeks and brow. Though her arms are broken and dislocated, her hands have been placed neatly on her chest, fingers laced. I approach and discover that her nest has been prepared so carefully, only the harmless undersides of the sawgrass touch her body. Her skin in the pallid light seems to glow, and though death sits on her delicate features, it's possible to imagine her lying peacefully on a bed far softer than any she's known.

I kneel by Rachel's side, touch her cheek. The sawgrass rustles in a breath of marsh wind, a soft sound like a mother hushing her child at night. Aaron might have hushed me so, when I first came to him. My eyes sting at the thought of Rachel's mother and father, two who trusted their child to the Sensorship, two who'll never see her again. And Rachel herself, the girl who just days ago was alive enough to lead Isaac into the wild, to help me heal his wound, to palaver with him over the Ecosystem's ways. Every Sensor knows that death is never far, life never wholly won from the destroyer. But did Rachel truly believe that? Did my mother? Did I?

On the far side of the circle where Rachel lies, another trail has been cut, one that veers sharply out of sight behind the sawgrass screen. I know I'll have to walk that trail soon. I've recovered enough of my wits to realize that some other human being must have done this, though who or how remains a mystery. Why the stranger left me by the swamp while he dragged off my companions, I can't guess. What I'll say to him if I find him beside Isaac's body, I can't imagine.

I rise from Rachel's side and approach the opening. As I draw near, I steel myself for what I'll find, let all hopes and fears sift from me like a dawn drizzle sliding from my skin. I tell myself I'm prepared. Then a quiver in the new trail touches my Sense, and I stop dead, waiting for the stranger to emerge.

He steps from the sawgrass, and it's Isaac.

The blade's in his hand, a load of freshly cut grass in his arms. Without the cloak, he's naked to the waist like the day I met him, and though he's holding the stalks lightly, soft undersides down, thin signatures of blood stripe his chest and arms. For a moment, we do nothing but stare at each other. I've just started to move toward him when he drops both his blade and his burden and strides across the clearing. We meet in the middle, stand facing each other for another spell. His hand rises to my cheek, and I don't resist as he pulls me toward him and kisses me.

It should feel wrong to touch him like this, to let him touch me. But it doesn't feel wrong, just strange and new. His lips move against mine, softly pressing and releasing, while my mouth remains open in the startled circle it took when I first saw him. I try to match his movements, and eventually I settle into the rhythm of it, though I can't help thinking we're like two fish breathing underwater. Still, it makes my heart race, this closeness, this contact I've never known. The connection we've shared since he joined me in the forest is so intense it's almost painful, a tangle of impressions too total to identify one by one. It feels as if nothing is secret about him anymore. As if he's the entire world, and I have it all to myself.

But that feeling doesn't last. Through the battery of images that leap from him to me, I see the face of the girl we're seeking, her eyes wide and wondering. And then it's as if I *am* that girl, and I can no longer tell who he's kissing, me or her. I grip his hands, pull them from my face.

"Don't," I say. "Please."

His soft mouth retreats, his heat melts away. I stand staring at his lips, and when I raise my fingers, I can still feel their touch on mine.

"Sarah," he says.

"You were dead," I say stupidly.

The corner of his mouth lifts in a rakish smile. "Slowed my heartbeat and breathing," he says. "An old healer's trick. To keep from drowning."

At the word *drowning*, I'm brought back to the reason we're standing here, in this funeral circle carved from living grass. Shame courses through me as I think of the frail girl whose pyre lies mere feet behind us.

"Isaac," I say. "We can't."

"I know," he says. "Not with…."

His head gestures toward Rachel. But his eyes say more.

"Oh, Isaac," I say.

"Help me pick this up," he says, nodding at the pile of sawgrass at our feet. His deep brown eyes nearly stop my breath, but their stricken look is finally enough to pull me from these last moments' trance.

"You shouldn't have cut it," I say, trying for gentleness. "The Ecosystem won't forgive."

"I couldn't leave her for the swamp."

Together we stoop, gather the blades, and stand. His fingers touch mine one last time, maybe by accident, and I jump back as if I've received a static shock. I'm flooded with a pang so dizzying I stumble as we walk the few short steps to Rachel's side, where he kneels to complete his work.

I don't expect such delicacy from his large, seasoned hands. Blade by blade, he lays the sawgrass upon her body, forming a pyramid that covers all but her restful face. Once he's finished, she looks like a girl asleep in a teepee of green, awaiting the summons of playmates to wake and embrace the day. While he tends her body, I retrace the path in the sawgrass and come out by the bank of the swamp, setting off a flurry of fear in the mangraves that stand dark and twisted by the water's edge. "Boo," I can't resist whispering, and they quail from me, trunks straining to escape. I wade ankle-deep in the mire, pluck white water-liliths tipped with pale rose and gold. Like so much else in the Ecosystem, the liliths' beauty belies their danger: I wouldn't pick them to crown any but a dead girl's brow. But Rachel, some feeling that doesn't come from my Sense assures me, would have loved these flowers. She would have nurtured them, braided garlands from them, thrown dried petals in the air, if her fate had been to live in any world other than this.

By the time I return with the water-liliths, Isaac has cut more stalks to put the finishing touches on his sawgrass bier, a series of rings curving gracefully over Rachel's broken body. I place three liliths in a circlet around her forehead and step back, admiring how the creamy petals stand out against her dark skin and hair. I try not to think about what this lovely adornment will do to her if we wait too long. Isaac kneels by Rachel's side, head bowed, hands clasped to his forehead. I wait a respectful moment for him to say his farewells, but the moment drags on, and I'm forced to intervene.

"Isaac," I say, tentatively laying a hand on his shoulder. "It can't wait."

"There are ceremonies," he says.

"Those are for the village. Not here."

"The healers learn them," he insists. "We're required to perform them."

"Isaac," I say, and a wave of pity and tenderness washes over me. "You can't heal the dead."

"No," he says. "But you can heal the living."

I hesitate only a little before dropping to my knees beside him. I duplicate his posture and wait for him to begin.

His voice starts, a low and melodic chant, using words I don't know, sounds I doubt my lips and tongue can form. I listen as intently as I did to the Ecosystem in the days when I first learned its language, when I first heard in its many-throated speech the measure of its fierce, ancient existence. Isaac's dirge is no less fierce and, I think, no less ancient: the words, if they're words at all, crackle and hum like the silent tune I've known as long as I can remember. I realize he's singing Rachel's body into the earth, beseeching this far greater being to accept her tiny and completed life. I think back to the lessons I learned as a girl, lessons of the Ecosystem and its ways, the lives of men and women, our place in its order. And I wonder: is there more to learn than those lessons had to teach?

Isaac keeps singing, a lullaby, an ode. My Sense is silenced, yet I feel, I know, that so long as the song lasts, we're safe from the Ecosystem's wrath. Maybe it's listening, too. Then Isaac's hand reaches for mine, and his song flows through me, and I understand.

I looked and saw the girl escorted, the
living to the dead: I saw them bear her.

When she was lost in blinding dark-
ness, then was she led homeward.

Knowing the world of living beings, tread-
ing the path which lies before her.

The speed of rivers, the waters' gall:
cool and refresh the spot which
has known her life and death.

Here let the water-lily grow, the
tender grass and leafy plant.

Here is one light for you, another
awaits: enter and be united.

Let soul joining with body be lovely,
safe in its house of earth and stone.

There let neither hunger nor thirst beset you.

Prepare yourself for your final journey: let
not your limbs, your frame be left behind.

Follow to its repose your resting spirit: go
to whatever spot of earth you love best.

The song doesn't end there. It continues, timeless as the lapping of water, the rushing of reeds. Long before it's done, I'm singing with him, the words streaming from his thought to mine in such perfect union my lips never miss a phrase. It feels like Sensing, this singing. It occurs to me that I've never sung before. We in the village have so little cause to sing, Sensors least of all. Why should we sing, with death all around us?

But I know the answer now. I know why Isaac sings. And I hope, while his song survives, that I'll not soon forget its teaching.

At last it ceases, our voices fading like the final whispers of wind on water. The sun's light, directly overhead, tells me we've been here half the day's length, but I have no memory of all that time. I can't even remember the words of the song we sang.

"What does it mean?" I ask Isaac.

He startles as if rousing from a dream. "I don't know," he says. "It's just something we do."

He pinches wet earth between thumb and fore-finger, sprinkles it over Rachel's pyre. I do the same, and my reawakened Sense detects a wince from the Ecosystem as if my fingers have defiled it. Isaac leans down to kiss Rachel's forehead, just below the liliths. I see to my grief that in the time we've spent singing, her complexion has dulled, the spot where his lips touch her cheek puckering like a damp rag. I rise from stiff knees and think Isaac will follow, but he huddles beside the body, wraps his arms around himself, and cries. His tears are mostly silent, but his shoulders shake with the force of his sorrow.

"Isaac," I say. "We have to finish the ceremony. Before she begins to…."

"I know," he says, his voice muffled. "But can't we wait a little longer?"

"No," I say firmly. I crouch by his side, free his arms, then lean forward and kiss his tear-stained cheek. "If you care about her, you'll help me do this now."

He nods miserably, looks around him as a new thought strikes. "Fire," he groans. "How are we sup-posed to start a fire?"

He's right. Our branches and flints were swallowed by the swamp, and there's nothing dry enough from which to coax a spark. We might wait for nightfall and search for flameflies, but by that time, Rachel's body will have become a pestilence. A Sensor deserves better: a clean burn, not a slow, withering corruption.

"We could bury her," Isaac suggests. "The healers

have always thought we should do that. If the Sensors would allow it."

"No," I say. "Not yet. We have to burn her."

He doesn't object, only looks at me as if for a solution. I have none to give.

But the sky sends me the very thing I need. Like a single ripple spreading over the face of the swamp, I Sense the Ecosystem bracing for the jolt. The next moment, my body channels what my Sense has already perceived: a tingle in my arms, the raising of hairs at the nape of my neck, the weak scent of ozone on the stiff breeze. I tug Isaac's arm, pull him from the circle of sawgrass to the swamp's edge. In my haste, I brush against the grass and wince as my skin opens, but I don't stop. The clouds are delivering a much-needed gift, and we have to be there to receive it.

We are, though barely. We emerge from the sawgrass as a thunderclap rocks the ground and a tongue of dry lightning arcs out of the sky, touching the top branches of the mangrave that assailed us. The wood sputters, wet and rank to its core, and I fear it won't catch. But then, with a silent shriek from the tree, a branch sparks to life and pulses with yellow flame. The mangrave twists in agony, and I Sense its roots about to rise from the depths in an effort to extinguish the fire.

"Don't you dare!" I call out to it. The roots halt in their tracks, and if the tree had teeth, they'd be chattering. "Hold still and I'll take it away."

The mangrave does as I command. It waits, motionless, while I swim out to it; waits, cringing, as I set hands on its trunk and climb. It howls with pain as I snap the burning branch from its crown, then relaxes and breathes a thankful sigh. It grows agitated when, in my one-handed descent, I fail to keep the flame as far from its cancerous bark as it prefers. Only when I'm standing once more on muddy ground does it recover its composure.

Isaac has disappeared into the sawgrass to wait for me. I set my foot on the trail, but before I go, I turn to the swamp and bow.

"Thank you," I say spitefully. Then, to the sky, with all the sincerity I can muster: "And you."

And I race with my prize back to Rachel.

WHEN IT'S DONE, we sit by the shore in the ebbing day's glow and try not to talk about the morning. Which means we don't talk about anything at all.

I've recovered my spear from where I dropped it, and if there were any purpose in doing so, I'd spend the time before nightfall hunting: frogs, turtles, the lone marsh crane that wades past, sizing us up with its fixed reptilian eye. But we've surrendered our burning brand to Rachel's pyre, and whatever I could catch, I couldn't cook. Short of another lightning strike, it'll be roots, nuts, and berries from here on out. It's a day at best before we reach the swamp's end, and already I'm feeling lightheaded from lack of food and water, even more so from the swamp sludge swimming in my gut. Isaac looks fit and hale—his limp seems to have vanished entirely—but I know from stray images I picked up when we kissed that his strength is mainly for show. We'll have to move soon, and move fast, if we're to make it out alive.

And yet, we don't go. Isaac sits on the bank, absently tracing circles in the muck with one of Rachel's fallen sticks. The red light of sunset cuts through the swamp haze. The only things more silent and anxious than I are the mangraves, which wait at rigid attention for us to leave. We're spent, yes, and heartsick, and my wound burns dangerously despite the efforts I made to clean it and refasten the binding. But none of that is what keeps us here, unable to look each other in the eye.

Rachel's funeral, I realize, gave us purpose, tasks to perform, a shared sorrow to replace the need for speech. Now that it's over, I feel stuck in the middle, farther from a decision or an answer than I've ever been.

The sun has met the swamp's rim when I put something to words. "We shouldn't wait for night."

Isaac shrugs, listlessly.

"The mangraves might recover," I try. "Especially if they perceive us as being too passive."

"They won't," he says. "They're terrified of you."

I wait for a further response, but there's none. He's right: the mangraves won't attack me again, not if I knock myself unconscious and float out to their root-tips. Making small talk will get us nowhere, and not only because I don't know how to do it. Everything I can think to say leads back to what I can't bring myself to say: my mother's life and death, the mysteries of a world I thought I knew so well, the ache in my heart when I think of the boy who might help unravel those mysteries with me. Everything has brought us to this point, and here we'll remain, until I find the right words.

I stand and walk the two short steps that separate us, sink to the ground in front of him. He won't look at me, not even when, my heart beating so hard it strangles my breath, I reach for his hands. At the touch of his flesh, images from his life race through my mind, and for the first time, I think I can see myself in it.

"I want to learn," I tell him. "What my mother knew."

His head lifts, and his eyes melt with wonder and pity. "Sarah...."

"Not for you," I say quickly. "For me."

"We can't," he says. "Not now."

I don't know what's changed between then and now, other than all the things I can't say. But I try, in words I never thought I'd offer him or any other: "I need you to help me."

"It's too late," he says, and his chest releases a sigh loud enough to make the mangraves squirm. "You were right. Daniel set me up to this. When he heard about the progress you were making with Miriam, he said," and his voice catches, "he said we needed you. He planned to train you in the healer's way, before...."

"I'm ready," I say. "I'm ready now."

He shakes his head. He hasn't withdrawn from my touch, and the images that flow from him to me flicker like the beat of my heart, the answering beat of his. Yet while I listen to the rhythm of his desire, I realize my mistake. This choice isn't mine, not entirely. It's his, too.

And it's not me.

"Sarah," he says, his voice as gentle as Aaron's. The tips of his fingers pull loose from mine. "I just feel like...maybe this isn't the right time. Or maybe you weren't the one after all. You're still so angry about what happened to your mom, and—"

"I've changed," I say. "Truly, I have."

"People don't change like that," he says. "And healers can't be burdened by the past. I feel like you need more time, more...I don't know."

I watch numbly while he stands, retrieves his sopping cloak. The stone blade slides into its sheath with a sound like my heart's strings snapping.

"Anyway, I don't think we should stay together," he says. "Miriam's my responsibility, not yours. You can go back to the village, and I—"

"No!" I say, and reach for him, but he pulls away. "Isaac, you'll never make it by yourself. You don't even know where to go...."

"I've got a pretty good idea," he says. "And I'm getting better at Sensing. I'll be okay."

His voice is expressionless, as if he's talking about a walk across the village, not deeper into the Ecosystem. As if he's talking to someone he's never met, not the girl he kissed earlier today. "Isaac, I'm sorry," I say. "We shouldn't have...I shouldn't have...."

"*I* shouldn't have," he says. "But that's in the past. I'm leaving now. Please don't follow me."

He stands above me. I look into his eyes, but there's nothing to see. No anger, and certainly no love. I wrap my arms around myself to contain the trembling that's overtaken my body. "Isaac," I say, "if you leave now, you'll die."

"That's a chance I'll have to take," he says. "Goodbye, Sarah."

His fingers touch my brow, but it's not a caress. I

feel the hollowness in him, and for an instant, I know what it is to feel death. Then I feel my head spinning, dipping into darkness. I think I hear him say a final word before the shroud of sleep enfolds me.

SARAH STRADDLES THE *mangrave's topmost branches. Her hair flickers with a corona of blue flame like a lit candle, but her eyes are calm. She speaks to me soothingly, telling me of everyday things, the world I've yet to discover.*

"We'll walk in the meadow, Ruth," she says. "And chase ruby-throated huntingbirds. Even the Sensors are too slow for them, but we'll run after them all the same. Maybe we'll be the first to catch one!" And her eyes shine blue with excitement.

"What does it," I start to say, but something blocks my throat, making my tongue thick and clumsy. I try to say what's on my mind, but "hum-burr" is all I can manage.

She tosses her hair, and the flame tumbles like a wave. "It doesn't hurt, my darling," she says. "You'll see."

I reach for her as she stands at the mangrave's peak with her arms poised like a diver, the dark swamp reflecting her blue halo. The tree shudders with fear, but Sarah steps lightly off its crest into nothing but air. "Mama," I say, as the flame consumes her.

DAYLIGHT WAKES ME, if anything does. Daylight and hunger and thirst. I'm lying in the mud where I fell, and Isaac is gone. His tracks are all that's left of him. The sun has yet to show itself above the field of sawgrass, so I know that whatever he did to me kept me asleep for the rest of yesterday and the whole of the night. He's counting on that being enough of a head start that I'll never be able to catch him.

He's left the canteen behind, most but not all of its contents spilled when I dove into the swamp. What he'll do for water, I can't guess. Beside the canteen sits a small pile of blood-red berries my bleary Sense tells me won't kill me. I don't want to touch this final offering, but I have to put something in my stomach or I'll faint on my feet. I clutch a handful and jam them in my mouth, swallowing without chewing. They're raspberries, one of only a few edible types the Ecosystem produces, though true to their name, they rasp against my throat and cause coughing and choking. Their juice should sustain me for now, leaving what remains in the canteen for the rest of the journey.

I stand and scan the swamp for Isaac's Sensory

imprint, but as with my hunt through the sawgrass the day before, I can't detect a trace. That can mean one of two things. It's possible he's learned to block me, masking his presence the way a Sensor hides from the Ecosystem. Or he's already dead, killed by the mangraves or any of a thousand things like them. He's a novice alone in the Ecosystem. Without me, he has little chance of surviving.

The thought of his death tears at me, but I remind myself that, dead or alive, he was lost to me the moment our kiss ended. Maybe before it began. With most things in the Ecosystem, I'm connected yet detached: I Sense their lives, and my Sense warns me away. With Isaac, it's only when I touch him that we're truly connected. And I'll never touch him again.

The wind has picked up in intensity since yesterday, blowing steadily at my back, tossing my hair before my face. The mangraves await my departure. I face the swamp, the place where Rachel died, and mouth a silent farewell. Then I shoulder my spear and start off eastward, but before I take a single step, I realize there's something else I can't Sense.

Miriam's trail no longer lights my mind. It's gone cold at last.

WITHOUT ISAAC TO cumber me, I make good time. There's only one way to go, unless I want to slice a trail through the sawgrass with my spear—and seeing that it took an experienced thresher a whole night to carve a clearing suitable for a small girl's burial, I'm not eager to give that a try. Plus the pain trees lie beyond, their venom kept clear of my lungs only by the wind that blows at my back. No, for as long as the swamp holds, my path leads due east.

One thing brings me comfort as I jog along the shoreline: Isaac's tracks remain visible in the mud. I've kept my Sense open for snares he might have triggered, but the swamp stays docile, and I conclude that the mangraves are unwilling to risk what I might do to them if I found him dead. They've guaranteed both of us safe passage to the edge of their domain, but it'll be up to each of us alone to face what lies beyond.

It's late evening when I exit the marsh, my leg throbbing furiously with every step I take. As is common in the Ecosystem, one habitat yields to an entirely different one in an almost palpable line. I Sensed this final boundary the day I laid hands on the sward to search for

Miriam, knew that I'd leave marshland only to set foot on desert. Now that I'm here, I find myself longing for the company of the mangraves.

I've never stood before an ecozone like this, and it's ghastly. Not barren, for no part of the Ecosystem is barren, but filled with forms of life that mimic death. The flat land is sparsely covered with patches of short, dusk-colored grass, brittle as dry leaves yet sharp as needles. Upon contact, it breaks into invisible fragments capable of penetrating any but the toughest sole. *Glassgrass*, my Sense tells me it's called. There's no avoiding it, for the wind and the passage of other creatures have spread the particles so finely, my Sense can detect them but my feet can't navigate around them. Sprinkled throughout the spiky grass are organisms I might call flowers, if flowers were gray, broken things, drooping stalks with buds as ugly as a fist. They writhe against the soil as if groping for something they've lost, though I know it's unwary insects and rodents they're hunting for. When daylight comes, they'll neither lift their heads nor open their petals to the sun.

The greatest contrast in this trackless land comes from the solitary trees that seem to stand upside-down, with bushy nests of roots erupting from the earth and spiny appendages sprouting toward the sky. Though immobile, these gash trees are deadly to a range of fifty feet, able to launch their killing barbs at anything that walks or flaps by. The only creatures they don't attack are the huge black raveners that roost in their branches, for in the dryness of the desert air, these scavenger-crows help break down the food the trees kill. Here and there, humped shapes tear at the skull or ribcage of a recent victim. If Isaac passed this way, his imprint is as dead to my Sense as the things that lie rotting on the plain, his physical track obliterated by shifting sand. I'm forced to admit I'm not going to find him, if I ever was.

Still, I have no choice but to press on. The last light of day is leeching from the land, and maybe I'll Sense something I can't see. I'm hungry again, famished really, the morning meal of berries being the only food I've touched all day. There's no longer any doubt in my mind that the leg's infected. My throat is parched, and where I'll find water in this arid land, I have no idea. But my canteen sloshes with a few final sips, and I'm determined to continue if I have to crawl the rest of the way.

The impressions that rush up my legs when I step onto the margin of the desert are entirely different from those of the swamp. There, I Sensed lush, watery life crouched and ready for the attack. Here, I register an advanced state of decay, life not growing but giving up, breaking down, letting go. There's anger in the gray earth, but it's directed not solely at me but at anything that clings to survival, anything that refuses to accept the fate of all things. There's a song in the desert as well, sung by insects called grassharrowers that congregate in the glassgrass, their numbers as great as our own cicatrix, their sharp-spurred legs scratching out a tune so piercing it seems to penetrate the bones of my ear and skull. Listen to it long enough, and disorientation will follow; stray from one's path, and confusion will give way to hallucination. Then the trees will reap the reward, and repay the executioners with dead bodies to nourish the silty soil from which the glassgrass grows.

I stumble forward into the sorrowing land. Within moments, my feet are torn and bloody, my eardrums afire as if the grassharrowers' legs are rubbing directly against them. Their song doesn't relent. It tells me things I already half believe. It forms words in my mind, and I struggle to remind myself it's only illusion. It invites, not threatens, me to join it in death.

Life grows, blooms, dies.

Ruthless, heartless, the cycle never changes.

*Deep in the forest, tree begets leaf, leaf
begets worm, life yields its own undoing.*

*Root and branch and trunk and
flesh obey this one great law.*

Freedom is an illusion, love a young girl's dream.

Lie down, lie down, embrace the escape I offer.

"No," I say out loud, as I set one plodding foot in front of the other. With every step, the glassgrass sends shivers of pain up my legs. "Never."

You won't find her, the song shifts its tune.

You won't find either of them.

*Or, if you do, you'll find them
together, complete without you.*

Save the girl and you lose him.

Lose him and you lose every-
thing, everything but death.

Your own mother knew this: she died for love.

Now her daughter can do the same.

"Stop it!" I cry, and press my hands against my ears. The gash trees can't turn their heads to look at me, but I Sense their spikes straining for release. The song of the grassharrowers sharpens, forces its way past my defenses.

You can deny me, but I'll be here.

Long after you're gone, long after the boy is
nothing but sand and bones, long after your vil-
lage is tumbled and cracked by time, I'll be here.

For I'm the only thing that lasts.

All your generations, what are they to me?

You breed, you live, you die, you think you love.

But you're already dead.

You've been dead since the
moment you were born.

"I hate you," I whisper. The song has a ready answer.

Hate me? You are me.

I bred you in my womb, nursed you at my breast.

Every breath, every heartbeat makes you mine.

Traces of my pattern sprinkle your skin like stars.

You know what you are.

What you've always been.

I stop, aim my spear at soil I can no longer see in the moonless night. I plunge it downward, feel it stick. The Ecosystem does less than shrug, and the song of the desert never stops.

I'll tell you a secret: I don't hate you.

I don't think about you at all.

Your lives pass so quickly, I can't see them.

You think to hide from me, spend ten long years learning to disguise yourselves.

Ten years you might have been chasing boys or butterflies or babies.

Run openly beneath my eye: I won't notice.

You think I hate you because you kill?

That's the only thing you do that makes any sense at all.

A bird's choked scream and a body thudding to earth tell me a gash tree has found its mark.

Do you hear that? the song of
the Ecosystem croons.

We're killers, you and I. Cold-hearted killers.

*How many have you killed, starting
with the one who gave you birth?*

*You kill in the act of living, live
in the act of killing.*

*You earned a fresh kill just yes-
terday, a girl like you.*

But you're no different from me.

*You spend a life denying it, but in the
final moment when flesh at last unknits,
this one truth is all that remains.*

Don't you know it?

The song falls silent. Perhaps the grassharrow-ers have gone to bed, or perhaps their final word has been sung.

Without their voice to goad me, I'm more lost than before. I proceed randomly, my Sense no longer able to pick up anything, my stomach a knot of emptiness and my head a fog of dismay. My spear's the only thing that keeps me from pitching headfirst into the grass. I haven't been able to recover Miriam's trail, haven't detected a snare of any kind since I entered this realm. If I could see anything, all I'd see are my own bloody footprints smearing the sand.

At last, my legs give out from under me, and I fall.

Glassgrass penetrates my hands, my thighs, my face. I try to rise, but I'm too weak to move. I lie there and listen to the silence, a depthless silence without the shuffle of my feet to break its pall. I remember my resolution to crawl, and I make it a few feet, but then I collapse and roll onto my back, staring up at a darkness so profound even my Sense is muffled.

It's torture to move, but my hand inches toward the hidden place within my shirt, just above my heart. I find the token even the waters of the swamp were unable to take from me, close my fingers around it, feel its cool solidity against my palm. I raise it before my eyes, but I can't see it, much less Sense it: it's a bit of my mother's life long past living, and I can't Sense what's not alive. I touch it to my lips, warm it with my breath, this chill sliver of the woman who once warmed my body with hers. I hold it before me in the deepest dark of night, not knowing what it is I wait for. Still I wait, and hope, and beseech it not to leave me without an answer.

"Mother," I whisper. "Show me the way."

Before my doubting eyes, the shard pulses, weakly the first few tries as if it's finding its fire, then with an inner radiance that lights the blue-veined tracery branching across its surface. It's like a gem, a spark, a flame I hold in my hand. I raise the beacon to the sky, feel its power flushing me with warmth and strength as it must have done to the one who held it before me. Like a train of flameflies dancing in the night, the path I thought I'd lost reappears, spots of light hovering above the desert sand as far as my eye can see.

Painfully, I push myself to my feet and take a shaky step forward, holding the fiery shard high like a candle before the night. As I do, I hear a voice speaking in words I thought I'd forgotten.

My darling Ruth, it says. *You've taken your first step. Now take the next.*

"Mother?" I say.

I'm here, she answers. *I'm just ahead. Come to me.*

Hunger and thirst are forgotten. My head and heart feel equally strong. I step forward, seeking my mother's arms, walking without thought of disguise beneath the Ecosystem's watchful eye.

Then the ground opens beneath me, and I'm swallowed in the gloom.

I DON'T KNOW where I am.

I KNOW WHERE I am.

THIS IS THE place.

I OPEN MY eyes. It's utterly dark, and so cramped I can't free my arms from my sides. I'm lying on my back on spongy dirt, and all around me, I smell the moist aroma of earth. How far I am beneath the surface I can't tell, but my body feels bruised and battered, as if I've slid for some distance before coming to rest. I also feel, though I'm not sure why, as if I've woken from a long sleep. Maybe I lost consciousness when I fell. The darkness is so absolute, it makes no difference if my eyes are open or closed. But my Sense is beginning to stir, and it tells me all I need to know.

I'm in the tunnel of an urthwyrm.

We also call them borers, and sometimes landpreys, though no Sensor in our village has seen one. They don't dig their tunnels near us, probably because we've dug so many tunnels of our own, pitting the earth with firewells. Mostly, they're spoken of in nighttime tales to frighten apprentices. The Conservator spoke of them that way, when he was teaching me and the other novices the Ecosystem's laws of death. Some Sensors have doubted their existence, or thought the tales exaggerated. If I'd told Isaac of the monsters that guard his beloved, if I'd described to him the thirty foot long wyrms whose blunt, eyeless faces gape with spears of teeth that can consume flesh as easily as soil, he might have thought the tales false too. Or he might have feared to come with me at all.

But I've never doubted the truth of those tales. I believed them as a child, and I knew them to be true the moment I set out on my journey. I knew because I'd laid hands on the Ecosystem and Sensed the dark burrow toward which Miriam was borne, her prison cell as deep beneath the surface as I am now. I knew in that moment what awaited her. I knew they were real. And now that I'm here, I know I can't escape them.

Deep, deep beneath me, the earth groans with the torment of their motions, their slow, agonizing digging, inch by inch, foot by foot, through the caverns of the soil. In my initial contact with the Ecosystem—days that seem years ago—I saw the wyrms, but couldn't determine the size or shape of their burrows. I'd thought, or at least hoped, that when I got here I'd be able to stand, turn, walk—and, when the time came to free Miriam, run. I'd also hoped the tunnels might be less steep than the one in which I'm trapped, that when I needed speed, I'd be able to keep my footing while I angled upward toward sunlight and air. I realize now that if I'm able to extricate myself from the spot where I'm currently stuck, the best I'll be able to do is wiggle blindly through the tunnels, moving no faster than the wyrms themselves and lacking both their knowledge of their home and their ability to dig new pathways with which to climb and descend. If I can find Miriam in what's sure to be a maze of crisscrossing tunnels, there's no hope I'll be able to get either of us out. At most, I'll be able to mother her, even if that means nothing more than dying with her in my arms.

I wonder, now that I've reached the end, why my own mother's presence feels so strong in this place. I've accepted the fact that the signs I witnessed aboveground—the glowing shard, the path of light, the sound of her voice—were counterfeits spawned by the grassharrowers to mock me even as they killed me. But my mind is free of their song now, and yet I feel her more powerfully than ever before, an aura as solid and real as the token I grip in my fist. She can no longer speak to me, but I have the strongest notion that she's here.

Yes, here. I understand. I feel her here because she *is* here. Because it was here that she died.

I'm lying in my mother's grave.

A rush of sorrow fills me. I know now that Aaron lied to me about her death, just as he'd lied to me about her life. Maybe he thought his lies would comfort me. But my mother's body never returned to the village, never received the burial of fire that Isaac and I accorded to Rachel. On the night Aaron saw the first signs of the Sense within me, a ceremonial burning took the place of her body, as it did for Barnabas and Samuel. She herself had ventured too far, so far that, though Aaron must have found her token when he went in search of her, he couldn't reach the place where she'd met her end. The Ecosystem's final joke is this: to bury me in the ground beside my mother, where the bodies of two Sarahs will mingle and be lost forever.

I've faced death too many times to fear it. But I won't die like a beetle flipped on its back. If this is the end, I'll meet it as I know she did. Fighting not only for my life, but for something greater. As Sarah, the brave and strong.

"Mother," I say softly. My voice sounds flat and alien in the tomb's silence. "Wait for me. We'll be together soon."

My eyes are worthless here. My Sense is uncharacteristically fuzzy, as if it's wrapped in a bundle of silken threads. I don't know if that's because I hit my head when I fell, or if it's a combination of exhaustion, hunger, and the infection creeping up my leg. Whatever the case, I'm having trouble locking onto the life that surrounds me. But I have my ears, and my nose, and my skin. If I can't Sense, I can use my surviving senses.

What they tell me is that the tunnel is barely wide enough for my body, but that the soil is porous enough to scoop out space to move. My fingers scrabble against the dirt, and my nails, depleted as they are, easily cut into the walls. In no great time, I've shoveled away enough soil to pivot, pull my knees to my chest, and reorient myself, turning onto my stomach and facing back the way I fell. I tuck my mother's token in its pocket for safekeeping, then reach upward, try to grab a handhold.

My hands return empty. The same looseness that enabled me to remove the dirt prevents me from getting a firm grip. If I'm to travel down here at all, it'll have to be horizontally, at least until I find a tunnel that slopes more gradually up or down.

I reverse the process, turn myself until I'm lying, stomach to the floor, in the opposite direction. From there, I'm able to crawl forward, my elbows tucked beneath me and my back scraping the roof. It's a tight squeeze, but it no longer feels quite so much as if I'm stuck in an urthwyrm's gullet.

The air down here is humid, not cold as I'd imagined, and the smell of soil permeates my nose. There's definitely oxygen passing through, because I have no trouble breathing. I remember what Aaron told me, years and years ago: one of the borers' principal jobs within the Ecosystem is to excavate the soil, to keep air flowing underground to serve the needs of the countless organisms that inhabit this world-beneath-a-world. Now that I've become one of those organisms, I'm thankful for how well the wyrms have done the work they're designed to do. Even if, as Aaron also told me, their other principal job is to devour and excrete any organic matter they encounter in their endless wandering through the earth's crust.

For a long black time, I wiggle forward like a hatchling wyrm, the rich smell of decomposing matter in my face, the movement of my giant cousins shaking my stomach as they prowl the levels below. My Sense flickers like a flamefly's lantern, at times drawing a fragmentary diagram of all the things I can't see, at others turning as opaque as the wall of darkness before my face. Accustomed as I've become in the past week to relying on my Sense even in the darkest night, I'm frustrated that it won't cooperate. I want to be able to anticipate what's ahead, if only to avoid wriggling into one of the monsters' mouths.

But no nemesis comes. So far as my fitful Sense can tell, nothing down here's shown the slightest interest in the small, tunneling creature making its slow way through the earth. Maybe the Ecosystem's in the process of laying a trap for me, or maybe it's too busy with other things to pay me any mind at all.

My elbows are rubbed raw when I feel a shift in the air on my face, a lessening of the wet stuffiness. I explore with my fingertips and find that the tunnel splits in two, the air issuing from the right-hand fork somewhat fresher, almost like a surface-level breeze. I draw a deep breath, and though there's nothing to smell but soil, my lungs fill with greater ease in that direction. I grope inside as far as my arm will reach, hoping I might find that the tunnel angles upward, but to my disappointment it tends, if anything, deeper down. With an effort, I gather my Sense and send it pulsing down the tunnel, but nothing responds. I test the left-hand passage with my fingers, feel another downward slant. Doubting I'll be able to map where I came from or where I am, I opt for air and plunge inside the tunnel to my right.

It turns out to be a good decision, given my circumstances. It's a bit less cramped here than the tunnel I came from, and the air is unquestionably moving, bathing my face and making the sweat that's formed on my brow feel almost cool. The tunnel does descend, but not steeply, and I encounter no other branches in the road, which makes me think, rationally or not, that this might be a main corridor out of the den. Even more encouraging, I Sense definite life readings up ahead, too foggy to name but not, I'm confident, coming from the giant wyrms. When I realize my back is no longer polishing the roof of the tunnel and I'm able to creep forward on hands and knees, it's not only my sore elbows that are thankful. The sound of the wyrms has receded, and it's possible, I think, that in the total dark, what I took to be a downward slope is actually tending up.

The next moment, the tunnel floor vanishes, and I land in a heap before I have time to wonder or worry how far the fall is.

It isn't far at all, though it's still far enough to make my bruised body object. When I collect myself, I realize that nothing hems me in any longer, no walls of dirt straiten my skin. I roll to a sitting position and strain into the dark, send my stuttering Sense in all directions around me. A rebound effect suggests that I've landed in a place more like a cavern than a tunnel, spacious enough for me to stand at last. I'm receiving only snatches of Sensation, not a steady enough stream to plot the cavern's dimensions. The life readings have grown stronger, but what or where they are, I can't say. I do learn that gash tree roots dangle from the ceiling, so I'm not as far beneath the surface as I'd feared. The roots transmit the first clear indication of the Ecosystem's mind I've received since arriving here, and what I detect doesn't surprise me. It's gloating, coldly calculating that it has me trapped. I decide not to let it have the last word.

"This is the best you could do?" I shout, and my voice comes out throaty and clear, though without the echo I thought might help me determine the dimensions of this place. "I'm disappointed."

The roots waggle invisibly above me.

"Really," I say. "I'd counted on something a little more, I don't know, gory."

The silence hangs over me. If I thought I was going to get a response—and truthfully, I didn't—I'm obviously not about to.

Or then again….

A sound comes from the darkness in front of me, a faint scratching. Not a wyrm; this is much weaker than the booming, pealing vibrations they send through the soles of my feet. With my hands out, I walk forward until I touch a solid wall. The sound issues from there, as if something is scraping at the soil. My Sense stubbornly refuses to get a read on it, even when I lay my ear against the wall. But it's definitely more than dirt falling unaided to the floor. It strikes me that the walls of this cavern might be hollow, or at least riddled with holes by the wyrms. Whatever's on the other side is trying to get out, to enter my cavern. I put my mouth to the wall and call in a soft voice.

"Who's there?"

The scraping stops. I place my ear against the wall and hear something new, a muffled hum, deeper than the scratching. It enters my ear more as a pulsation in the dirt than an audible sound. Still it seems familiar, and I return my lips to the wall and lift my voice louder.

"Is someone there?"

Again, the muffled response. It pauses after it's had its say, as if waiting for me to answer.

"Miriam?" I call, as loudly as I can with my lips pressed against the dirt. "It's Sarah."

This time, I'm sure it's a human voice I hear. The words it says are impossible to interpret.

"Hold on," I say. "I'll...."

I give up on the worthless conversation and attack the wall with my all-but-spent fingernails, scraping and tearing. My invisible partner I hear do the same. I have no idea how thick the wall is that separates us, and in the back of my mind, I envision a cave-in that buries us both. I'm driven by desperation to remove the barrier that divides me from the girl on the other side. If I've truly found Miriam, even if I can't deliver either of us from this place, I'm determined to make contact with her before the end. I want to see her, though I don't know what I'll do then. Tell her my story, tell her I'm sorry.

I can't see when the two of us break through, but I can feel a rush of air, fingers touching mine. My mouth opens to deliver a speech I haven't begun to formulate, but before the words are freed from my chest, an image arcs through my mind like a flash of lightning in the dark.

"Well, well," Isaac says. "Couldn't keep away from me, could you?"

NOW WOULD BE the time to laugh, or cry. Time to apologize. Or time to confess, come clean, admit everything that's happened to me the past week with him, the past day without. Now would be the time to tell him how much of his life I've seen through our snatches of contact, how much of *my* life I've seen anew in the feel of his skin against mine. I know it's not me he loves. Yet I long to spill my guts to him, here in this most private of places, where all the secrets I tell him would be swallowed by the earth. Even the Ecosystem, I have the feeling, wouldn't release those secrets. It would let them sink deep and take root, and maybe, in ten or fifty or a hundred years, it would let something grow out of them to mark this place, this moment.

But I don't laugh, or cry, or tell him anything. All I do is wrap my fingers around his, and feel his life flow into me, and hold on.

IT'S ISAAC WHO breaks the silence. "Let's try to knock the rest of this wall down," he says. "At least, enough to get through."

Immediately, I drop his hand and attack the wall with fingers and fists, sending clods of dirt flying, feeling my nails sting where they scrape rock. Isaac laughs, the warm sound filling my chamber.

"Easy," he says. "I asked you to break through, not pound it into submission."

I laugh. Or not laugh. I honest to grabgrass giggle. "Sorry."

I force myself to slow down, concentrate on widening the hole we've started. His fingers flick against mine every so often, and I thrill to his touch, relishing the images that rush to my mind. It strikes me as odd that I feel only one of his hands, since I'm scooping and carving with both of mine, but I say nothing. The hole grows large enough that I could see his face, if I could see anything. It seems to me that if I could see anything, his face would be the only thing I'd see.

But then I strike rock. Hard, unyielding rock. It's lodged in the wall between us, and though I can't trace its outlines, I know it's much larger and thicker than the chunks that have come loose at my fingertips. I try to get my hands around it and pull, but it feels as if it *is* the wall, a solid sheet of bedrock in which the opening we've dug is the only fault. I tug, and when tugging doesn't work, I push. But I'd have to be a full-grown urthwyrm to dislodge it.

Isaac has stopped digging, too. Through the hole in the rock, I hear his heavy breathing. "I was worried about that," he says.

"We'll try another spot," I say. I don't like the resignation in his voice. I want to hear him laugh again and make light of this dark place. "There's got to be a way to dig under, or over—"

"I don't think so," he says. "I'm kind of...well, trapped. Rock all around. I think there must have been a rockslide when I fell. And my left hand is...."

I reach into the hole to touch him, and I feel what I should have before: his pain, the contortion of his body as he crouches there, entombed in rock and blanketed in darkness. "Can you move at all?"

"It would help if I could see anything," he says. "But my hand's wedged tight. I can't really feel it, which is probably a good thing."

"I'm coming to get you," I say. "I'll dig...no, I'll find a way to the surface. If you fell down, there must be a tunnel...."

Through the gap, his hand clenches mine. "The tunnel's closed, Sarah. There's a ton of rock an inch above my head. I wasn't sure what would happen if I tried to dig my way out. But then I thought I heard your voice, and I had to try."

I open my mouth to protest, but realize I have nothing to say. I wrap my fingers around his hand, feel the difficulty he's having drawing breath. But I also see the thought in his mind, and the words rush from me without my bidding. "How did you and Miriam meet?"

"Me and Miriam?" he says in surprise, and gives a short laugh. "Well, everyone in the village knows everyone else, right? I mean, it's not like you can avoid anyone."

Unless you're a Sensor, I think. "But there must have been some special moment," I say. "A moment when you knew…." I can hardly bring myself to utter the words, but something deeper than Sense tells me they're the right thing to say. "When you knew you loved her."

"Oh." He falls silent for a long time, and I fear I've misjudged. Maybe he thinks I'm angling for a disavowal of his love for Miriam. Or maybe he doesn't want to think about her at all, doesn't want to remember what could have been if not for me.

But his voice returns, and I detect no bitterness in it. "Well, we're second cousins. I mean, everyone in the village is related. If being a Sensor is in the blood, we all share the same blood." He squeezes my hand, and though he's trying to disguise it, I can tell his grip is growing slack. "My dad died when I was pretty young, so me and my mom moved in with her cousin's family. And Miriam was…well, she was always there. She was always a part of my life."

This doesn't sound like the stuff of great romance, but

what do I know? I try to think of something to say, but the words that come to mind fall short of what I feel. I reach both hands through the hole in the rock and clasp his single hand, my thumb caressing his wrist. Wordlessly, I send the message through my skin: *You are loved, Isaac. Your life has been touched by love. You may have been too embarrassed to admit it, but it's true. Even if today is the end, you have lived a lifetime, for you have known love.*

Whether the message gets through or not, his voice resumes. "Everyone else thought there was something wrong with Mimi. She'd drop things, and burn things, and get all flustered and tongue-tied. You've seen her, you know what I mean. But to me...."

I stroke his wrist, try to ignore the fact that it's growing cold.

"Well, I thought she was beautiful," he says. "Because she was so different. She had this inner strength that no one saw but me. She didn't even see it herself. She could have been a healer, you know."

"Really," I say, and hope I don't sound too surprised.

"That's how I joined the order," he says. "Daniel had gotten wind of this girl who couldn't do anything right, and he thought—Daniel's really good at this—maybe she needed something other than the normal routine to inspire her. So he came to our house and talked to Miriam, told her all about the healing profession, practically begged her to join. But she was too...."

"Shy?"

"Something like that," he says. "I tried to convince

her, I even went to talk to Daniel, but you know what he said?"

I wait for him to tell me.

"He said, each seed blooms in its own time. He said her time would come. Meanwhile, he got more than he bargained for. He got me."

He tries to laugh, but his laugh ends in a wince. Through our touch, I feel what's happening to his arm, his body, as the cave squeezes him in a vise of stone. "And you got her."

"Pretty much," he says. "I went home and told Miriam about joining the healers, and she was totally excited for me, and she gave me a big hug, and then we...." He pauses, and his next words come in a rush, as if that's the only way he can bring himself to say them. "We kissed, really kissed, like the kind of kiss you've been saving for years but didn't realize until that moment. And the next thing I knew, we were pledged."

I know that kind of kiss. "Pledged?"

"To be married," he says. "She was only fourteen, and I was about to start my training with Daniel, so we knew it would have to wait. But it's a pretty binding thing. Sensors don't know about pledging, huh?"

"Sensors don't know about anything that has to do with love," I say, and unlike him, I can't keep the bitterness from sharpening my words.

He tries to squeeze my hand, but his strength fails. He's been trapped, with no food or water and virtually no air, with a crushed arm and a weight of stone at his back, for at least a day. Digging the hole to me was his last hope, and his last effort. This isn't the time to dwell on what I've lost.

"What happened then?" I ask, gently massaging his hand, hoping he can feel my touch.

"I blew it," he says. "I didn't realize how much becoming a healer would change things."

"The training must be difficult."

"It wasn't just that," he says. "Daniel opened a new world to me, and I guess it went to my head. I told Mimi she was missing out on something amazing, that she was being a coward not to try. And I told her...I told her I wasn't sure...."

"That you loved her anymore," I whisper.

"Yeah," he says.

"Isaac," I say. "Miriam knew you'd never stopped loving her. Deep down, she knew. It was just her lack of confidence. Her feeling that she didn't deserve your love. That's why she joined the Sensors. Not because of what you said."

"Yeah," he sighs, in a weak voice I never thought I'd hear from him. "But if I hadn't said it, she wouldn't have had any reason to doubt, would she? She wouldn't have joined the Sensors, and we would've gotten married, and none of this would've happened. And she wouldn't...we wouldn't...."

His voice ceases, and through the passageway that connects us, I hear the sounds of his grief. His hand has gone limp in mine, his sobs seeming the only thing he has strength for. I draw his hand as far as I can toward me, and with my face flush against the opening, I can just press my lips against it.

"I'm going to save her," I say. "She's going to return to the village, and she's going to become…what my mother was. A Sensor, and more than a Sensor. She's going to live in the Ecosystem without fear. Like a seed that's finally bloomed."

He gives no sign that he's heard me, and I fear he's gone. But my fingers find the flat beneath his thumb, and his pulse still beats there. "Isaac?"

"Sarah," he says in an almost inaudible whisper. "I know what this place is. I know about the wyrms."

In my focus on him, I'd forgotten the creatures that surround us. "How?"

"You talked in your sleep," he says. "When I stitched you. Rachel knew, too."

So he knows. He's always known. Yet knowing, he chose to follow. And now, I have to let him go.

"I'm going to save her," I say again. "For you."

"For me," he says, and though he's too weak to laugh, I feel him smile.

"I have to go now," I say.

"Sarah," he says, and his next words are broken as the cave takes his breath. "When I left the village. With Rachel. It was to find Miriam. Not to spy on you. You've got to. Believe me."

I'm not sure I believe him, I'm not sure I want to believe him, but what does it matter? "I believe you."

"Good." His fingers flex feebly, and with a final kiss,

I let them go. "Now find Miriam. She'll make. A great Sensor. You both will."

"Isaac," I say into the dark.

There's no response.

"Isaac," I repeat his name, and even if he's gone, I have to say the words. "I love you. I promise. I'll find her. I love you."

I step back from the wall, and for the first time, I'm conscious of the tears that wet my cheeks. I stand for a moment, listening. Not for his voice, for I no longer expect to hear that. To my own heart. It beats loudly in my throat, so loudly it's as if the cavern echoes its pulsing sound. And then my Sense ignites, and the cavern grows as bright to my inner eye as a sky blazing with stars.

I can't see, but I can Sense everything. I Sense the roots of the gash trees waving like slender fingers from the ceiling high over my head. I Sense the millions, no billions, of things too small to see, the things that thrive in this place where life meets death. In the stone chamber just out of reach, I Sense the boy who braved the Ecosystem with me, his arm shattered, his heart beating its final few notes. I Sense the network of living tunnels that snake through the ground, the ones that plunge, the ones that climb. I Sense, so far below it's as if they're swimming in the depths of a bottomless sea, the urthwyrms turning in their course and rising, slowly but steadily, toward the two-legged creature who's dared to enter their home.

And I Sense her.

She lies amid a squirming mass of borer brood,

yard-long creatures that nip but don't bite, their maws not ready for food such as her. She's always been thin, but now she's gaunt as a chick, the result of her long wait without food and only the few drops of water the cavern's roof allows. My Sense scans her face: eyes shut, lines etched in a mask of exhaustion and pain. For Isaac's sake, I linger on that face, try to find its beauty. But more important to me are the slow rise and fall of her chest, the weak but steady thrum of her heart. She's unconscious, but I can Sense her holding on, with the strength only he could see in her.

I fling the slimy brood-wyrms from her arms, her belly, the knots of her hair. That black tangle is the only part of her that hasn't suffered from her ordeal—the only part, I can't help thinking, that couldn't get any worse. My own strength has returned with my Sense, and it's no burden at all to lift her child's body in my arms. As I do, the shiver I've felt only at Isaac's touch races along my skin, and I see her dreams, know that she dreams of him. It's an effort to stop the flow, to focus on my task; I succeed only by shifting her body so my hands touch clothing and not flesh. The map of the borers' tunnels imprinted forever in my mind, I run for the passageway that leads up and out, a main artery more than wide enough to accommodate us both.

I've no sooner set foot in the tunnel than the cavern shakes and the urthwyrms emerge.

I'D THOUGHT THEM slow. But that was deep down, where they were carving trails, forcing their massive bodies through tons of soil. Here, in the open, they strike with a speed my eyes couldn't follow, if I were using my eyes.

Fortunately for me, I'm using my Sense. Four of the monsters lash out at once, and it's only by retreating into the tunnel with Miriam in my arms that I'm able to avoid their tails and teeth. One of them slams the ceiling, the dirt it dislodges a reminder of what it would have done to me. Another, in its recoil, blunders against the wall where Isaac lies buried, and I scream as the rocks of his tomb shift and grind. Without thinking, I release Miriam and leap at the creature, pound its back with my bare hands. Its rubbery skin repels my blows as if they're love taps. My hand finds a sharp stone on the cavern floor, and with this weapon, I slice the monster from blunt head to a third of the way down its back. It has no throat to make a sound, but its body buckles in agony, the viscous liquid that passes for its blood spraying me as it writhes across the floor. Not dead, though. Urthwyrms can suffer far more damage than that and live. Cut them in two, and you've only doubled your enemy's strength.

Isaac is beyond my help. I have to fulfill my promise. I avoid a third borer's lunging maw, scoop Miriam into my arms. Adrenaline coursing through my body, I race up the tunnel.

My leg sears. The monsters are everywhere. My Sense registers dozens of them, all converging on the path of my escape. The vanguard from the cavern have squeezed into the tunnel and are sliding toward my heels, their speed no less than my own. Others have dropped their underground construction projects and are racing to cut me off where the main artery meets theirs. The Ecosystem orchestrates them all, animating their normally torpid bodies with will and strategy and anger, turning them into an avenging army bent on me alone. This must have been how they overwhelmed my mother. They possess a brute power I'll never match, and I doubt whether cunning can defeat them.

I stoop low as two urthwyrms explode from the tunnel, one from either side, their bodies crossing in a spray of dirt. Had either hit me, I'd have been crushed to powder. While they free themselves from the walls, I duck past, leap over the tail of another wyrm that flashes up from the tunnel floor. The roof rumbles with the weight of a particularly massive wyrm, and I Sense its intention the moment before it acts. I skid to a halt as the creature's head bursts through the ceiling and curls to receive my body. Its mouth is so broad there's barely room to squeeze past, but I shove myself and the girl in my arms through the gap that opens as it swings its head back and forth like a giant pendulum. My skin scrapes the wall, my arm sticks against its squelching hide, but the only thing that goes down its gullet is the dirt I kick up as I resume my flight up the tunnel.

Ahead, my Sense maps a maze of passages as intricate as a spider's web. Wyrms slither through them all, and if they force entrance into the main tunnel, they'll block my way for sure. With an extra spurt, I dodge three wyrms that erupt from the tunnel floor, leave them in a tangle of teeth and tails. By the time they extricate themselves, I've opened up a lead ahead of the main pack, though I Sense others cruising toward me along the route I have to travel. My lungs and thigh burn, and Miriam's body no longer feels quite so weightless, but my legs pump mechanically, and my Sense doesn't miss a thing. It tells me of the Ecosystem's anger, but also of its doubt: it fears it's miscalculated, given me a chance to escape. Its frenzy doubles the urthwyrms' speed. They course through the tunnels like arrows from a bow.

One tries to trap me from beneath, but I leap the hole it's opened, land on solid ground beyond its snapping maw. I stumble, catch myself against the floor with the one fist I can spare, and gasp as pain lacerates my ankle, the prostrate wyrm's parting gift. Another wyrm tries to barricade my path with dirt from above, but it doesn't count on me racing through the landslide, clods of earth raining on my shoulders while I hunch over to protect my precious burden. I'm grateful the creatures haven't realized they could collapse the entire underground city, ruin their handiwork in the short term for the much more lasting reward of burying their second Sarah. I'm thankful, too, that the Ecosystem can't read my thoughts. If it knew my mind, it wouldn't be so eager to spring its next snare.

The floor of the tunnel dissolves, then rises again as the wyrm that hollowed it out surfaces directly beneath my feet. I ride its length until I gain its midsection, then straddle it, gripping with bloody thighs, clutching Miriam to my chest with a single hand. With the other, I plunge the stone I've saved from the cavern floor into its back. The wyrm struggles, internal fluid slopping over my hand, the smell pretty much what I expect from filth trapped for ages within the planet's crust. I hack at it until the wyrm divides raggedly midway between snout and tail, two half-wyrms falling apart with my body and Miriam's between. Its head turns back to strike what it thinks is me, only to discover I've dropped beneath its severed hindquarters. As it latches onto its own body, I shoulder the coils aside and run on. I'm far less interested in what's going on behind me than what's coming up ahead, but I can't help Sensing the creature's baffled pain as it ingests itself.

Running has become its own reason for existence; the only thing that keeps me going is my streaming legs' stubborn rhythm. Light refuses to penetrate this subterranean world, but I know I'm nearing the surface, know that at this pace, it's not long before I spot daylight. For it's the coming of dawn I Sense beyond the tunnel's end, gash trees basking in the glow, the wings of insects translucent in bright spears of sun. Though everything appeared a wasteland when I fell into the urthwyrms' lair, I know there's light up above, a living world to walk and explore. Isaac will never see it again, and neither will my mother, and as for me....

Miriam stirs, her breath changing from the steady cadence of sleep to a series of soft, confused moans. I slow for the briefest moment to set her on her feet, then clutch her hand and drag her behind me, trusting her Sensor's instinct to keep her upright before wakefulness returns. She stumbles, emits a louder moan, then her legs heed her mind's instructions and we're running up the tunnel as fast as we can manage. Through our touch, images flow, cloudy with sleep but with Isaac at the fore. I have little breath to spare, but I talk to her as as we run.

"Miriam. It's Sarah. I'm getting you out of here."

"Where are we?" I haven't heard that plaintive voice in a week, and it's oddly uplifting to know it hasn't changed.

"No time," I pant. "Just stay with me. Don't slow down."

"I dreamed..." she says blearily. Her free hand brushes at her arm as if to clear the borer brood away. Then, with an edge of panic: "Where's Isaac?"

There's nowhere near enough time for that, but I can't lie to her. "He's gone. He came with me. He told me...he told me to tell you he loved you." That's basically true, and though her breath turns to a broken wail, she stays on her feet.

We've gained on the wyrms now that I'm no longer slowed by my companion's weight. The darkness seems good for Miriam, minimizing distractions for her nascent Sense, enabling her to keep up a pace I wouldn't have thought her capable of. She's crying softly, but maybe it helps that she isn't completely aware of what's happening. If we survive, she'll rise from her bed a day from now to realize he's truly gone. I can only hope she has the strength Isaac said she does.

A sharp bend in the tunnel falls behind us, and I see it at last: the exit, a pinpoint of light against the cave's gloom. After so long underground, even that puny spot of brightness makes me squint. Miriam sees it too, and her legs and lungs pump harder to reach our goal. I'm too exhausted to feel anything anymore, but I suspect she's pulling me as much as I was her. In thirty rods, maybe less, we'll reach the exit.

We're going to make it, I think. Emerge into sunlight. Leave the memory of this place behind. Or carry it with us, in hopes of a better day.

Then the tunnel ahead collapses, eclipsing the growing circle of light.

We stop, test the wall of soil with our fingers. I know instantly that we can't break through. My Sense is as clear as before, and I can't understand how I failed to divine the creatures' plan. Maybe my focus on Miriam stalled my wits long enough for them to spring their trap.

The monsters in our rear will reach us in no time. The ones that caused the cave-in will chew through the soil and pin us against the ones behind. There'd been a moment when I thought I might be able to avoid this. But I can pretend no longer. I can't save us both.

"Miriam." I grip her arm as hard as I can without hurting her. "There's another way out. It's smaller, narrower. You'll have to crawl. But it leads straight to the surface. And it won't be guarded."

I perceive her panic. "How do you know?"

"Because they only want me. They'll take me as soon as you go."

"You're coming with me," she says.

"Then we'll both die."

"I'm not leaving you here."

"Yes, you are," I say. "I made a promise, Miriam. To Isaac. I told him I'd get you out of this. I don't plan to go back on that now."

"But if you die…."

"You'll live," I say. "Here." I withdraw my mother's token from my shirt and, before I have time to reconsider, press the shard into her hand. "Go back to the village. Find Aaron. Tell him I've given this to you. Then find Daniel and ask him about the seed. He'll know what I mean."

In the dark, I feel her clutch my hand. "I can't make it without you," she keens.

"You can," I say. "If you move fast, you'll pick up the trail we took to get here. Sense for sprung snares, traces of our passage. You'll Sense anger, and fear, and hurt, but no menace. Keep a firm grip on the token, and the Ecosystem will let you pass." An obstruction rises in my throat. I swallow it down. "You're a Sensor, Miriam. The village needs you, now more than ever. This is what we do."

She's silent, the tears having dried on her face. She lets go of my hand and wraps both arms around me, squeezing with all the strength in her bony frame. I fend off the flood of images that wash over me, bite down on my lip, and accept her last goodbye. When she lets go, I touch her cheek and feel it glowing with warmth and strength.

"Go now," I say, and I don't need to shoo her toward the side tunnel, but I do anyway. Before she enters, she gives me a lightning quick kiss on the forehead, then drops to a crawl. I listen to her hands and knees scraping across the ground as she starts upward, then silence returns.

The urthwyrms behind me have nearly reached the spot where I stand. The ones in front press against the wall they created, the sharp gashes of their heads threatening to burst through. My energy is all but spent, and I know I can't elude them. I have a moment to myself before the end. I drop to my knees on the tunnel floor, lay my hands in the hot soil, and speak to my enemy.

"Take me," I say. "Not her. Take me. Let her live."

The Ecosystem rumbles, shifts. Its mind registers surprise, suspicion, doubt. The wyrms it was on the verge of dispatching to intercept Miriam waver, turn their blind heads back and forth as if waiting for further instructions. I sink my hands deeper, let the Ecosystem feel the steadiness of my pulse, the cool waves flowing through my skin.

Peace, I think. *Let there be peace between us at last.*

All at once, I Sense the wyrms halting in their tracks, the ones before and behind stopping short as if some greater force has caught them by their tails. My Sense spreads through the caverns of the soil, and what it detects is quiet: an enormous quiet, so new to one who's heard its voice so very many years, I wonder if my gift has fallen deaf. But no. The earth is simply and everywhere silent, as if I'm Sensing the Ecosystem before its rise, before it developed a hatred of my kind and a will capable of carrying out its bloodlust. The gash trees nod as they return to their original sleep, the mangraves drift into placid dreams, the bloodbirds settle serenely to roost, the cicatrix song skips a beat for the first time in millennia. The Ecosystem rests, and seems content.

Only one thing moves in it: Miriam, doggedly making her way through the tunnel on hands and knees, my mother's token mated to her palm and the memory of the boy she loved a sweet sadness in her heart. She's almost there. Just another yard, another foot, another inch....

Her head breaks the surface, and she breathes the fresh air, blinks in the sunlight.

I take a breath of my own, a single breath, and the urthwyrms swarm.

I'VE KEPT MY promise. The village will have its Sensor, and more. The seed will bloom. Neither Isaac nor I will be there to see it, but the new day we lived and died for will dawn.

I wrap my arms around my shoulders and brace for the onslaught. Then pain engulfs me, and my Sense flutters and dies as they drag me down.

Book Four: Shard

There are occasions when you can hear the mysterious language of the Earth, in water, or coming through the trees, emanating from the mosses, seeping through the undercurrents of the soil, but you have to be willing to wait and receive.

—John Hay,
The Immortal Wilderness (1987)

SARAH LOUNGES IN the forest glade. Sunlight kisses her brown limbs. The smell of witch hazel permeates the air. A few steps away, the greensward glistens, the village of stone brooding beyond the charred circle. But there's no one to warn her of her peril, no one to chastise her for straying from the stone's embrace. She's young. She's in love. She can't imagine that, in time, this pretty place will claim them both.

"Which one's your favorite?" she asks.

He smiles. "I like them all."

Teasingly, she swats his arm. "We have to decide."

"So soon?"

"Days will turn to weeks, and weeks to months, before we know it," she answers. "And things like this have a timing of their own."

"All right," he says. "I like Deborah."

Her face falls. "Really?"

"You picked it."

"As an option," she says. "To get our thoughts flowing."

"All right," he concedes. "How about Lydia?"

"This isn't a game," she says. "It's not, 'he loves me, he loves me not.' We have to choose."

"Well, I'm stumped," he says, but he's smiling, too.

She stands and takes a step toward the village. Beneath her breeze-blown hair, her face is etched with anxious lines.

"My master will be calling soon," she says quietly, almost to herself.

"So?"

"So he'll know. He always knows."

"He can't possibly know."

"He'll know."

Her partner is silent. The forest buzzes with life unimaginable. The village beckons, shelter of stone. She listens to both, and her Sensor's heart is pestered with the choosing.

Then she turns to him, all worry erased, her smile as bright as the sun.

"Her name is Ruth," she says.

LIGHT STABS MY eyes. A hazy face floats above me. Fingers stroke my forehead, and though their touch is gentle, I feel pinched and lanced with pain. The face moves from view and returns, and this time, something moist soothes my brow. The smell reminds me of him, and another pain, sharper than the light, pierces my eyes. I blink, and the already blurry world wavers like images seen through a rainstorm.

"Child," the face says. "Can you hear me?"

I blink again, and the image clears. I recognize the face. It belongs to Judith, the village midwife. That she's here with me seems the unlikeliest of possibilities, unless what I dreamed is true and I've been born once more. Or unless I'm still dreaming, my body not yet consumed in the belly of the urthwyrms, not yet prepared for its final resting place in the soil that holds both my mother and the boy I thought to love.

With that memory, the tears flow freely, and I know this is no dream.

Judith waits while I cry myself empty. There's a severe line at the bridge of her nose, and if I look at it one way it seems disapproving, if I look at it another, concerned. The line helps me focus, helps me bring to a close this cascade of tears. When the ache in my chest finally releases its hold, Judith springs back to business, removing the rag from my forehead and reaching behind me to help me sit.

I look around me. The house seems no different than any other: stone walls and floor, stone chair for Judith, stone bed piled with furs. A basin of water rests beside me, the source of the witch hazel smell. The rag, a slice of animal hide, curls like a limp reed within the milky fluid. The only thing out of the ordinary is the adornment that protrudes from an earthenware jug on the windowsill. The sunlight streaming through the window makes me doubt my eyes, but there's no mistaking: it's a flower, a bright yellow hub ringed by a symmetrical ruff of oblong white petals. Instinctively, apprehensively, I reach out to it, only to discover the second thing that's out of joint in this place.

My Sense fails to stir.

Discomfort rises in me as I struggle to exert something that's never required exertion, something, I remember telling Isaac, that's always been as basic as breathing. I want to believe that my Sense is only slumbering, away in the country of my dreams. I strain until sweat stands on my brow, but nothing happens: I can see the flower, smell its faint fragrance, but no more.

"My Sense...my Sense is..." I stammer.

Judith lays hands on my shoulders to contain the shaking. "You've been near death, child. As near as a body can be. You'll need time to mend."

Guided by her touch, I lie down. But her words bring no comfort. Who am I, without my Sense? *What* am I? How can I face a world where all about me is as silent and dead as stone?

"Where am I?" I ask Judith, and try to keep my voice from betraying my heart.

She nods approvingly, convinced, I suppose, that her ministrations have brought me back to reason. "You're in a house of the healers," she says. "For a time, we feared you might never come to. But you rallied last night, and the worst, we expect, is past."

"Last night?" I say. "How long have I been here?"

"Most of a week," she answers. "Six days and nights, to be precise."

"And how," I begin then pause, because this part seems wholly unaccountable to me, "how did I come here?"

"That's what we'd like to know," Judith says with a frown, as if she thinks I'm withholding information from her. "You were found on the village stone at dawn six days ago, with your legs stitched and wrapped. And this after you'd been missing nigh on two weeks. You and Miss Miriam."

My heart leaps at the mention of her name, falls at the name Judith fails to mention. "Miriam…."

"Was found by your side," she says. "Though in far fairer shape than yourself. She's told us of your adventures," a word she says with obvious distaste, "but she can make no account of how the two of you happened to return, nor of Miss Rachel's whereabouts. As for the young man—"

"Isaac," I cut her off, barely daring to hope. "He's alive?"

Her frown deepens. "He returned not two days ago. Delivered, it seems, by the same means as you and Miss Miriam. As for that—"

"Can you take me to him?"

Exasperation sours Judith's normally affable face. "You're not to be up and about. You've no idea how narrow a scrape you've had. And as I was saying, the young man—"

"I must see him," I say, and despite my agitation, I nearly laugh to think what Judith counts as a narrow scrape. "Can you take me to him?"

"He's poorly, child," she blurts. "He's being cared for in a house set aside for the gravest of cases. He's to have no visitors, except—"

Her voice ceases as I struggle to sit. She crosses her arms over her matronly bosom and exhales sharply, stirring a strand of gray hair that's deserted her bun. The look she gives me suggests she'll throw her body across mine and pin me to the bed if that's what it takes to make me stay put.

But then, for no reason I can tell, she relents. Standing, she reaches out and helps me wiggle to the edge of the bed. I feel desperately weak, a mere child in her hands, and I realize that if she were unwilling to let me go, no efforts of mine would avail to fight her.

"If you won't lie still," she says primly, "you may be of some use, at least."

She bends by my side, unwraps the bandages that sheathe my legs. I tighten with fresh pain as the material pulls against my skin. When she's done, Judith straightens and gives me her arm.

"You've lost much blood, child," she says as I slide from bed to floor. "And your wounds may come as a shock to you."

They do. The legs on which I stand—with considerable assistance from Judith—have wilted like dying stalks. They're scrawny and puckered, skin hanging loose over bones once clad in muscle. Countless black threads crisscross my thighs and shins and knees, completely obliterating what was left of Isaac's sewing. The borers bit deep, and though they stopped short of taking my legs off, it's evident that contagion followed the damage they inflicted. Gangrene and death would have come next, if someone hadn't saved me.

Someone. Not the village healers, for they were clearly as baffled as Judith by my return. Not Miriam, for it seems she failed to navigate the Ecosystem and was delivered along with me. Someone else. Someone who dragged me from the borers' lair, treated my wounds for as much as a week's time, and then brought me home for the healers to nurse back to strength. Someone who clearly had no wish to be seen, for our savior left me and Miriam during the night and fled before the light of day. And, days later, brought Isaac home, too.

That's the thought that lifts my heart, even if the

effort to stand spins my head. Someone dug Isaac out of his tomb and brought him home—sick and weak, but alive. I may never run through the forest again, but I can walk, my arm draping Judith's shoulders, to the place where he waits. I can see his face again. Touch him again. Heal him again.

"There now," Judith's voice interrupts my thoughts. "We'll take it slow, child. It's a long way to the Sensors' meeting-house."

I stop, almost trip. My legs refuse to cooperate with my brain. "I thought you were taking me to see Isaac."

"And indeed I would," she says, "if it weren't for the question of your old master."

"Aaron?" It shocks me to realize how little I've thought of him these past days, how I didn't ask about him when I woke. "Is he sick?"

Judith shakes her head, but her arm tightens on mine. She leans close and speaks in a low, conspiratorial tone, all the breeziness of the village gossip vanished. "Your old master's gone mad, they say. Won't leave the meeting-house, won't let anyone come near. Bellows at those who try, threatens to do who-knows-what-all to himself or any other who sets foot in the room. Master Nathan's had to move the meetings to his own home. Not that there's much time for meetings, busy as his ranks are in the field."

There's no accusation in her voice, but guilt gnaws me at her words. I can't tell which is worse, the knowledge of what's become of Aaron or the knowledge that, even now, I long to see Isaac first. So much has been undone by my acts: the lives of my peers, the sanity of my mentor, the safety of my village. I'll have to tell someone soon what's become of Rachel, and it's likely the ones I'll have to tell first are her parents. But I know, without Judith's prompting, where I belong now.

"Take me to Aaron," I say. "Maybe he'll listen to me."

"Of course," she says gently. "That's best." Then, her voice still gentle: "The young man won't lack for company, child. As I was trying to tell you, Miss Miriam hasn't left his side since he came in."

WE SHUFFLE FROM the healer's hut, and for the first time I can remember, I cast eyes on an Ecosystem I can't touch with anything but my five senses.

In every way those senses can tell, it's the same. The trees tower above the low roofs of the village, and I know each one by name: ache, hexlox, sickenmore. As before, the shapes of bloodbirds circle lazily, red against blue. The world hasn't changed. Perhaps, like the song of the cicatrix, it never will.

But I have. I know it the instant my eyes fall on the bloodbirds and nothing stirs inside, no hint of the rotten, clotted hunger that used to emanate from them like a fume. I spy the pustules on the sickenmore trunks but can't detect their digestive juices; I watch the leaves of the ache trees fall but take no part in their dizzying descent. Countless snares surely lie waiting beyond the village stone, but I can neither identify them nor intuit their will. Whether my Sense will return, I don't know; I hope that, like my palsied legs, it merely needs to learn to walk again. But for now, a world I know to be overflowing with danger appears blandly inert, the droning of the cicatrix masking a deeper silence I never thought the Ecosystem could hold.

I take a deep breath to steady my pounding heart. *I can be a healer*, I say to myself. *Healers don't need to be Sensors*. But thinking about my future only reminds me of everything I've lost. If healing is to come, it will have to come in time.

As if seeking to distract me from the pain she sees in my face, Judith embarks on a recap of everything I've missed in the past weeks.

"When the four of you young ones vanished without a trace, the village was thrown into a tizzy," she says. "Nothing of the kind had happened before, much less with four such as you: our newest Sensor, two who were training for the post, and a boy in whom we all placed such high hopes. Isaac was chief of the threshers' crew, you know," she says with obvious pride. "The youngest such we've had."

I nod absently, wondering why Judith says nothing of Isaac's work with the healers. Maybe I'm not supposed to know. Or maybe his purpose was familiar only to Daniel's inner circle. That would be consistent with his secrecy, the impression he conveyed that recruiting me to the healers' cause was a mission known only to a select few.

"But there was little we could do except wait, and watch, and hope," Judith continues. "Master Nathan was consulted, of course, but he couldn't spare any more of his forces to traipse after you young ones. Times have been lean enough with the few Sensors we have left.

Young Levi was rushed into service, and he's been busy as ever a body was. Why, just yesterday, he brought in a string of tricky vultures, mother and young, and in so clever a way! It seems the chicks...."

I half-listen as she describes something every apprentice knows: tricky vulture poults will follow their mother anywhere, even into a Sensor's kill sack. Yet it gives me a fresh pang to hear that while I deserted the village on a mission of my own making, Levi was dutifully filling the vacuum I'd left.

"...and Master Nathan has done wonders to keep the supply of wood, water, and meat flowing," Judith chatters on. "He's lengthened the shifts, while training the younger Sensors in the use of the bow. And he's approached the Chief Warden about coordinating the threshers and firestarters and all the others under the Sensorship, to make all run more smoothly. The Brotherhood of the Sensorship, as he calls it," she says with a laugh. "Imagine that!"

"Really?" Despite my wobbly legs and drifting thoughts, this grabs my attention. The Sensorship, so far as I know, has never meddled in civil affairs. "And what has Daniel said?"

"I'm sure I'd be the last to know," Judith replies with a sound halfway between a laugh and a sniff. "But something had to be done. What with the trouble with Master Aaron and all."

My heart clenches at the reminder of where we're going. "Is he really that bad?"

"We're all wishing for the best," Judith says, heaving a sigh. "But you'll see for yourself."

And we walk on toward the Sensorium, the eye of the Ecosystem watching invisibly from behind the trees, Judith holding me up with her strong, lined hand.

FROM THE MIDWIFE'S ominous tone, I expect his howls to shake the foundations of the Sensorium. Instead, the building's eerily silent. I leave Judith a few paces off and approach the door, fearing at any moment to hear his voice groan from the interior, to see his furious face emerge from the doorway. My sickly legs tremble with more than weakness as they take their first few unassisted steps. If he's really turned violent as Judith claims, even his age won't protect me from him now.

I reach the doorway and peek inside. The gloom momentarily prevents me from seeing what he's done to it, but when my eyes adjust, I'm shocked at the sight of stone benches overturned and scattered about the circular space, the central platform streaked by fire. Upon the blackened stone he sits, hunched and motionless, his gray locks dangling to the floor, his thick cloak enveloping him. His staff, reduced to near nothing by the fire, lies beside him. I can't tell if his eyes are open, but I can see that his mouth hangs slack, his chin shiny with saliva. The cloak makes it impossible to detect his breath.

I step into the room. The stone chills my feet. He doesn't move, but I think I see his eyes dart to the side.

"Master," I say softly. The room magnifies my voice to a roar. "It's Sarah."

This time, he lifts his face to mine. Through the tattered drapery of his hair, I see that his eyes are empty, and when he speaks, the sound is like that of a man dying of thirst. "Sarah is no more. Her body lies rotting in the grave, food for wyrms."

I wonder which Sarah he means. I take another step, and he shifts in his wrap like some wild creature prepared to spring. My hands reach out to him, though I'm too far away to touch him.

"I've come home, Master," I say. "Your Sarah has come home to you."

He cocks his head, dead eyes wandering my face. I can't guess what he sees, but I know it's not me. I can't think what to say or do to bring him back.

Before I can try, he rises in a swooping motion and lunges at me. I stumble back, my legs giving out, his hand finding my throat. With a strength I'd never have thought he yet commands, he lifts me from the floor and holds me at arm's length, my legs kicking like a bug's. Veins and creases in his face make him appear overcome with rage, but his marble eyes remain flat and unseeing.

"Aaron," I gasp. "Master—"

He says nothing, but his hand tightens at my throat. I clutch his fingers, try to tear them from me, but he's too strong. I have no more breath for words. Drowsiness fogs my mind, and the room darkens.

Then I hear his voice, as if from a great distance: "Sarah?"

His hand releases my throat and I land, gasping and coughing, on the frigid stone. The floor shudders beneath my cheek, and when I force open my eyes, I see Aaron's cloak spread before me. It's only with a great effort of mind that I realize its owner has toppled with it. I claw the ground, dragging myself to the heaped furs, and climb them to search for Aaron's face.

It's there, bundled in the fur, frail and motionless. My hands shake uncontrollably as I sweep curls from his forehead. His lips can't move, but his eyes flick just enough to find mine. My head screams at me that I can heal him, restore him to life as I did Isaac, but my heart tells me it's too late. Yet before the light in his eyes goes out, his hand twitches, his fingers lace with mine. A rush of sensations flows from my fingertips to my palms, from there to every inch of my aching body. In a flood of images, the life of my dying master washes over me.

I see a man with Aaron's face but dark hair, piercing eyes, strength and vitality in his limbs that had begun to diminish by the time I came into the world. I see the man, this much younger Aaron, reach out to touch the belly of a woman I don't recognize, a woman with strange skin as pink as a poisonrose bloom and long yellow hair like strands of moonlight. Her plumpness is that of a woman with child. Next, I see my youthful master plodding through the Ecosystem, the bundled form of an infant in his arms, the silver trails of tears on his cheeks. I see the pale-skinned woman no more, and I know that her life ended the night her child's began. I watch as the child grows, a girl with her father's dark eyes flecked with her mother's uncanny blue. When she turns three, Aaron takes her from the houses of the healers, this girl whom all in the village believe to be a foundling abandoned to the forest by some nameless mother. He trains the girl, watches with pride as she joins the Sensors' ranks, though he knows he can never claim her as his own, never admit, to her or any other, that her gift came from him. When, like the man she doesn't know is her father, she finds a love forbidden to those who walk in the Ecosystem, I see the meeting in the Sensorium where she stands with the mark of her shame evident in her growing belly, hear the ugly words of Nathan rising above Aaron's defense to rob her of the title she proudly bore. In the few short years she has left to live, I see through Aaron's eyes the child in her arms, the laughing girl she names Ruth. And when she dies, when she strays too far from the village on an errand of the healers and Aaron finds nothing but the token she lost on her final voyage, I see him return to her daughter, give the child his own child's name, and raise her to be what his own child was.

Sarah, the brave and strong. A Sensor, and a healer. The one who was never meant to be, the one from whom he learned to shield himself all his life lest her childish hands discover the truth. The one who, in that life's final moment, finds and holds him at last.

I look in his eyes. Their light has died. "Grandpa," I say.

MUCH AS I long to see Isaac—to touch him, to heal him—I know I can't with Miriam at his side. And I know there's one more visit I have to make.

I've had enough of the lies. They kill as surely as the Ecosystem. How many Sensors must we sacrifice—my mother, Rachel, Barnabas, Samuel—before we face the truth? If I succeed in what I seek, then come tomorrow, the Sensor named Aaron, father of Sarah, grandfather of Ruth, will be laid to rest in the earth where stone yields to sward, and all will know him as he was.

And then, there will be time to search for the other truths that have been kept from me, from all of us. The hidden life of the Ecosystem. The power of the healers. The presence of another village beyond ours, home of my mother's mother, with her weird yellow hair and blue eyes. Could the stranger who freed me and Isaac from the borers' lair have come from the same village? A village of healers, perhaps, with knowledge of wyrms and wounds we lack? I don't know, but I vow to find out.

But first things first. While Judith bustles off in search of Daniel, I steady myself and, wishing for a fleetness of foot I may never find again, make my way along the lanes to the Chief Sensor's home.

IT SITS ON the eastern edge of the village, at some remove from the other Sensors' huts. For as long as the Sensorship has existed, this lonely spot has been kept for the Conservator of our order, and it's always been treated as unapproachable by any but a fellow Sensor; the Chief Warden never visits, even the threshers being barred from the area except in times of greatest need. As a result, the grabgrass has grown so long it's overlapped the charred circle. When Nathan became Chief Sensor, he remained here, though by rights he could have taken Aaron's home. If he was watching from his window the evening I left in search of Miriam, he'd have seen me slipping into the shadows of the trees. No doubt he'd have mouthed a curse and shuttered his blinds.

But I need to do this. I didn't start it. It began years—millennia—before I was born. But if there's to be a change, it'll have to come from me, the blood of Aaron. I need to talk to Nathan, alone.

"You're not my enemy," I say softly as I approach his door.

A light glows through his window, orange on the gray stone. I search for the shadows that will show me he's inside, but see nothing. Still, I doubt a Sensor would be so careless as to leave a fire burning when there's no need. Not with fuel so precious. Not this Sensor.

"Nathan?" I call. My voice sounds as feeble as my legs feel.

There's no response. I lean my head in the door, eyes and ears attuned for the slightest sign. The firewell throws off flame and aromatic smoke, but aside from its crackling, the hut is silent. It's been years since I've seen its interior, since I sat on its floor with the other apprentices and listened to Nathan's stories of the Sensorship. Within the secrecy of these walls, his tales were far different from those he recited in public: heroic tales of glory and renown, his private lessons pictured the Sensors as superhuman figures who blazed through the forest like meteors while the foolish commoners gawked in awe. I was pleased by those stories then, my child's pride fed by them. But now I see only a small, empty hovel, a stone cage that bars its prisoner from touching a friend's hand, holding a lover's body. Pity fills me at the thought of his stunted life, but it's mingled with anger that he would impose such a life on us all.

"We're not enemies," I say again, too softly for any but me to hear.

A sharp *thunk* from behind answers me. I turn to find the evidence that he's been watching: a black-feathered arrow protrudes from the cobbles, so close to my feet I can't convince myself it was a bad shot. A moment later, he steps from behind an ache tree at the edge of the sward and stands facing me, a second arrow nocked to the string. Disdain rides on his brow, power sits in the majestic sweep of his shoulders. He raises the bow and lets the arrow fly, and though it's another clean miss, I flinch as it embeds itself beside its fellow.

"Do you mean to shoot me?" I call, seeing the third arrow ready on the string.

"That wouldn't be sporting," Nathan responds. "Not without giving you a fighting chance."

"I won't fight you, Nathan."

"Then you'll die where you stand," he says, and sights along the shaft.

The bowstring twangs, and the third arrow whizzes past my ear. Again, I'm not fool enough to think it a missed shot.

"The tyranny of the Sensors is coming to a close," I say, much more bravely than I feel. "The people will wake soon, and you can't kill them all. Or will you hunt to feed your belly alone?"

Nathan pauses with a fresh arrow on the string, and his face does something I've never seen it do: it smiles. I like that a lot less than the stony imperiousness I've always seen there.

"I rejoiced when you fled the village," he says. "Rejoiced that the weakness you carry in your blood was blotted from the ranks of the Brotherhood. But I will do now what the Ecosystem failed to do. And you will play along."

Again the arrow leaps from his bow, and this time, its point sears my cheek like a red-hot brand. My fingers fly to my face, return blood-tipped. The bloodbirds scream in the treetops, settle on the nearby branches, and my thought returns to the day of my investiture. I reach to the ground and yank one of the arrows free. Nathan's smile sets as if he thinks I've decided to play his game, but I have something else in mind.

I place the arrow's point to my lips, test the dried blood with the tip of my tongue. Then I snap the shaft and throw the pieces to the ground.

"This must be the one that shot Barnabas," I say. "The trees kept the one that shot Samuel. But where's the one that shot my mother?"

I see from his startled look that I've guessed right, but his composure quickly returns. "That one I keep in a place of honor. I have not loosed it since that day, and will not loose it again, save to bring down her child, or all whom her child loves. One death or many. This the daughter of Sarah must choose."

Again the bow rises, the archer sights, the arrow flies. Again my cheek is scored with fire. I have little time to choose. I try to summon hatred for him, but all I feel is a great sadness. My mother was killed by the borers, but now I know that she was weakened by Nathan's arrow long before she stumbled on their lair. Barnabas was consumed by watermites and Samuel by the arachnard, but only after blood drawn by the Conservator's bow attracted the Ecosystem. What his purpose was in these latter two deaths I can only guess: to punish Barnabas for past transgressions, to weaken Aaron's authority, to press for the total control of the village he sought to engineer in my absence. If I choose to fight him and die, all his purposes will be achieved. But if I refuse, the deaths of Miriam, and Isaac, and many others are sure to follow.

I pull the second arrow from the ground, point it at him like a blade.

"Good," he says. "Now I'll give you a head start, and we can begin."

"We're not enemies," I call to him.

His face twists. "No?"

"No," I say. "But I'll meet you if I must."

"That's the spirit," he says.

He sets a final arrow to his bow, and though I can't taste the blood on it, I know it's my blood as well.

"I will enjoy this, girl," he says. "Even more than I enjoyed the hunt for the bitch you call mother." His eyes meet mine. "Now run."

I run.

A WEEK AGO, my instinct would have steered me toward the forest. Now I break for the center of the village. Nathan hasn't established the rules of this hunt, and if I can lure him toward other human beings, maybe I can stop him without further blood being shed.

But he's too smart for that, and far too quick. I've gotten nowhere before he sprints across the sward, cutting me off from the village center. His bow's at his side, and a stone knife flashes in his hand. I try to dodge, but my legs tangle and I fall, a long hot streak of red painting my shoulder. He sheathes the knife and kicks me, and I scramble painfully away on hands and knees.

"On your feet, girl," he snarls.

I get my legs under me and stagger in the only direction he'll allow: across the pavilion, toward the blackened turf that borders the sward. From there, he'll drive me deep into the forest, far beyond sight of the village, where he can kill me at his leisure and leave my body for the scavengers to dispose of. No one will hear of me again, and most will assume what they did of my mother: that I made my last, doomed voyage of my own foolish pride. But I have no other recourse; when

I risk a backward glance, he lopes easily behind, with no one else in sight. I move as fast as my brittle legs can carry me, but I'm no match for him now, if I ever was.

My feet crunch across the charred circle. The next moment, they meet the margin of the sward, and I Sense what I hoped I wouldn't, what I feared I would.

Nothing.

There's no response, no hint of the life that lies there. I feel the slightly springy blades of grass, smell their weak scent on the breeze, but that's all. The will of the world is closed, while the man who pursues me is processing everything I can't, his nerves expanding with each stride to embrace the whole of the living earth. He's one with it, shielded from its hunger, while I'm a tasty tidbit limping before its million and more wakeful eyes.

The sounds of the wild assail me as I duck under the first tree limbs: prowler monkeys throatily hooting, fellcats screeching in delight. The song of the cicatrix rises to a jarring cacophony, and I realize they've zeroed in on me, their homing devices no longer muted by a Sensor's power. My chest beats wildly, my breath quickens. I try to calm my vital signs, but I can't remember how to do it, can't remember learning how. All I can remember is the way I ensnared Isaac, the cicatrix swarming his scalp while I stood safely by. So many tricks. So many secrets and lies. And all will end today.

An inquisitive bug lands on my hair, mandibles flexing, but drifts away when I swat at it. Up ahead, vines rise tentatively from the forest floor, nosing the air at my approach. Another roving cicatrix nests in my hair, and another. I brush both away, but one returns, droning lazily beside my ear. Not hungry, it seems: just curious. Branches scratch my face, and though I emerge with scrapes, none burns with the telltale sign of poison. The nettles coil and sway like wary serpents as they judge the distance between us, trying to decide whether I'm worth killing. For now, they let me pass.

An arrow screams past my cheek, embedding itself in a hexlox tree, which writhes and jerks the barb loose. For a moment, I think Nathan's missed, but then I come to my senses: he couldn't have missed, not from so close, with me moving so slowly. He's merely toying with me, delivering deadly messages to herd me deeper into the forest. He might even be laughing at me, but with the wind howling in my ears, I can't hear it.

And then it's the wind no longer; it's the cicatrix, hundreds of them coalescing into a swarm. I clamp my teeth shut to contain my breath, but it makes no difference. The uproar of their wings drowns out my frenzied heart as they descend. Sensor's instincts gone, I duck.

Something slams into my shoulder with such force I gasp and pitch face-forward onto the forest floor. The cicatrix, disoriented, break formation and sail over my head. I try to get my hands under me, but pain and nausea flood my body, and my left arm collapses. It's then I see the point of the black arrow protruding from my shoulder, coated in my own bright blood. The smell is so strong I nearly swoon. It's my blood, and my mother's, and Aaron's as well. It oozes from my shoulder, stains the leaves beneath my body.

Nathan has let loose his final shot. Aimed, no doubt, at my heart. Ducking the cicatrix saved me from the death he'd planned. But my arm's impaled and useless, and my legs have no strength to lift me. It's all I can do to roll onto my side and face my killer.

He steps from behind an ache tree so fluidly it's as if he's parted a curtain of air. The bow is hitched to his shoulder, its work done. His breath is easy, his brawny arms and chest free of perspiration. His face is stern, the scowl of a teacher who takes no pleasure in disciplining a wayward student. Then he smiles, and I know that what he said before was true. He's going to enjoy this.

His knife describes a short arc in the air. I must be lying in ache leaves, because my head spins at the motion, the blade forming a helix of blades that weave before me. He kneels at my side and grasps my hair, jerking my head back. The knife twirls about his fingers before he lays it against my throat, its edge so keen my flesh parts at its touch.

"Where is it?" he hisses in my ear. "Where do you keep it hidden?"

My fogged brain can't make sense of his words, so I shake my head, the knife-point digging into the soft skin of my throat.

"The token!" he says. "Where do you keep it?"

"I lost it," I say. My words sound strange, as if I'm hearing them through a long tunnel filled with wind. "In the cave of the borers. It's gone."

He holds the knife steady as he searches me. His inspection is brief, for while the taboo remains, he won't touch my skin with his bare hands. Whether he'll search more thoroughly after my death, I don't know. For now, though, he seems satisfied. He leans forward, the point of his knife pressing against my throat.

"Your blood draws the Ecosystem," he whispers. "It was the same with the whore who gave you life. And now, I let the Ecosystem drink freely of it."

It takes all the effort I can muster to stare into his eyes. My head spins under the influence of the ache leaves, but I'm determined to face him as he kills me.

"May you gag on it," I say.

His leering face swims before me a moment more, then snaps into sharp focus. The tip of the knife rests on my jugular, and I feel its point with an intensity as perfect as Sense. Something other than ache leaves, I realize, forms my bed. I can smell it around me, just as I did that night in the forest. I guess—no, I *know*—that he can neither smell nor Sense it. Of all the things in the Ecosystem, he's brought me down on the one thing where I'm the master and he less than an apprentice.

It's witch hazel.

My right arm shoots out with a strength and will all its own, catching the wrist that holds the knife. My fingers rip the blade from his grasp, drive the point into his shoulder where it slopes to his neck. It's not a killing blow, but he staggers away from me, trips on creepers, sprawls on his back. The knife protrudes from his neck, dripping gore. He glares at me in feral rage. "You bitch—"

He reaches for the knife and tries to stand, but puzzlement replaces bloodlust. The vines have found him, this wounded creature that's entered their domain, and they've gripped his arms and legs with a strength that dwarfs his own. He struggles, strains, pulls, but succeeds only in attracting the notice of other vines, which wrap his torso, his throat, his eyes. He's mummified in the Ecosystem's green. The vines flip him onto his back and squeeze. His mouth opens in a howl before a creeper clamps down over it and silences him for good.

The cawing of bloodbirds fills the air, a flock of at least a hundred settling on the branches around us. They shift awkwardly on their roosts, open their sharp beaks, flap their blood-tipped wings. Their eyes gleam golden and black as they cock red-tufted heads. They smell blood, but not my own. What attracts them is the bundle of vines that lies a short distance from my nest, a bundle that flops and thrashes in a weak and unnatural way.

Their enormous leader is first to investigate. It lands on legs that barely seem strong enough to support its bloated body, pecks at the Chief Sensor with a beak far sharper than his buried blade. It takes a moment to work through the coating of vines in the area of his shoulder, but when it does, it finds something it likes. It lifts its head and caws sharply, its red breast swelling like a bladder. Then it plunges its beak to the meal.

The others shrink back while their leader feasts.

As the vines slicken with red and the victim thrashes more violently, they grow bold, taking short bursts of flight to land on the blood-soaked green. They fight over Nathan's body, pulling at vines and flesh and hair, nipping at each other's wings and beaks. Attracted by the commotion, other bloodbirds are circling, circling, seeming to come no closer with each lazy loop but then plopping from the sky to join the melee around the Chief Sensor's body. Soon, I can't see either the vines or their prisoner beneath the tumult of red feathers, which cover him as completely as a wildfire raging.

With a convulsive tug, the bloodbirds lift their trophy from the forest floor, hoist him by beak and claw till he hangs six feet above the ground. Perhaps they mean to drag him to their roosts. But there are too many of them, and so he hovers there, his body dripping and dwindling as the flock darts in to carry off morsels of flesh. The vines have been eaten away, and I see him clearly, what's left of him: his savaged body, jaw dangling by a thread, throat so ripped by talons there's nothing left to produce a scream. His eyes have been torn from their sockets, and his blank face glares with exposed tooth and bone. His body no longer moves of its own will, but twitches reflexively as it's battered this way and that by the furious swarm. Beneath him, a pool of blood darkens the forest floor.

Finally, they drop him. Bones fall in a clattering heap. The birds have been so thorough they've licked his skeleton to a spotless shine, perversely perfect against the red. Shrieking, they dive to the ground to lap up the last traces of blood, scattering his bones as they do. In their mania to get at his flesh, they've consumed even the furs he wore. The only other evidence they've left of the Chief Sensor's existence are his weapons, which lie amid the pile of bones like relics of a vanished time.

A hurricane of wings signals the bloodbirds' departure. Their caws fill the air, then the sky empties of them and all falls silent.

Slowly, stiffly, I creep from the witch hazel to inspect Nathan's remains. As soon as I move, the torment in my shoulder returns, making my good arm quake. I drag myself to the cairn of bones and sift through them, seeking the one last thing I think the bloodbirds might have spared. When I find it, tears start in my eyes.

It's such a small thing, so small it's slipped through his ribs and fallen to the turf. But as soon as I touch it, I know it's the real thing, the final shard that remains of my mother's life. Aaron found her token and passed it to me, but he didn't know she bore another charm, one given to her by the healers. Hers is the same as Isaac's, except it's carved from an opalescent pink stone, so finely wrought the scales of the snake seem to undulate beneath my touch. I hold it to my lips and think I detect her scent on it, though the aroma of witch hazel and the tang of the blood we share are so strong I can't be sure.

I wonder how Nathan came to possess this charm and not the other. Perhaps he thought it was her Sensor's token, though he learned later that he was mistaken. Did my mother trick him, bartering her healer's mark for the sign of the Sensors? In the end, when she knew she couldn't keep both, which did she wish to bequeath to me? Which did she hope would guide her daughter's path?

I don't know, and maybe that's why I cry.

My legs quiver and my gut heaves, but I rise to my feet and breathe as deeply as my ruined shoulder will allow. Miriam can keep the shard that belonged to the two Sensors called Sarah. We'll need her kind for years to come. But we may need my kind even more. I will live in this world fully, and I will be my mother's child at last.

It's a long walk back to the village, but I walk it without fear, for I know no unfriendly thing can touch me now.

THE DAY OF Aaron's funeral dawns bright and clear. I rise at sun's first light, peer out the window at the greening day, then attempt to perform my morning rituals one-handed. My wounded arm's in a sling, which means of the four working appendages I had two weeks ago, I'm reduced to one. I manage to get the fire started, the water boiling, only to realize my larder is bare. Probably a good thing, since any morsel that might have been in it would have developed a life of its own in the time I've been gone. I'm baffled as to how I'll change my clothes, but I decide I'm not too proud to ask Judith for help. Maybe she'll have something for me to eat as well.

There's a gentle breeze blowing in my face when I emerge from my hut, and that along with the sunlight diffusing through the branches lifts my spirits for the challenge to come. I've been so focused on planning, I've barely stopped to think what today means for me. On this day, I'll bury the man whose face forms my first memory, the man who housed me, fed me, taught me. Loved me. Today I'll bury my grandpa, and I've not yet taken the time to cry.

My heart catches at the thought of his body not

burning but descending, his dear face not vanishing into smoke but darkening as the earth's shroud covers it for all time. Would he grieve to be buried this way, as he mourned his own daughter's earthbound burial? It strikes me that when my grandfather laid hands on the Ecosystem in search of Barnabas, it wasn't the first time he'd done so, nor was it the first time he Sensed the missing one to be beyond his reach. I only hope that, when the villagers leave the stone circle to watch this man be lowered into his grave, they'll understand what his life and death meant. That they'll not be too fearful to walk where I lead them, too cowed by the Ecosystem's mystery to hear what I have to tell.

My heart catches again at the sight of a figure inching across the stone toward my door. He's far distant, creeping like Aaron in his latter days, supporting himself by one hand with a long wooden staff. But I know him instantly. I'd know him if it were pitch dark and I couldn't see him at all, if all I could feel was the touch of his hand on mine.

It's Isaac.

I never visited him as I intended. There was the small matter of removing an arrow from my shoulder, which left me too weakened to resist Judith's order of bedrest. Now that I see him, I'm at once elated that he's alive and stricken that he's been brought so low.

His left arm is bound at his side, mimicking my own sling. Where Judith promised me that my wound would heal, there's something about the way he holds his ruined limb that tells me he'll never use it again. His progress is painful to watch: he plants the stick before him then takes two miniature steps, as if it's pulling him along and he struggling to keep up. Even so, seeing him here, now, makes me giddy with warring emotions: joy, guilt, jealousy, hope. I struggle to compose my face in the eternity it takes him to close the distance between us, but I have no idea what finally settles on me when his journey is done.

What he presents to me, though, is simple enough: a small smile. Haggard though his face is, I can't help smiling back.

"Well, hello there," he says. Then, while I try to untangle my tongue: "I'm sorry about Aaron."

"Thank you," I say. "How are you feeling?"

"Like hex," he says, his grin broadening. "Daniel says I'm lucky to be alive. I'm not sure I agree with him."

I try to smile back, but the thought of what could have happened to him is too strong. The next thing I ask is the last thing I want to know: "Where's Miriam?"

"Sleeping," he says. "After nearly a week without, from what they tell me. Judith filled me in on all the details."

"*All* the details?"

"And then some."

"No wonder you look so tired," I tease.

"Yeah." The smile falls, and without it, his face looks terribly old and worn. "I'm actually here at Daniel's request," he says. "He would have come himself, but he thought you'd listen to me. This is all happening very quickly, and he wanted to make sure you heard us out."

"Of course," I say. Though this is not at all the kind of thing I'd thought would be our first topic of conversation.

"Daniel wonders if you might reconsider your decision and let Aaron be cremated in the traditional fashion," Isaac says. "He's had reports of the Sensors marshaling their forces, and he's concerned about what they might do. They're pretty tough customers, as you know." A pained smile crosses his face. "If they decide to take on the village, there could be all-out war."

I feel my spirits deflate, yesterday's victory and the riot of anticipation it spawned seeping from me. "Is it Esther?"

"She's one of the few who seems to be on our side," he says. "But that makes her a target for the ones loyal to Nathan. The ones he was grooming to take command of the village."

"Like Levi," I say.

"And Ezra. And there's concern about Jarrod, especially after what happened to Rachel. The two of them were really close. He's been in contact with her parents, and it seems he's planted some…ugly ideas in their heads."

I'm stunned by this development, though I should have seen it coming. I'd not resolved what to say to Rachel's family, and while I dithered, Jarrod struck. Not out of malice, I realize. Out of love. He'll never admit it, not even to himself, but he was in love with Rachel. And he'll fight, even kill, to tamp down the pain I caused him.

"I didn't mean to start a war," I say.

Isaac looks at me hard. "Maybe not. But you were ready to fight it if you had to."

We walk in the direction of the healers' huts. To see us, one might think we're an old couple as we hobble across the stone. Isaac hasn't so much as glanced at my legs, but he can't help noticing what I see in his emaciated frame: if a war comes, neither of us will be up to fighting it.

As if he's guessed my thought, Isaac resumes, "Daniel believes a funeral might be the wrong place to start the healing process. Funerals are…well, they bring up lots of old stuff. Bad stuff. He's been working for years to siphon off candidates for the healers, and he doesn't want that work to be undone. He even recruited a few who failed the most recent Sensor trials—like Caleb and Noah, if you can believe it."

"I hope they're better healers than Sensors," I say.

"They are," Isaac says, and his voice is serious. "They're like so many of us: people who've felt all along that something wasn't right but couldn't figure out what. In time, we might have enough of those people to face the Sensorship. But for now, Daniel wonders if there might be a better way to build support."

I nod slightly, warily. "Such as?"

"Such as another kind of ceremony," he says. "One that promotes the union of Sensors and healers without opening up old wounds. Not a funeral, but—"

"A wedding," I say. "Joining Isaac the healer and Miriam the Sensor."

He stops, and his eyes won't meet mine. "How'd you guess?" he says with a weak grin.

"Come on, thresher," I say. "You can't hide from me."

He looks up, and his eyes hide nothing. He shifts his walking stick to the crook of his bound arm and reaches for my hand, and as our fingers knot, I feel the full force of his love flooding my skin for the first and final time. It's like a landscape, a forest, alight with fire. I curl my hand around his, draw it to me, try to smile. To myself I say, we'll have to learn to hide these feelings in the days and months and years to come.

"Miriam's a really good person, Sarah," Isaac says. "And she's—I don't know how else to put this—she's not affiliated with any faction. The Sensors won't be crazy about one of their own marrying, but Daniel thinks the rest of the village will be more willing to accept it. Especially since…."

"You were pledged," I say. "I understand, Isaac. The villagers won't question the marriage the way they would…another. It'll just seem like the way things were meant to be."

His face is so miserable, I wish I could kiss him and make his troubles dissipate into sunlight and air. But that's not for me to do any longer. It's risky for us to be seen together, much less holding hands. With as much firmness and gentleness as I can manage, I loosen my fingers from his, return the walking stick to his grasp. A paroxysm of pain or hurt crosses his brow as I step back to restore the space between us.

"There's something I have to tell you," he says.

"There's nothing you have to tell me."

He doesn't listen. "At the swamp. When I left you. I was just so torn up about losing Rachel, and then... well, me and you...."

"That's behind us now." The thought of all that's behind us makes my throat tighten, but I swallow and get through what I need to say. "We have to look to the future. My training. Your marriage. The new world we're trying to build. So all this hurt won't have been for nothing."

He's quiet for a long time. At last he smiles, and it's like sunlight warming the village stone.

"I have to be getting back," he says. "Daniel will want to know your decision, and Miriam...."

"Will need you by her side."

"We'll be working together, Sarah," he says. "You and me. No matter what, we'll be working together to build a better world."

There's much I could say to that, much I could demand. But I say none of it. I have no right, and the world of which we both dream won't allow me.

We walk the remaining distance to the house where Miriam sleeps. All around us, the Ecosystem sings its endless melody, threnody, carol of birth and death. At the doorstep, Isaac opens his mouth as if to say a final word, but thinks better of it and simply smiles. I stand on the threshold as he turns from me and enters the house of stone.

THE END

Acknowledgments

Ecosystem has been a labor of love for many years. My thanks to the people who helped me turn my dream into a reality:

My agent, Liza Fleissig of Liza Royce Agency, for encouraging me to follow my heart.

Readers Jen Rees and Allison Wortche, for providing valuable feedback at various stages of the book's genesis.

Christa Yelich-Koth, for giving the manuscript a final run-through before publication.

Fellow YA authors Kat Ross and Stephanie Keyes, for advising and inspiring me.

The authors cited in the book's epigraphs, for reminding me why eco-lit matters.

Ralph T. H. Griffith, for the 1895 translation of a funeral hymn from the Rigveda from which I've derived Isaac's song.

My children, Lilly and Jonah, for offering some very cool ideas for monsters.

My wife, Christine Saitz, for patience befitting a saint.

And finally, my readers, for following me on this strange and magical journey. Hope you like this one.

About the Author

Joshua David Bellin has been writing novels since he was eight years old (though the first few were admittedly very short). A college professor by day, he has published three science fiction novels for Young Adults: the two-part Survival Colony series, *Survival Colony 9* and *Scavenger of Souls*, and the deep-space adventure *Freefall*. In his free time, Josh likes to read, watch movies, and spend time in Nature with his kids. Oh, yeah, and he likes monsters. Really scary monsters.

To find out more about Josh and his books, visit his website and sign up for his newsletter. He promises not to send it to you more than once a month!

www.joshuadavidbellin.com

Also by Joshua David Bellin

SURVIVAL COLONY 9

SCAVENGER OF SOULS

FREEFALL

Available in print and ebook formats
from Amazon, Barnes & Noble, and other retailers.

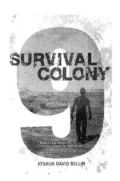  

Made in the USA
Lexington, KY
17 April 2018